Summer of Supernovas

Summer of Supernovas

Darcy Woods

CROWN
New York

This is a work of fiction. Names, characters, places, and incidents either are the product of the author's imagination or are used fictitiously. Any resemblance to actual persons, living or dead, events, or locales is entirely coincidental.

Text copyright © 2016 by Darcy Woods
Jacket art copyright © 2016 by Vincent Besnault/Getty Images
Jacket design by Liz Casal

All rights reserved. Published in the United States by Crown Books for Young Readers, an imprint of Random House Children's Books, a division of Penguin Random House LLC, New York.

Crown and the colophon are registered trademarks of Penguin Random House LLC.

Visit us on the Web! randomhouseteens.com

Educators and librarians, for a variety of teaching tools, visit us at RHTeachersLibrarians.com

Library of Congress Cataloging-in-Publication Data
Woods, Darcy.
Summer of supernovas / Darcy Woods.—First edition.
pages cm
Summary: As the daughter of an astrologer, Wilamena Carlisle knows the truth lies within the stars, so when she discovers a rare planetary alignment she is forced to tackle her worst astrological fear—The Fifth House of Relationships and Love—but Wil must decide whether a cosmically doomed love is worth rejecting her mother's legacy when she falls for a sensitive guitar player.
ISBN 978-0-553-53704-8 (trade)—ISBN 978-0-553-53705-5 (ebook)
[1. Love—Fiction. 2. Astrology—Fiction.] I. Title.
PZ7.1.W66Sum 2016 [Fic]—dc23 2014048932

Printed in the United States of America
10 9 8 7 6 5 4 3 2 1
First Edition

Random House Children's Books
supports the First Amendment and celebrates the right to read.

FOR DAVID.

WHOSE LOVE MAKES ALL THINGS POSSIBLE.

(THE PROOF IS IN YOUR HANDS.)

Chapter 1

Be humble for you are made of earth.
Be noble for you are made of stars.
—SERBIAN PROVERB

Two fears have plagued me from the time I was little, and today I must face one of them.

It's not the clowns. A lot of kids get squeamish around clowns, I know. But no one else at Jessica Bernard's seventh birthday party screamed bloody murder and wet their pants at the sight of one. That's when I earned the nickname *Wila-pee-na*. The nickname is quasi-forgotten—thank heavens. Though the fear of clowns is not.

Still, what I'm about to tackle is worse. *Way* worse.

Carefully I take my place at the top of the water tower, letting my bare legs dangle. The early summer breeze rushes to greet them. One hundred and twenty feet stretch between me and the ground. My pulse doesn't even flicker. I wish it did. Because heights are a perfectly reasonable fear.

Beneath and around me, the water tower spikes like a bulbous-headed nail from an otherwise tidy landscape. The aging white reservoir once proudly proclaimed CITY OF CARLISLE. But since most everyone, except me and the elements, has forgotten the old tower, it now reads: ITY OF CARL.

I adjust the wrinkled towel underneath me since the metal of the six-foot-wide circular platform is equal parts rust and chipped paint. It's not as if I planned on coming here—and certainly not in a dress—but driving by on the way to Hyde Park . . . well, I just *had* to stop. Because for all the structure's imperfections, it does manage to get one thing right—the view. From here the world is utterly perfect.

Unfolding the yellowing paper, I smooth it over my lap. My astrological birth chart's intricate and faded markings offer nothing I haven't seen a million times. I do it out of habit, because the placement of every planet and its degree is as well-known as the location of the nose on my face.

And there it is: The queen mother of all my fears. *The Fifth House.*

Relationships.

Romance.

Love.

Much as I'd rather bury myself in the study of astrology and its role in the human experience, I can't avoid reality any longer. Because the clock is ticking. I have precisely twenty-two days.

Twenty-two days of planetary alignment to find my perfect match. If I don't, it will take another decade for the stars to produce conditions this ideal. And by age twenty-seven, I could be a whacked-out spinster with eleven cats and a raging case of agoraphobia.

Well, that's a risk I can't take. Especially when born with an ill-fated Fifth House that already tipped the scales toward a dysfunctional love life. So help me, if I don't find my match now, I am staring down the barrel of ten years of falling for the wrong guys. Ten years—*or more*—of heartache, heartbreak, and widespread astrological malaise.

I have no choice. I must swallow my fear and seize this cosmic opportunity.

Eyes closed, I inhale deeply.

From the moment my mother cast it, I have *never* deviated from the guiding wisdom of my chart. After all, its importance is as genetically predisposed as the blue color of my eyes. Failing just isn't an option.

So I set to work. I dig out my notepad, pen, and iPod, slipping the latter in my dress pocket. Popping in my earbuds, I press play, letting the music take me higher. But even the upbeat song isn't enough. I stand and pace the platform. Movement of body breeds movement of ideas—gospel according to Gram.

I begin my brainstorming by compiling a list of the twelve zodiac signs, placing stars next to Aries, Gemini, Libra, and Sagittarius for their intellectual-mindedness and passion for adventure. I add a couple more stars with question marks to the signs that are possible matches. Scanning the list, I cross off Taurus and Scorpio—too possessive; Leo—too outwardly absorbed; and Cancer—too feely. I don't mesh with the emotionally upheaved. And then there is Pisces. *Absolutely* out of the question. Why did I even write it down? I scribble until the word is an unreadable inkblot.

But this measly list doesn't scratch the surface of the daunting research ahead. I'll have to consult the astrology books tucked under my bed and, of course, my best friend, Irina.

Irina says she has a surprise for me. Something I'll find *quite* valuable in my search. *Hmm* . . . a surprise from my dear Russian comrade doesn't exactly lower my blood pressure.

I lean back, resting my elbows on the waist-high railing. Cumulus clouds drift overhead, their undersides ironed and starched. One of my finger waves has come loose and slaps the lens of my cat eyeglasses. I tuck the chin-length wave behind my ear, and lose myself in whirling thoughts of sun signs, decanates, and cusps. *How in the world will I narrow my search? Where do I even—*

All of a sudden vibrations carry from my feet all the way up my legs. And there's another noise. Faint at first, but growing louder.

Confused, I yank out an earbud.

"—it! Okay?" a voice bellows from the ground.

I spin around, searching for the source. A guy stares back. The distance between us is too great to make out much more than that. I glance toward the outer part of the platform and spot a second guy racing up the ladder as though he's being pursued by the hounds of hell and his rump is a beef-flavored chew toy.

A pickle-colored station wagon idles beside Gram's Buick. The driver's-side door hangs open.

"Help is coming! Stay where you are!"

Help is . . . *coming*? Then it occurs to me how this must look from far away—lonely girl at the top of a tower, unresponsive, manically scribbling while leaning over the rail. For the love of zodiac, they probably think I'm writing a suicide note or something! Oh my—

"Hey!" I shout, waving my arms. "No! No! There's been a mistake!"

"No mistake is that bad! Just . . ." The guy's head lowers, as if he's searching the crabgrass-and-dandelion ground cover for wisdom. He then lifts his gaze again, cupping his hands to the sides of his mouth. "Just don't jump!"

So much for wisdom.

The wind awakens with a violent gust. I try to situate myself in line with the shouter so I'm better heard. "Look, I'm not trying to—" I inhale sharply as my foot catches on the strap of my bag. Stumbling forward, I slam into the rail, folding like a rag doll over the metal piping.

"Ahh!" ground guy yells. "Grant!"

Powerful arms latch around my middle, reeling me away from the edge. We stagger backward. The guy hits the tower's siding with a resonating *bwong!*

I topple against him, feeling the punch of his heart at my back. His arms remain shackled around me.

"It's . . . okay." The climber's ragged breath blows the hair at my neck. Heat radiates from his body, carrying the scent of sweat and something clean like dryer sheets. "I've . . . I've got you. I won't let you fall. I won't let you fall." Despite the insane strength of his arms, the rest of him shakes.

I wriggle in the stranger's grip. "Let me go!"

His heart continues jackhammering. "Only if you promise to keep away from the edge."

"Okay, I promise! Now loosen your death grip before you shatter my ribs!"

He immediately drops his arms.

"Thank you." I heave a breath of relief and turn. His eyes are first to demand my attention. They're brown. Brown isn't always memorable, but his are. It's as though something lights them from within. But maybe it's just the glow from the setting sun.

"What are you doing up here?" I ask.

"I'm saving you, *obviously.*" The last bit comes out in a wheeze as his tall frame doubles over to brace his hands on his knees. His back sags with another heavy exhalation.

"Saving me," I repeat with a bemused smirk. "Which is why you're the one needing CPR?"

Ignoring my remark, he squints down, pushing the damp hair at his forehead. "Um . . . It's really high up here." The guy doesn't appear to be trembling anymore

6

but remains less than steady. He slides down to a sitting position against the tower.

"Well, yeah. That's sorta the point."

The breeze shifts, plastering my vintage yellow dress to my body. Sure, there was a time I felt self-conscious about my curviness. But the hourglass gene wasn't something I could alter with diet or exercise. It was simply a force of nature—easier to accept than fight.

His face flushes darker and he quickly looks away. "Look, whatever it is, this *can't* be the solution. Because if you think jumping off a tower is going to be—"

"I am *not* a jumper!" I cry. "How many times do I have to tell you guys? Sometimes I come up here to think, to clear my head, not . . . *flatten it.*" My gaze wanders the vista. I don't need daylight or twenty-twenty vision to know how Carlisle's homes and businesses align in static rows. Or how the railroad tracks suture the well-to-do east side to the blue-collar west. There's the hazy outline of the three smokestacks guarding the south, smokestacks that watch everything with winking, tireless eyes. There is place and purpose to every single thing if you're high enough to see it.

"Being up here gives me a different perspective, you know? Sometimes it's all a person needs." I bend to collect my scattered belongings, shoving my papers into my bag before he can question the scrambled charts and lists of signs.

"Whoa, whoa . . . wait." His dark brows knit. "You seriously climbed all the way up here just . . . to think?"

I nod.

He scratches his head; dark hair sticks up every which way. Somehow I get the impression his hair is a serial misbehaver.

"Well, I came to think and for the Milky Way." I tap the mini telescope in the side pocket of my bag. "I'm referring to the band of stars. Not the candy bar."

"So I gather." He gives the ladder a sideways glance and gulps.

"Summer's the best time for viewing, and up here, it's easier to see without all the light pollution from the city." I squint. "Sun should be fully set soon; then it'll be spectacular. Hey, did you know some Native Americans believed the Milky Way to be a pathway for departed souls? Like a sort of astral skyway they traveled until they found a star to inhabit. And you know what's even more amazing?"

He shakes his head.

"Some scientists are predicting a supernova will be visible inside the Milky Way within the next fifty years! Can you imagine? Witnessing a star going supernova in our very own galaxy! That moment a star dies, it explodes and emits the most brilliant . . ." My smile collapses when I find him staring like I've just declared the moon made of cheese. "Sorry. I, um, didn't mean to go all tangential on you. I'm Wil, by the way." I offer my hand. "Wil Carlisle."

Yes, the same Carlisle our fair Midwestern city is named for. Some quadruple great-uncle or other founded it back in 1847. Which is reason enough for Gram to live and die here.

He rises before taking my hand in his. "You're kind of an unusual girl. No offense, Wil."

I grin. "Yeah, well, I tried ordinary once and got bored."

"I'm Grant, Grant Walker. And somehow"—he gives his head a small shake—"that doesn't shock me." When he finally smiles, it is for real. It shows in his eyes and where his skin touches mine.

My pulse unexpectedly flutters. "So, Grant Walker"—I pull back my hand, wiping my palm down my dress—"mind calling your friend off suicide watch? As you can see, I'm pretty intent on living." I notice four lines of orangey-brown where the metal rail has left marks across my midsection. I look like a grilled banana. Awesome. I brush at the unmoving lines.

"Yeah, about that. Unfortunately, I think it might be—"

Wee ooh, wee ooh, wee ooh.

The distant wail draws nearer. I jerk my head up.

"Too late," he finishes with a grimace.

Several police cars and a fire truck barrel down the side road, red lights whirling, sirens screaming. Rocks spray, ricocheting off the base of the tower as the truck screeches to a halt. I watch in horror as firemen and emergency personnel spill from their vehicles. They're barking orders while unfurling a large trampoline that bears a striking resemblance to the Japanese flag.

This. Can't. Be. Happening.

A nasally voice projects over a loudspeaker. *"Wah-wah, wah-wah-wah. Waaaahhh!"*

I can't make heads or tails of what's being said because

the guy is smothering the mic with his mouth. I'll assume he's telling me not to jump.

I bury my face in my hands, sending my glasses askew. All I wanted was a little peace and perspective. Instead, I get a circus. My only consolation is there aren't any clowns.

Stars in heaven, Gram will kill me. *Kill* me. I've gotten myself in some pretty bizarre twists, but this one's a cake-topper.

"Damn!" Grant rakes his hand through his hair. His expression offers the apology his mouth doesn't deliver. Giving his hair a rest, he asks, "So what do we do now?"

I shake my head and blow out a breath. "Now we go down there and explain what a huge misunderstanding this was. *Is.*"

Grant starts inching over to the steep ladder, back flat to the tower's surface. The color has completely drained from his face.

I stand beside him, following his line of sight down the hundred-plus rungs. "Grant?"

His eyes are unfocused. "Huh?"

"Are you . . . are you that afraid of heights?" There's an affirmative bob from his Adam's apple. "Well, what on earth *possessed* you to come charging up here?"

"Adrenaline," he snaps. "I *thought* you were about to jump. And you were pacing. And *you*"—he points—"you wouldn't respond to anything we said!"

"I had earbuds in!" I cry with a flap of my arms.

"Ooh, well, *now* I know you're a music aficionado!"

Grant shouts mockingly over the whooping sirens. He holds up a hand. "Sorry . . . I'm sorry." Working to un-kink the lines of panic on his face, he adds, "Look, I'm not phobic or anything. Heights just make me a little"—he sways—"uncomfortable."

I take his arm to steady his teetering form. "Easy there. Hey, look at me." I give him my most reassuring you'll-live-to-see-another-day smile. "Stay with me. It's gonna be okay, Grant. I promise. I've been up and down this ladder more times than I can count. We'll just take it one step at a time. I'll even go first. All right?"

The nasally fireman is making out with the mic again. I wish he'd stop. It only agitates Grant.

"No," he says, sliding his hands up and down on his jeans. Grant grips the top rung as his nostrils flare with determination. "I'll go first."

I pat the tense muscles of his back, doubting there's a soft spot on him. "Okay, you've totally got this. You can do it."

His mouth twists in a grim line. "Yeah."

I wait until he's made decent progress before I climb on. He's moving, slow and steady . . . well, steady enough.

"You're doing great!" I holler. We clamber down the ladder as I continue to shout random encouragements. I'm not sure if it helps. Grant's been funeral-procession quiet for a while now. I squint, trying to assess the remaining distance. "Almost halfway there!" I report. Give or take.

The breeze, which had the civility to die down, notches up again. My dress flutters. I've been so preoccupied with keeping Grant from full-on freak-out that it doesn't sink in. It takes me all of four rungs to realize why I feel so airy.

No. I freeze.

Why? Why today? Because it's laundry day, *that's* why. And I was out of clean bikinis. So I had to opt for the scrap of beige lace balled in the back of my drawer. Emergency use only.

A thong.

An effing thong.

My forehead thunks to my arm. When I consulted my daily horoscope, it said to consider new prospects for current obstacles. Nowhere, repeat, *nowhere* did it tell me to consider my prospect in undies!

"Wil? What's wrong? Why'd you—"

"Don't look up!" I shriek.

"Why, what's . . ." Silence. *Blaring* silence.

I squeeze my eyes shut. "If you're finished with your study of my backside, can we keep moving?"

"I, uh . . ." Grant clears his throat, snapping his head down. "I don't know how to answer that without being offensive. But thank you," he says over the resuming creak of the ladder.

"Don't mention it. Seriously. Ever."

"No, I just mean"—he chuckles nervously—"for a second there I almost forgot my fear of—"

CLUNK!

"Grant!" Twisting my neck, I see he's missed a rung completely and has slid down to the next. There's a groan of rusted metal giving way. Part of the ladder is breaking. I scramble to close the space between us, to try to catch his flailing arm. "Grab my hand!" Knees slightly bent, I lean back. All my muscles quiver as I strain to reach him from above. "Grab it!"

Shouts erupt. Sirens woot. The firemen jostle to position.

Grant's brown eyes are wide and terrified as his grip loosens. In sheer panic, he reaches out. His hand clamps around my ankle.

I am not prepared for that.

The bottom of my ballet flat slides, slipping effortlessly beneath me. Corrosion scrapes my palm. My knee gongs against the metal. I scream.

And Grant is falling.

Correction . . . *we* are falling.

We sink like graceless stones through darkening sky. My yellow dress flaps—useless, broken wings at my sides. For a nanosecond, I wonder if I'm flashing the world my full moons. Butts aren't meant to be seen moving at this velocity.

Then it hits me. I could die!

And here I am, traveling at the speed of ass, and I can't form a single profound thought. Pray. Yeah, I should pray. . . .

Dear God, please don't let me die. I promise to be a better person and be more efficient with my laundry and . . . and to never wear these devil's panties again.

"Aaameeennnnn!"

Grant yells, too, but I doubt he's bargaining with God over his choice in Skivvies.

He touches down first with a muffled thud.

My impact closely follows. *"Uuuhhh!"* The trampoline stings my skin; all the air is slapped from my lungs. I bounce and my head strikes something hard.

I see stars. I blink to clear my vision.

Faces hover in a frantic circle above, red lights streaking across them. Mouths are moving, but I don't hear what they're saying over the ocean in my ears. A fireman with a push-broom mustache is directly over me. He spittles when he talks. He needs a bigger mustache.

If this is heaven, I want my money back.

There's a dip in the fabric as someone moves. His face appears inches from mine. Full lips, prominent straight nose, and those striking brown eyes all volley for my attention. *Lush.* If Webster gave me only one word to describe Grant's features, that's the one I'd pick. Did I notice that before? Yes. No. Maybe. My head is fuzzy. It's made fuzzier by his concerned gaze. His lips compress in a tight line. I want to tell him not to worry. I'm alive. Honestly, I've never felt more so. And my heart is slamming so hard, I'm sure it registers on a Richter scale somewhere.

"Wil?" My name tumbles from his lips; it is the only sound I hear. Like sound didn't exist until this very moment. "Wil? Are you hurt?" He brushes back the hair at my cheek, inspecting my temple.

The grin on my face feels crooked, like a picture frame you tap this way and that, impossible to level. "Grant . . ."

He leans closer, eyes searching. I can smell the fabric softener and summer on him. His fingers continue to linger on my face. "Can you hear me? Are you hurt?"

"I hear you, Grant . . . Parker."

His shoulders drop as he lets out a shaky laugh. "It's Walker, actually."

"Whatever," I mumble.

The earth spins faster and faster, blurring the people and commotion around me. Dark clouds mushroom my vision, leaching color from the world.

I must be falling.

But how can you fall when you've already hit the ground?

chapter 2

"What do you mean, 'There was an incident at the water tower'?" Gram's got a shriek that rivals the sonar system used by bats; I instantly cringe. "Where's my granddaughter? I demand to know her condition!"

Letting out a soft sigh, I sink back into the flat-as-a-pancake hospital pillow. I know, without moving my blue privacy curtain a centimeter, that the lines on Gram's face have just carved themselves deeper. And I'm certain the silver hairs on her head are now outnumbering the black ones. She's probably even clutching the crucifix that rarely sees the light of day because it's buried in her cavernous bosom.

How many times have I been the reason for Gram's hold on the cross? Sadly, too many to count.

My fingers gingerly probe the lump on my head. It isn't *so* bad. At least, my hair provides a nice camouflage. Except for the dull headache—which I attribute less to the lump, and more to the suffocating lemon-scented hospital disinfectant—I really can't complain.

"Now, Mrs. Carlisle . . ." The doctor's calm, authoritative voice drifts from the hallway as he attempts to smooth Gram's ruffled feathers. Yeah, good luck with that. Gram is all Taurus, all the time. And while she can be slow to rile, once she does—well, it's best to batten down the hatches and ride out the storm. Because you don't have a prayer of stopping it.

When the doctor's finally able to get a word in edgewise, he explains the procedural CAT scan and physical exams confirmed everything is normal, other than the small knot on my head and sizeable contusion on my left knee. But seriously, I would take countless bruises and knocks to the head, just to avoid facing Gram right now.

In true Genevieve Carlisle fashion, she bursts into another litany of questions. "How did this happen? Doctor, young girls don't spontaneously drop from water towers! Just who in the name of Hades was responsible for this?"

Who in the name of Hades? Despite the gravity of my situation, my mouth forms an involuntary grin. That is a phrase Mama used with regularity. Maybe she inherited it from Gram, or Gram from her, but I always thought of them as *Mama's* words.

And Mama's words are something that will stay with me forever. Like the smell of her burning sage—pungent, herbal, and sweet—and the beat-up card table she made mystical with a scrap of brilliant purple satin.

My mother always had a fondness for vibrant colors. Colors just like the ones in the van Gogh print hanging on the hospital wall. In fact, I bet I could pluck the exact shade of yellow from those swirling sunflowers that was the color of her favorite dress.

I close my eyes, letting my mind drift to the last time I saw her in that dress. It was an event I'll never forget. Because it was the first time I ever saw my astrological chart.

There it was. My entire destiny neatly confined to $8\frac{1}{2}$ by 11 inches of paper. Every cell in my six-year-old body fizzled like a shaken-up can of soda ready to explode. And my wide eyes devoured the paper with its scatter of funny shapes sprinkled about the wheel-like image. I didn't know what any of it meant.

But Mama did.

"Tell me what you see, Mena?" Mama asked. Her eyes sparkled like sapphires in the candlelight.

"A chart! Like the ones you read for people. And it shows where all the planets were in the constellations the very minute I was born," I proudly announced.

Mama held her finger to her red lips with a look of warning. "We must keep this our little secret. Your gram wouldn't understand."

The small, forgotten space on the third floor with its stacks of sealed boxes and dusty sheets was made for keeping secrets. I was not. But I would try.

"One day you'll be fluent in the language of the stars," she said. "But for today, I will read them for you. Okay, sweetheart?"

"Yes!" I squealed. Then quickly clapped my hands over my mouth.

Mama went on to explain how the pair of zigzaggy lines meant I was Aquarius—a truth-teller and seeker of life knowledge. How I must be careful not to let my free spirit and tireless need for independence cause me to push others away. I wasn't judgmental, nor did I put on airs, but *horns of Taurus,* I could be as persistent as the itch of poison ivy.

"These wedges"—she tapped at the pie-like sections of my chart—"are called houses—there are twelve total. And each house represents a certain aspect of our lives. For instance, the First House is the House of Self, *who you are.* The Second, right here"—she pointed beside the First House—"is the House of Money and Possessions. Then we have—"

"*Ooh!* What about these symbols?" I asked, skipping a few houses around the wheel.

Mama quieted for a moment; her dark brows pinched together. "That's the Fifth House. The House of Creativity and . . ." The word seemed to get stuck in her mouth. Clutching the chunk of amethyst on her necklace, she began rolling it between her fingers as she stared at my chart. And whatever stared back made the frown stretch lower on her face.

"And what, Mama?" My ballet tutu felt itchy. Or maybe I was just itchy to understand why the squiggles on my chart made her so full of sadness.

"Come here, Mena," she said, quickly brushing her fingers under her eyes.

"N'kay." I slid from my seat. The creaky attic floorboards moaned as my feet touched them.

Mama then lifted me, setting me on her lap. She always smelled like rain mixed with flowers. "The Fifth House is also the House of Love—of Heart," she explained. "And I now see that this will be your greatest challenge to overcome. Just as it has been mine."

I fiddled with the stone hanging from her necklace, trying to understand what could possibly be hard about love. Because it was pretty clear to me boys were gross and should be avoided like black jelly beans.

"You see, sweetheart, there was a time I thought I knew better than the stars. When I fell in love with your daddy, I thought it could be enough. But"—her head shook—"fate doesn't always follow our heart. It follows this." She tapped the paper. "Our astrological chart holds the key to all the answers. But you must *listen* to this wisdom, Mena—*especially* in matters of love."

I gazed up at her. "I'll listen, Mama. I promise."

"And"—she frowned once more—"beware of Pisces. That is a poor match that would only bring you heartache."

My head bobbed.

"Good girl." Mama kissed my forehead and took off her necklace, placing it around my neck. "I want you to have this."

I blinked. "But . . . it's your favorite." And of all her pretty, sparkly jewelry, it was my favorite, too. "How come?"

"Because I love you."

Throwing my arms around her, I pressed myself like a second skin to her sunny yellow dress. "Love you, too, Mama."

"For longer than the stars will shine above," she whispered.

The snap of the curtain as Gram flicks it aside with the force of a matador tugs me out of the past. And while the subtle ache of missing my mother still lingers, I force myself to focus on my present quandary.

"Mena!" She throws her arms around me briefly before pulling away. "What in heaven's name—let me have a look at you, child." Sure enough, the lines on her face grow more determined as she inspects the bruise on my knee and the small bump on my head. Now, last I checked, there wasn't an MD after her name, but I have the good sense to keep quiet and let her finish. "Hmm." She holds my chin, gently directing my head left then right.

"Gram, I'm fine, I swear. *Gram*"—I end her exam by retreating back into the pancake pillow—"I'm *okay*. See?" I smile widely, proving once and for all I'm alive and well.

"Well, I'm delighted to hear it." She places her hands on her hips. "Because you've got a lot of explaining to do, young lady. What in blue blazes gave you the notion to scale that tower?"

I consult the hospital wristband on my arm, which offers no helpful answer. "Uh . . ." I gulp and squirm under Gram's steady gaze. "The Milky Way?"

Her mouth puckers like she's swallowed vinegar. "*Tell me* this does not have to do with *astrology*. Because I believe I've made myself quite clear about spending too much time with your head stuck in the cl—"

"It's astronomy," I correct under my breath. I mean, technically, I *was* up there to see the Milky Way. Gram doesn't need to know the superfluous details.

"Oh? Is that meant to be amusing, Wilamena Grace?"

To avoid digging myself deeper, I answer with the only response she's keen on hearing. "No, ma'am."

"Good. Now start talking."

Gram's not mad. Not anymore anyway. Following last night's hospital discharge and my glowing health pronouncement, I was forbidden by Gram *and* the city of Carlisle from ever climbing the water tower again. Which is tantamount to telling a bird not to fly. I memorize their exact words and vow to find a loophole once the ladder's repaired.

But I won't be curtailed by yesterday's debacle. No way. I reason when you survive a forty-something-foot drop, things have nowhere to go but up.

And it's Sunday—an auspicious day for an Aquarian. The card in my hand confirms today's stroke of luck. His signature is scribbled on the front, along with the words "admit two." I flip over the Carlisle Community Hospital business card, rereading the compact slanted writing on the back.

Wil (aka Gravity Goddess),
   Deepest apologies. Please accept this olive branch.
   I hope you can come.
                              Grant (aka Gravity Amateur)
PS This is your ticket.
PPS Absinthe—Sunday 8 PM

Absinthe is a hot music club on the city's west side, featuring up-and-coming indie bands. It's damn near impossible to gain entry without having an in, which I've never had . . . until now.

I tap the card on my thumbnail, ignoring the unexpected swell of nervousness. But I have no reason to be nervous. The day could not be better aligned. I pocket the card the nurse had discreetly given me, and smooth on a layer of my signature red Parisian Pout lipstick—the only makeup I wear most days.

"Gram?" I shove my keys and phone in my purse and heft the overnight bag onto my shoulder. "Gram? I'm leaving!"

"Hold on!" she hollers from the kitchen, moving to the entryway as fast as her arthritic knee allows. She pushes a basket into my hand. "You be sure and give these to Irina. Lord knows that girl could stand to have some meat on her bones." Gram's convinced all the problems of the world can be solved with baked goods. As the aroma of banana-nut muffins funnels to my nose, I'm not inclined to argue. Really, who doesn't find peace in simple carbs?

"Thanks. I'll be back in the morning. Oh, and bleed 'em dry at bridge club." I turn to leave.

"Mena"—she catches my elbow—"you certain you're well enough to be out and about?"

Okay. Subtlety isn't Gram's modus operandi, but it's recently dawned on her I'm graduating in a year. I'm not a kid anymore, which . . . she knows. Still, it's a massive change in her thinking. *Change.* Nothing is more excruciating to a Taurus.

"We've gone over this already, Gram. The doctor said my vitals are perfectly fine. I've rested all day and can report zero headaches, blurred vision, or dizziness. Now, I'm gonna be late. And so are you if you don't finish up that order."

Carlisle Confections has been Gram's business for over three decades. She makes delicious designer cupcakes and treats for the overprivileged who can afford them. She's a sort of Monet of the baking world. And, not to brag, but I know my way around a baking tin. Gram's had me assisting since my motor skills were reliable enough for precise measurements. Too bad I don't possess one iota of Gram's decorating panache. Nope, I leave that in her capable hands.

I kiss her soft cheek, perfumed by cinnamon and toasted nuts. "You worry too much."

"You give me plenty to worry for, child," she barks as I skip down the warping front steps of our old Victorian. "You keep away from that water tower!"

"I will!"

Which for today is the honest-to-God truth.

Adjusting the bag at my shoulder, I wait as traffic clears the crosswalk. My eyes fix on the freestanding single-story brick building. Its neon sign flashes: INKPORIUM TATTOO & PIERCING. Wexler Street isn't the slums, per se, but it also isn't the side of town where you want to look lost. Yes, Gram knows I come here. But Gram also remembers Wexler as it *was,* not as it *is.* Now it's a mix of pawnshops, bars, and check-cashing facilities that get seedier the farther west you go.

The bell chimes as I push through the glass door. Heavy guitars assault the speakers, and the vocals sound like someone with a wicked case of stomach flu.

"How's the sheep, Bo Peep?" Crater calls without looking up from his artistry. His string-bean frame is hunched, vertebrae poking from beneath his T-shirt.

The burly customer in Crater's chair quickly wipes the pain from his expression. While he might be wearing a brave face, his complexion is paler than milk and he's squeezing the life out of the armrest.

"Crate, I wore that dress *once* and it was adorable," I holler over the metal music. "Just because it was white and had crinoline, it does not make me a sheepherder!" But arguing's a lost cause. Once Crater names you, it's as permanent as his tattoos. Could be worse. I could have Irina's nickname. "How'd you know it was me?"

"Because." Crater adjusts the volume before turning around to swap out vials of ink. Then he flicks the overgrown Mohawk from his eye and grins. "You smell like a bakery. Dead giveaway."

I grin wryly. "Hazard of living in one, I guess."

"Least you're not the old lady who lived in her shoe. Imagine if you had to go around smelling like a foot."

I laugh, then peer down at the sample tattoos in the portfolio that lies open on the counter. The page shows off every ornate dragon tattoo Crater has ever done, along with every place he's ever put them. *Oh . . . eww.* I can't fathom a reason to tattoo *that* part of my body. I swiftly close the book.

The guy in the chair squirms and grimaces. "How much longer, man?"

"Hour," Crater snaps. "Maybe more if you keep up your worm-wiggling." Good thing what the twenty-something tattoo artist lacks in charm, he makes up for with talent.

Crate glances back to where my hand rests on the portfolio. "Just promise when you finally decide to ink that virginal skin, you'll come to me. Don't trust anyone else. I'll practically do it gratis."

"I promise." And it's a promise I have to reaffirm virtually every time I step foot in Inkporium. Crater, in his way, is very sweet. He's also very Leo, so I forgive his fixed and headstrong ways. He can't help that his ruling planet is the Sun.

The electric needle whines as Crater resumes his work on Worm-Wiggler. "The harpy's in back." He means Irina. "Hey, you got anything in that basket for me?"

I take out one of the muffins and set it on the counter. "You're lucky I'm feeling charitable today."

He pauses, sniffing the air. "Banana-nut?"

"Yep."

"Right on. Later, Bo Peep." Crater winks—lion through and through. The incessant buzzing drowns out the sound of his chuckle at my annoyed expression. Stupid nickname.

I head for the narrow hall toward Irina's private studio. The exposed brick on my right is littered with leaflets for local bands, local support groups, and local . . . well, you name it. I slow at a flyer for Absinthe showcasing a band called Wanderlust. Nice name. A lot better than Charred Biscuits or Pocketful of Lint.

Irina's door is ajar. About now I'm really hoping Crate didn't send me down here if she's with a client. I'd pass out if I walked in on a piercing in progress—not to mention those south-of-the-border ones. Seriously. Irina's pierced everything you can imagine, and a whole lot you can't.

"Knock, knock?" I give the door a little push. I gain more confidence when I see the reclining chair in the center of the room is empty. Thankfully, Irina's alone. The studio itself is small and well lit, with a perpetual scent of rubbing alcohol.

Irina holds up a finger. She then points to the phone in her hand and rolls her eyes. It's her *tetya,* her aunt. My friend replies in an equally loud stream of Russian. Irina is first-generation Russian American. But I suspect the shouting will be multigenerational.

"She's mad," Iri translates in perfect English as she hangs up. "When am I going to settle down, find a nice American man like she did—blah-blah-blah. What's new, right?" Irina has this theory that her *tetya* talks for two since her uncle rarely speaks. "Oh, and fair warning, she's making borscht for dinner. Which you're going to have to pretend you *love* unless you want to start another cold war."

My toes curl. "Then I'll love the hell outta that icky pink soup, because your *tetya* is scary."

"Yeah." Irina plucks a few platinum strands of her long hair from her tunic. "But better than my mom."

The fact that she's brought up her mom is more jarring than hearing her switch from Russian to English.

Iri *never* talks about her mom. Any more than she talks about why, at the age of twelve, she came to America with her aunt. But I've pieced together enough to know there was poverty. Neglect. And that it was likely her mom's drinking and the revolving door of men that caused Iri's aunt to assume guardianship. I also know it took almost five thousand miles to create a comfortable distance from that past.

I quickly change the subject.

"So, what's with the flowering cactus?" I ask of the tiny plant beside the sink, dumping my stuff on the nearest counter.

She smirks. "Oh, *that*. I had a consultation earlier with this guy. He asked for my number."

I pull out the doctor's-office-like stool and take a seat. "And? Did you give it to him?"

Her tall and thin form stoops as she restocks the cupboard beneath the sink with gloves. "I gave him *a* number. I think it was to some support group for the wheat

intolerant—Wheat Beaters maybe?" She shrugs. While Irina's only a couple of years older than me, sometimes it feels more like twenty.

"You didn't!" I laugh. "And he got you a cactus because you're so prickly? That's kinda clever and cute."

"Or maybe it's because I work with lots of needles. Either way, I don't think I could date anyone named Jordan Lockwood."

"Jordan Lockwood sounds like he wears a suit."

"Actually, he does—total stiff. Hey, what's the deal with you not texting me back last night?" Her kohl-lined gray eyes glint, competing with the diamond Monroe piercing above her lip.

"Oh. Last night was a *spectacular* disaster. I mean, I *really* outdid myself."

Her forehead immediately furrows. It doesn't take much to rouse Irina's protective-lioness streak. Not surprising she and Crater are always butting heads. Two Leos under one roof is one Leo too many. "Are you okay? What happened, *dorogaya*?"

So I tell her—everything. Right down to flashing my undies.

Irina stops the fretful turning of her diamond stud to ask, "Wait. Since when do you wear thongs? I thought they were your sworn enemy. You called them ass floss."

"Laundry day."

"Ah." Her head tips knowingly. She opens a drawer that contains clamps and a slew of medieval torture devices.

Looking at the hostile implements, I recall the exact

sensation of how my navel retreated to my spine the day I met my Russian friend. My belly button never did get pierced those two years ago, but we forged a close bond anyway.

"Really? That's your only question?"

"Well, the other things seemed to be more"—she waves her hand—"in character. Speaking of in character, you haven't even asked about my surprise. You're usually a curious kitten."

Before I can reply, Oscar—another piercer at Inkporium—appears at the door. His short black hair has a streak of vibrant blue in the front, similar to the color of Irina's shirt. Because of his bold appearance and carved features, people never expect him to be as soft-spoken as he is.

"I'm heading out." Oscar crams one of his infamous battered copies of Shakespeare into the outer pouch of his backpack. "Hey, Wil." He gives me a cursory glance. And I will never get why the Almighty would gift a guy such amazing eyelashes. Oscar's hazel eyes briefly pan back to Irina's fishnets as she bends to shut the bottom drawer. "So, Iri"—he cracks his knuckles—"the new seafood place on the riverfront is getting rave reviews. Can I interest you in—"

"Sorry, Wil and I already have plans."

"Oh . . . okay." Oscar toys with the ring on his lower lip, his thoughts as cryptic as his expression. "Maybe another time. Later."

"Bye," I say as he slips away.

The back door slams shut and I swivel to Iri. "Uh, ex-

cuse me, comrade, but did something happen between you two?"

Irina hefts her messenger bag, decorated with metal rivets. She waves her hand airily. "We might've made out at a party last night."

My mouth drops open. I fight gravity to pull it shut. Irina rarely breaks her own rules, I think because there are so few to follow. "But doesn't that go against your strict no-messing-with-coworkers policy?"

"Momentary lapse in judgment. Won't happen again." A wistful grin touches her lips. "Pity, though. Why is it always the quiet ones who make the best kissers?" She shakes her head.

"You and *Oscar*?" I'm going to need a crash helmet. "Sure, he's cute but"—I scrunch my face—"seems like a lot of hardware to negotiate."

Irina rolls her eyes. "And this observation would be coming from your extensive make-out experience?" She laughs when I give her a playful shove. "All right, grab your stuff and let's fly."

On the drive to her place, I'm quiet. I can't shake the joke about my "extensive experience." Of course, she's fully aware I've never had a serious boyfriend. I'm just not sure if she's aware why.

Irina pauses at a stop sign before rolling through. "What's wrong?"

I pull my gaze from the signs advertising liquor and lotto tickets outside the corner store. "What do you mean?"

"There's always something wrong when you breathe

like that. Like you inexplicably have an oxygen short-age."

How she could discern my breathing over the deaf-ening exhaust system of her '95 Ford Taurus—lovingly named Natasha—is miraculous. I angle toward her and take another breath. "Okay, I need to tell you something, but you have to promise not to laugh."

Her eyes veer from the road, measuring my seriousness. She holds up her pinky, which, in turn, I hook in mine. We shake.

"All right, here goes. Irina, I think there's a possibility I might be . . . *asexual.*"

She snorts, quickly clamping her lips together.

"Okay, that, that right there, counts!" I holler. "Asexu-ality is a very real and legitimate condition. I looked it up."

Irina works to regain the neutrality in her face. "You're not asexual, Wil. You were not given that body to be asexual. It would be a crime against nature."

I sniff, recalling how Brody Cooper had kissed me fresh-man year under the football-field bleachers. His tongue had done a full cavity search of my mouth. It was *disgust-ing* and totally pointless, seeing as how I already have a dentist and my own saliva.

And it wasn't like sophomore year had gone any bet-ter when I dated Dylan "The Dyson" Murphy for an eye blink. The guy took the phrase "sucking face" way too literally. If I'd ever sought proof of my ill-fated romantic endeavors, then those boys had delivered it.

"Yeah? Well, tell that to my underwhelmed teenage libido." I sigh, pushing shut the temperamental glove box. "Maybe I'm just being too picky. You know, Gram's got this theory that I'm a late bloomer. Which is sort of tragically funny given my measurements."

"You haven't met the right person, Wil. The right person will change *everything.*"

I shake my head. "I don't know. The fact is, I lack . . . *passion!*" The word explodes from my chest. "How am I supposed to embark on a search for the love of my life without *passion*? I'm so screwed." I poke her arm. "And I'm ending our friendship if you make a joke about that."

We stop at a traffic light. *"Dorogaya moya."* Irina gazes with a softness that can't be masked by heavy makeup or an abundance of piercings. Beauty this delicate and pure can't be hardened, even by metal. But she tries anyway. Her fingers close around mine. "You live life with more passion than most people I know. Just because you don't have the burning desire to hike up your dress for every guy with a line doesn't mean you have a medical condition."

"Pfft, you're confusing living and loving."

Her eyes narrow as Natasha lurches forward, tires squawking. "And you're an absolute fool if you think there's a difference." She mutters something else in Russian.

"(A) I'm not a fool. And (b) don't call me a hemorrhoid."

"I didn't call *you* a hemorrhoid. I'm talking to the Corsica who just cut me off." She lays on the horn and waves her middle finger. "And your Russian is far too literal, Wil. Hand me my bag."

I grumble my displeasure, but dutifully reach in the backseat, hoisting the bag between us.

She swerves in the process of her search. "Aha!" She pulls out a folded paper, tossing it to my lap. "Your birthday came early. *That's* my surprise."

I unfold it, pushing up my glasses. "An astrological chart?"

Her mouth curls up at the corner. "You know how you only have twenty-two days to find your perfect match?"

"Twenty-one now, but yeah."

"Well, I might've fast-tracked it." She smiles triumphantly. "Wilamena Carlisle, say hello to Mr. Right."

I snap my head up. "Is this . . . ?"

"You bet your sweet, star-obsessed ass. I discovered this program where you can upload your chart and cross-reference it with tons of potential matches. What you have in your hand is the one ranked most astrologically compatible."

"But . . . how did I not know about this?"

Iri shrugs. "Probably because your nose is always buried in one of your books. Repeat after me—*technology is your friend.*"

Of course I'd seen the sites that ranked the most compatible signs, but isolating it right down to the date of birth? This was taking matchmaking to a new stratosphere. My shaky finger traces the circle. "He's Sagittarius."

I should be jumping for joy. I'm not. Panic is making my arteries collapse like slashed tires. I am actually going to have to go through with this.

"You look scared shitless," Irina says.

"No I don't. This is my thinking face." She gives me a disbelieving sideways glance. "What? *It is*. I'm fine . . . really. Besides, this is my lucky day. I can't lose. And at least now we can narrow our search to a Sagittarius. So"—I clear my throat, gazing at the paper in my unsteady hands—"all we have to do is find him."

"Where should we start looking? Oh! I know a guy at the Vault who would let us in, no question."

Grant's card with free admission to Absinthe develops a pulse in my pocket. "Actually, I, um, I think I know the perfect place."

My match is out there somewhere waiting to be discovered.

And secretly I am hoping, hoping that by discovering him, I will discover the parts of myself that lie dormant.

I only hope it isn't too late to bloom.

Chapter 3

Our heels click in unison through the parking lot as we draw closer to the unremarkable cinder-block building. This is part of Carlisle's crumbling and forgotten warehouse district. Smack in the middle of the city's wasteland, Absinthe glows, a pale-green beacon in the night.

Irina stops to fish something from her high heel—heels tall enough to give me a nosebleed—then adjusts her black corset. "By the way, you look *smoldering.*"

"Oh." I frown at my button-down shirt and fitted pencil skirt. "I was going for understated, you know? Casual chic, nothing that screamed *I'm here and desperate to find my soul mate.*"

She bursts out laughing. "I'm sure you were. Unfortunately, there's no such thing as an *understated* naughty librarian. Textbook guy fantasy—pun intended."

I scowl.

"Don't be mad. Come here. I just need to make a minor wardrobe . . . there," she says as she deftly frees the second button of my blouse.

"Wh—"

"*Because.*" Her arm hooks in mine as we continue to the club's entrance. "I'd give my left ovary for breasts that magnificent, and you never even show them off. People pay top dollar for those."

I have to admit, I can breathe better. "Well, I don't need to show them off," I grumble. "They practically enter the room before I do."

The line to get into Absinthe snakes all the way around the side of the building, stopping shy of the trash bins in back.

Twenty minutes pass, and I'm still standing next to the same broken Bic pen and gum wrapper.

"This is asinine." Irina picks at her dark fingernail, a baleful eye on the scores of people ahead of us. "They can't possibly expect anyone to stand in a line this long. Let me see that card." Handing it over, she reads the back, brow raised. "Gravity Goddess?"

"He was being funny." I search for the moon in the dark sky before remembering it is a new moon. That's good, ideal for tackling new endeavors.

"You didn't tell me his name was Grant."

"Grant Walker. Why, do you know him?" I ask.

"I know *of* him." Iri flashes a Cheshire grin. I bump my shoulder to hers. "What?" She tosses her blond tresses over her shoulder. "It's *rumor*. I don't speculate on other people's personal affairs."

"Well, your face is doing an excellent job of speculating. Oh, come on," I goad, "tell me."

She's about to speak when the giggling girls in front of us drop the bottle they've been passing. It shatters, sending bits of glass and sticky sweet liquor everywhere. My stomach curdles at the smell of high-octane cherry schnapps.

Irina shakes her high heel. "*Dura!* We're outta here, Wil. I am *done* with the waiting." She pulls me from the line.

Her legs are way longer and I struggle to keep up. I also struggle to ignore the burning glares as we line-jump. Thank God I'm not flammable.

She leans close to my ear. "I'll do the talking. Follow my lead, okay?"

I push up my glasses and nod. "I hope you have a plan."

"Are you joking? We already discussed the plan."

"Not this part. Not the part about needing a plan just to get in the club."

We approach the more daunting bouncer of the two stationed near the door. He isn't a man; he is a wall—a wall of honed muscle. The greenish hue of the lights reflects off his shaved head. While this African American bouncer's stance is relaxed, his eyes are calculating, drifting from face to face in the crowd.

The other bouncer casually sits at Absinthe's entrance, checking IDs. I do a double take at the sign by the door:

YOU MUST BE AT LEAST 18 YEARS OF AGE TO ENTER.
NO EXCEPTIONS.

I gulp. My suddenly dry throat feels as if it's stuck to-gether like sheets of flypaper. Irina's of age, so it's not an issue for her, but me . . .

"Ladies"—the fortress nods—"is there a problem?"

My eyes round. Um, yes, yes there is. There's a pulsat-ing, itchy hive forming at my side, and the sensation that my tongue has turned itself inside out, and the goiter on my neck. I touch it, oh wait, that's my carotid. Good, be-cause I can't handle . . .

Irina grips my hand firmly and gives me a tight smile before responding. "As a matter of fact, there is"—her eyes drop to the label on the walkie-talkie clipped to his belt—"Lucien, and I believe you're the only one who can help us." Her barely detectable accent makes a sudden grand appearance. Just as it always does when she feels it'll work to her advantage.

And if following her lead means looking seventeen and terrified, then I'm doing awesome. I try to relax my shoul-ders and appear indifferent.

"Is that so?" the bouncer replies. His brows do a subtle lift, intrigue overruling his skepticism.

"Da." Irina passes him the card. "You see, Grant Walker was expecting us over thirty minutes ago. And"—she bites her lip in dismay—"well, you know how he gets before a show."

"Huh. He gave this to you, did he?" The bouncer holds the card up to the light, presumably studying the signature. "Looks legit." He hands it back, giving us another once-over; Irina and I are so opposite and mismatched we somehow go together. "Tell me . . ."

"Irina," she supplies.

His white teeth gleam in the shadows. "Irina, just how many piercings do you have?"

"A lot."

"Anywhere interesting?"

This is the moment I know she has him. He is a fly in her web. She steps closer, wrapping him snug in her silken spider thread. Her mouth rises seductively at one corner. "I never pierce and tell."

Lucien chuckles. "Go on, then." He nods toward the door. "Don't wanna be more late. And, hey . . . *hey!*"

Our heads cautiously swivel back. Iri's squeezing my hand and I've forsaken breathing all together.

"Be careful in there." He says to me, "That goes for you, too, school teacher. Better guard those apples."

Anger steamrolls my short-lived relief. "And just what the hell do you mean b—"

"We will!" Irina nearly jerks my arm clean from its socket. "You're going to blow this," she warns.

"Mudak!" I hiss with a hostile glare.

Lucien cocks his head as Irina springs into damage control. "Uh, yes, *mudak* is our special way of saying . . . 'thank you' in Russian. Let's go, *dorogaya.*"

Her brow rises a fraction higher once we've distanced ourselves from the bouncer.

I huff. "Don't *even* start. That was totally justified."

"*Mudak?* After a year of being exposed to my Russian, you've only managed to learn swear words?" Irina clucks her tongue. "I'd be disappointed if I weren't so damn proud."

The door opens. Thumping music echoes down the tunnel-like entryway. I peer uncertainly up to Irina.

"After you," she says. "Let the hunt begin."

Pendants float from the high ceiling in a staggering display of emerald lights. The lounge adjacent to the bar has a bohemian hodgepodge of sofas and overstuffed chairs, sectioned off by thick velvet curtains. For now, the stage is empty, and the DJ spins trip-hop and off-the-grid electronica that makes me feel drunk despite being stone-cold sober.

Irina's chatting up a couple of guys near the crowded dance floor. Bodies bounce and move to the relentless rhythm. I point to the bar and she lifts her chin in acknowledgment.

Operation Soul Mate has been in full swing for almost an hour. Irina and I have split up to check out the club under the guise of "research" for a cutting-edge book on astrology I'm writing. Part of why I picked tonight's outfit—contrary to Iri's naughty-librarian jab—is that it has a *literary* air. We have a totally plausible excuse for approaching complete strangers to ask their astrological sign and date of birth. Not that *I* really need to ask. My skills are finely honed. I can often pinpoint a person's sun sign with alarming accuracy—based purely on observation.

Take the trendy cute guy standing next to me. His posture oozes confidence, and when he speaks, his buddies hang on every word. And there are a lot of words. But they're thrilling tales of white-water rafting and skydiving. The guy might as well be wearing a pair of ram horns. But I asked his birthday anyway. You can imagine my nonsurprise when he turned out to be Aries.

I haven't been wrong yet.

But despite my star savvy, the plan has been . . . an epic fail. It doesn't help that the place is crawling with Scorpios, which I'm most certainly *not* in the market for. And it *really* doesn't help that many of my astrological questions have been met with "whatever you want it to be," some quizzical stares, and one guy proudly claiming he was the cock.

As in Year of the Rooster.

As in the Chinese zodiac.

As in this will be the longest night of my life.

I've been dodging that guy the whole evening. This is one of the few instances where being slightly below average height has worked to my advantage.

A server dressed in a green sequined shift dress squeezes by, tray in hand. The fairy wings at her back are coated with green glitter. Right, Green Fairy is a nickname for absinthe liqueur. Someone was a marketing genius.

"Watch it!" a tall redhead snaps when I bump into her.

"Sorry." Seems the club has given me a case of sensory ADD.

The Amazonian laughs, dragging her glassy eyes up and down me. "What are you supposed to be, honey? I didn't know it was theme night."

"Myself," I answer.

She giggles before disappearing inside a velvet-draped alcove marked RESERVED. "Ooh!" The redhead's squeal is followed by male laughter. I don't stick around to hear the rest.

Spotting an empty seat at the bar, I carefully pick my way through the people. And wouldn't you know, just as I reach the stool, someone else slides into it.

Clearly, this dude didn't get the memo that it's my lucky day. I tap his shoulder. "Excuse me?"

He turns. "Yeah?"

Wow. He's really cute. Dark eyes and dark hair that's mussed in a way like he tried but didn't. Despite my previous declaration of a sexual flatline, I still know a good-looking boy when I see him. And there's something terribly familiar about him, but I don't know why.

"Oh, were you going to sit here?" He stands. "Here, go ahead, you take it."

"Really?" I refrain from kissing him in gratitude. "You are an absolute lifesaver! These shoes are killing my feet."

"I know exactly what you mean. That's why I left my heels at home. I only wear them on *very* special occasions." He's grinning as I clumsily hop up on the barstool. This below-the-knee pencil skirt was much better in theory.

I blow out a breath, finally settled, and brush back a drooping wave. "So, tonight isn't special?"

"It could be," he replies, his gaze lowering. "Those are a really nice pair by the way."

I prickle as I recall the open button of my shirt. I consider tossing my drink on him and then remember I don't have one.

He inclines his head toward my feet. "Your shoes, I mean."

"Right, yeah, I knew that."

"Well, that's good, because for a second there I thought you were going to slap me. By the way, I'm Seth."

"Not the Egyptian deity associated with chaos and destruction, I hope?" I ask.

"Hardly," he chuckles, "but my mom might have occasion to disagree." He motions to a bartender with ambitious sideburns. "Most people just call me plain Seth—no immortal Egyptian reference. How about you?"

"No. No one calls me Seth."

"Witty, adorable"—he ticks off on his fingers—"*and* wears stylishly painful shoes. If *only* she had a name."

I grin. "Wilamena. Most people just call me Wil . . . except for my grandmother."

"What does she call you?"

I fold my arms and shrug. "Typically, Mena—unless I'm in trouble. Then there's a sliding scale of names proportionate to the offense."

"Wondered if you'd show tonight." The bartender reappears, setting a glass of amber liquid in front of Seth.

"Warms my heart to know I'd be missed. Thanks, Nico." He tilts the glass in a toast.

"Anything I can get for you, doll?" Sideburns, er, Nico addresses me. His five-o'clock shadow grows more shadowy awaiting my answer.

"Um, just a ginger ale, please."

"You can get whatever you want." Seth gives me a knowing look. "Nico'll take care of you."

"Ginger ale is fine," I repeat. My dabbling with drinking has often led to a vomitous end, and tonight, a clear head is essential.

"Your wish is my command," Nico replies with a slight bow.

Seth rolls his eyes. "Mothers, hide your daughters. You should know he's like that with everyone. The flirting thing's compulsive."

"I'm guessing it makes for better tips."

"You'd guess right." Seth takes a drink and squints. "So, Wil, I have to ask . . . are you here with someone?"

"My friend Irina, why?"

His face is pensive. "Because that guy's been checking you out since you sat down."

"Really? Where?" I crane my neck.

"Other side of the bar. Oh, uh . . . looks like he's gone now."

Nico returns with my drink, eyes lighting on something behind me.

When I reach for my purse, Seth stills my hand. "Don't worry, I—"

"It's on the house," Nico cuts in, giving Seth a funny look.

"Figures," Seth mutters, setting his jaw.

"What figures?" I ask. But before Seth can answer, my purse starts vibrating along the bar. "Oh, um . . . that's probably my friend." Unsnapping the clutch, I struggle to liberate my cell from the inside pocket. I've crammed in so much, it's a minor miracle I was able to close it the first time.

Seth chuckles. "Can I get you a crowbar or something?"

I grin with a touch of embarrassment. "Maybe. This is what happens when you downsize your purse but not the number of—" Suddenly I catch Iri bobbing up and down and wildly waving her arms. I drop my bulging purse back on the bar. "Seth, can you wait here just a minute?"

He sees Irina impatiently bouncing around as if she's composed of ninety percent rubber. "Sure."

I squeeze my way through the crowd, rushing over to her. "What is it? What's wrong?"

Her red lips curl, the telltale huntress gleam is in her eyes. "Did you get my text?"

"No, I couldn't get to my—"

"Never mind." Irina grabs my shoulders, swiveling me slightly to the left. "What do you think of him? Hot, yeah?"

"Of who?" The strobe light flickers on a cluster of guys.

"*Him!*" She points to the tallest, Hulkiest figure in the group.

I make a face. "I think I would not date someone who wears a Charlie Brown T-shirt. He's Sagittarius?"

Irina expels a breath. "Not for you. For me! And it's not a Charlie Brown T-shirt."

"*This* is your emergency? Need I remind you of the mission at hand? *Jeez,* Iri, *focus,* would you?" I don't wait to hear her line of defense.

Returning to my barstool Seth asks, "Everything good?"

"Yeah." I wave my hand. "False alarm."

Seth tosses back the rest of his drink, pushing away from the bar. "Listen, Wil, I'm sorry. Something just popped up I gotta take care of, but I hope I see you again. That is, if you're in the market for chaos." He winks.

Well, when he puts it like that . . .

"Wait, Seth." I catch his arm. He stares where my hand rests. I quickly let go. "B-before you leave, can I ask you a question? It's important." I bite my lip. I've asked the question an absurd number of times and *now* I'm nervous? I should just make an educated guess and be done with this.

His demeanor warms. "Ask me anything. No promises I'll answer."

"Okay . . . what's your sign?" I blurt.

Seth starts to grin, blocking the full smile with his hand. "That has got to be the lamest line *ever*. And I'm here a lot, so I've heard 'em all."

I hold my chin high. "I'm *serious*."

"You are, aren't you?" His grin falters. "Uh, I dunno."

He pulls out his cell and taps at the screen. Guys rarely know their sign, so I assume he's looking it up. Which is my mistake. I should've just asked for his birth date. But after a few moments, he answers. "Sagittarius."

A shock wave ripples through my body. *Of course.*

Seth leans close enough for me to smell a faint hint of his cologne. "But if what you really want to know is whether or not I'm interested . . . the answer's definitely yes."

Yes. The word holds the heat of his exhalation in my ear. More than the yes, I cling to the other word.

Sagittarius.

My preordained match.

I smile. Everything is coming together.

chapter 4

"You must get tired of that," says a familiar voice. "Every Tom, Dick, and Seth hitting on you when you least expect it." Grant wedges into the space Seth left moments ago. "Glad you got the card," he adds, "and that you're conscious."

"Oh, hey!" I brighten. My breath catches. Must be a by-product of the napkin. The napkin with the hastily scribbled digits Seth has given me. I fold the napkin and cram it in my clutch.

As the lights from the dance floor pan Grant's face, I realize another reason his smile warms me. It's the ever-so-slight overlap of his two front teeth. Why I'd find snuggling teeth endearing is a mystery, but I do. It's possible I'm smiling back like an idiot.

What is my deal?

I stare up at the hanging green lights, hoping to divine some conversational brilliance. He watches me and it's unsettling. "This place is incredible!" Not brilliance. Okay, move on. "Uh, so thanks for the ticket. You really didn't have to."

He shrugs off the gratitude. "I'm just glad you're in one piece. How are you feeling?" Tiny wrinkles crowd the center of his forehead.

"Good, good. Really good." I take a drink of ginger ale.

"Any more emphasis on the word 'good' and I'm taking you back to the hospital."

I grin. "Oh, you know, residual bruise on my knee but no permanent damage. How'd you fare? When I came around, there was nothing but distorted recollections and your note on a business card."

"Yikes, you make it sound so skeevy." Grant pushes up his sleeve, revealing little black tattoos that wrap around his forearm. Music notes? His other arm is bare, save for a distressed-leather cuff at his wrist. "Guess I didn't think your next of kin would take kindly to the person responsible for almost killing you. But I'm fine. Most of my bruises were to my ego. What?" He eyes the amused twist of my mouth. "You think it was lost on me that it was my idea to save you in the first place? If I hadn't intervened with—"

"Then I wouldn't be here right now. And we might never have met. Everything happens for a reason— cosmic forces and whatnot. Right?" I swirl the ice around my glass.

He doesn't answer. Instead, the small wrinkles have once again taken up residence between his brows. He flags Nico for a drink before resting his gaze back on me.

I lean forward, drawing the straw to my mouth. It's the intensity, the deliberateness in the way he watches me that's so unsettling. My pulse is doing that funny fluttering again. The heat in the pit of my stomach migrates to my cheeks. I swallow. "So, um, are you from the area?"

"Born and raised, east side. But don't hold it against me."

"I wouldn't." Though between the tattoos, nondesigner clothes, and imperfect teeth, I wouldn't have pegged him an eastsider either. Irina claims eastsider blood runs green from all their money, and that the sticks up their asses are actually dinosaur bones they convert into oil. She reasons this is how they stay rich. But loathing a group of people because of financial plentitude isn't Irina's style. Actually, I'm not sure why she hates them.

"Then you must go to Hartford," I say.

"Went," Grant corrects, resting his forearms on the bar. "Just graduated." There he goes again, studying me in that way he does that makes me fidget. And I'm not a fidgeter. "What about you?"

"I, whew, it's warm in here." I press my hands, chilled by the glass, to the sides of my face. "I'm from here, too. Being a Carlisle means I practically sprouted from the soil. I live over in the historic district and go to—"

"Alexander?"

I smile. "Yep."

Grant rubs his hand along his jaw. "Do I even want to ask how old you are?"

"I don't know. Do you?"

He braces himself. "Okay, hit me."

"Seventeen." I add, "And four months! Those four months are important, Grant. It means I'm practically halfway to eighteen, so why not just round—"

"All right, all right," he sighs, "but do me a solid. Don't mention this to anyone else—house rules—last thing I want is to see you get blacklisted. Got it?"

"Don't worry, no one ever thinks I'm under . . ." My eyes catch on a determined face in the crowd. It can't be. "Oh, for the love of Venus!" I slink from my stool and hunker beneath the bar. If this were truly my lucky day, the earth would indulge me by shifting its fault lines. Just crack open and swallow the problem.

"Wil?" Grant ducks his head under the bar. "Hey, I said I promise not to turn you in." He pauses. "Or is this disappearing act part of your Unusual Girl mystique?"

"Rooster!" I hiss.

"Ah, right, so it's the latter."

My hands curl around the edge of the bar as I slowly peer over the top. Sure enough, there's Year of the Cock, working his way toward me. He's momentarily derailed by one of the green fairies. I drop down again, inwardly cursing.

"I'm gonna venture there's an excellent reason why you're down here crouched in the fetal position. I'll be above sea level when you're ready to explain." He's choking back a grin. "Man, I can't wait to hear this one."

"Wait a sec!" I grab his shirt, yanking him back down. We are almost nose to nose. I get a whiff of the fresh laundry smell I noticed the other day. "Look, um, there's a guy over there laboring under the false impression that I'm interested."

"Did you say something that might've led him to believe that?"

"What? No! I mean, I asked him a couple of questions." Grant starts to pull back. "W-wait, okay, here's the thing." I take a breath. "I came out tonight to . . . find someone." Humiliated, I drop my hands from his shirt. "But, Grant, trust me, it isn't him."

"I see. So you want me to tell him to get lost?"

I shake my head. "Tried that. Not good enough. His arrogance is second only to his persistence. He is, after all, the Year of the Cock." I bite my lip, mind racing.

Grant blinks. "Uh, I'm sorry, you lost me at co—"

"Rooster," I interject. "You know, Chinese astrology? Ugh! This guy is relentless—like the social equivalent of a plantar wart." I rub my temples, grappling for an escape plan.

"Well, you could just pretend we're together."

I snap my head up, softly thumping it against the underside of the bar. "Seriously?"

Grant's indignation glows in the dark. "Now who'd have thought I'd be a worse alternative than someone born in the Year of the Pecker."

"I—I'm sorry. I didn't mean—"

"No, no, your plan is *much* better. Keep hiding till spring, little gopher." He stands up.

I stare at the frayed edges of his jeans. There's the silvery sheen of duct tape on the side of one of his Chucks. He's right. I can't stay here till spring, plus it smells like old alcohol and even older mops.

"It isn't gopher. It's groundhog," I say as I reluctantly poke up from my hidey-hole.

Grant eyes me warily over the rim of his glass.

Insulting him and correcting his rodent know-how isn't gaining me any points. Change of tactics. This calls for boldness. I twine my arms around his waist.

He lowers his drink and croaks, "What . . . what are you doing?"

"Mr. Walker, would you do me the esteemed honor of being my airbag?"

He clears his throat; the prelude to a grin threatens his lips. "Airbag?"

"Yeah, you know, a buffer? Only for a few minutes. Pretty please?" I plead.

"Why, Miss Carlisle, is this how you charm all the guys? Flattering as this is"—he glances over my shoulder—"I'm not sure we're really convincing as a couple. He's almost here. Spiky hair, black motorcycle jacket, am I right?"

I tense. Then press myself a bit closer, my body molding into the spaces between us. And it feels . . . oddly . . . *right*. I'm light-headed. Jupiter's moons, if I'm having delayed brain-scrambling effects from the fall, Gram will *never* let me hear the end of it!

Now *he's* tensed.

"Grant, if you keep standing there like a cardboard cut-

54

out, we're never going to be believable. Come on, I can't be that awful. I'm not asking you to eat Brussels sprouts or anything."

I catch a glimpse of his adorable front teeth. "I happen to love Brussels sprouts."

"Ha, and you thought *I* was the weird one."

He reaches out, letting the backs of his fingers follow the rise of my cheek. I'm having an overwhelming sense of déjà vu. "If we were really together, then I'd touch you back. Is this okay?" he asks.

Okay? "Okay" is for describing mediocre test scores, or milk on the day of its expiration. This was neither.

My entire body tingles. I blame it on the heavy bass traveling through the concrete floor. "Yes." I force a swallow. "Is he still coming?"

"Yeah, he's watching us."

I pull an arm from Grant's waist, looping it around his neck. My fingers graze the short hair at his neckline as I murmur in his ear, "Do you mind? I thought if it looked like I was whispering sweet nothings, then it'd look real."

He cups the back of my head and holds me like something priceless that was lost and now found. "It's perfect." Then we lapse into silence. And our language becomes one of heartbeats and irregular breaths. "You smell nice," he whispers into my ear.

I was thinking the same of him.

"Th-thank you. It's this French lavender vanilla soap. I'm . . . I'm mildly addicted."

I feel the weight of his inhalation against my chest, followed by a slow exhale. "Me too."

And now it's impossible to ignore the way our hearts thump together. The mutual rhythm moves faster.

The moment goes on for seconds that feel like hours. Until someone bumps Grant, bursting our bubble. The music and chatter and people all come flooding back.

His hand glides down my back as he chuckles. "I think it worked. Pecker looks pissed."

I push away, swept with an achy sort of exhaustion, and swill the remainder of my drink.

"You okay?"

"Sure," I say. "Why wouldn't I be? You've officially vanquished my stalker. I can't thank you enough. Guess I owe you."

"So, that entitles me to a dance before I go?" Grant's voice lowers. "In keeping with our façade, of course."

"Yes . . . of course."

His hand finds mine as he leads me toward the dance floor. He keeps glancing back like I'm going to bolt. Maybe I should, because something has definitely shifted. Like . . . this is suddenly more serious than a dance. His thumb brushes the back of my hand and I look down.

"Calluses," Grant explains, "from the guitar."

"I didn't realize you played." Which is kind of a silly thing to say, because I could fill a freakin' teaspoon with the things I know about him.

"Yeah, I—"

"Son of a bitch!" A short Latino guy launches at Grant,

who stumbles back, clutching him. After a couple of hearty backslaps they separate. "What the hell kind of stunt was that? Ryan told me you took a nosedive off the old tower. And since when were you a thrill seeker outside that phase of . . . well, *hellloooo,*" he says, turning toward me. "*¡Coooooño!* Grant"—he nudges his elbow—"who's the morsel?"

"Jesus, Manny, she's not a bucket of chicken. This is Wil Carlisle. Wil, this is our ill-mannered drummer, Manuel Rodriguez."

"Call me Manny. Pardon my ill manners, Wil." Manny rests a hand to his broad chest and dips his head in apology. "But I was raised in a barn, and you do look good enough to eat." He grins. He's wearing a T-shirt that reads: STICKS GET CHICKS. WANNA SEE MINE?

Grant flicks his ear.

"Ow! Hey! It's not like I said she was finger-lickin' good, even if it's— Ow!"

Grant flicks him a second time. "I *will* lock you back in the cellar."

Manny massages his ear. "Come on, *vato,* she knows I meant it as a compliment."

"In the sweetest, most disturbing Hannibal Lecter way," I say, smirking.

"See? She gets me." Manny punches Grant's arm and narrows his eyes. "Backstage in twenty, or I'm locking *your* ass in the cellar. Farewell, succulent Wil!"

I laugh. "Nice try, but flattery still won't get you the Colonel's secret recipe. Bye, Manny."

He smiles before staring deliberately at Grant. *"Hermano, es única. No pierdas esta oportunidad."* With that, Manny plunges into a cluster of girls with glow sticks. He snags a pair of orange ones, beating the air like a virtual drum.

"He's one of a kind," I say. "You didn't mention you were playing tonight. What's the name of . . ." I try to decipher Grant's expression as he watches Manny. "Hey, if you need to go now, it's no problem."

"No, I have time. Besides, you owe me, remember?" Grabbing my hand, he draws me to the floor and into the crush of the crowd.

The music transitions into something with a subtle Latin vibe, causing the dancers to thin out around us.

"Fantasma?" I ask.

"A girl who knows her music."

"I'm an aficionado, remember?" I tease, turning away.

"So that's it?"

I turn back, flummoxed. "You know how to dance . . . to this?"

Grant steps closer, his eyes intense as he draws my hand up to his shoulder and clasps my other hand. "Yeah." He grins. "And wow. Impressive you can still look so cute with your mouth hanging open like that."

I clamp my lips together, shaking my head. "No, it's just there aren't many guys who . . ." But I lose my train of thought as we find the rhythm and begin to move. It's a basic salsa, but if I don't concentrate on my steps, I'll tenderize his feet with these heels for sure.

Grant is a strong partner, and where he leads I follow, but he has a gift for making it feel like the other way around. Like *I'm* the one leading.

"You're fantastic!" I say.

Grinning, he twirls me. "Nah, you just make me look good."

That's a lie. Still, his feet are unscathed, and for that, I'm grateful.

Our bodies become mirror images of one another's movements. My head is spinning. My heart is racing. And none of it is from dancing.

Suddenly I have to know.

"Grant?" His hand grazes my hip, gently directing my movement. My back bumps against his chest. His other hand drops to my waist. I shiver. *Focus.* "Do you know much about astrology?"

"Zero. Other than it seems to snow every year on my birthday, but then"—his soft laugh rumbles at my ear—"I guess that's meteorology."

I'm having trouble stringing my sentences together. His proximity muddles my thinking. "Um, well, remember how I said I was looking for someone?"

"Uh-huh." He spins me so we are facing each other. One of my hands falls to his chest; his breathing is irregular like mine. "Did you find him?" Grant's eyes are dark, un-readable.

"I—I'm not sure. Astrology is a complicated study." Our swaying slows with the waning song.

"Ah, well, I don't put much faith in the stars." He casts

me into a final spin, tugging me back. I land solidly against his chest.

"Funny," I say, rather breathless. "I put all my faith in the stars."

His left hand splays over my back. The other hand is gripped firmly to mine. I can feel his guitar calluses. His gaze lowers to my mouth; his breath sears my skin. "I put mine in people."

The cinder below my navel explodes in riotous flames. Every square inch of my skin tingles with our connection. The ebbing bass lures me closer. Closer. My head tilts.

I'm not broken! It isn't too late.

He could be the one! He could be . . . and then the realization hits me, as certain as the earth's next revolution. Grant is charming, intelligent, passionate, sensitive, and creative, and it often snows on his birthday. Taken as a whole, these facts could only mean one thing. Oh God!

He is . . . he must be . . .

Pisces.

I gasp.

Instantly the fire dies. Winter ravages my blood; my veins fill with ice.

My mother's sweet voice echoes in my ears, *"Beware of Pisces . . . Beware of Pisces . . . Beware of Pisces . . ."* Her ghostly voice repeats until I'm dizzied by her words.

My legs weaken and buckle.

"Wil!" Grant catches me, holding me upright. "Wil, what—?"

"I can't . . . I can't breathe." Suddenly the amethyst stone throbs at my neck and feels like a million pounds pulling me to the concrete floor. As if the weight of my promise to my mother has become a tangible thing.

And I'm suffocating. Choking. Everything presses in at once. To fall for a Pisces would be unforgivable. Because it would go against . . .

"Come on, I'm getting you out of here." Grant loops an arm around my waist, supporting me. "Move!" he roars as we push through the onlookers.

The crowd shifts around us. Faces stretch in nightmarish images. The green lights make everyone look ghastly and sick.

I'm panting, hiccuping, and still I can't gain my breath.

"Wil!" Irina appears, placing a hand on my clammy face. Her expression twists in fury. "What have you done? I will gut you like a goddamn fish if you've done anything—"

"I didn't hurt her," Grant snaps. "She needs air. She just needs some air."

But as I stumble, gasping in his arms, I realize what I need is way more complicated than oxygen. I need to overcome the pitfalls of my fate . . . realign the stars. And in order to do so, Grant Walker must become as invisible to me as the very air I cannot breathe.

chapter 5

I draw in a breath; the paper bag crinkles loudly, deflating and sucking flat against itself. Crap. And there he is again. *So not invisible.* Grant's staring at me with those anxious eyes while twisting the leather cuff at his wrist until I worry the hand attached will pop off.

"Guys, this is totally unnecessary." My muffled words inflate the bag like yeast in dough. I sink back in the folding chair. The thumping from the club feels light-years away from the second-story fire escape.

This is awful. *Humiliating.* If I thought I could fit more than my left foot in the paper sack, I'd crawl in. There's nothing worse than pitying looks.

Irina frowns, turning the diamond stud above her lip. It's as if she takes being "wound up" literally. "It *is* necessary. You were hyperventilating. Wil"—she crouches, placing her hands carefully on my knees—"what happened in there?"

Oh, but she knows me too well. Knows it would take something catastrophic to send me reeling off my axis like this.

I lower the bag. "I just . . . it was the heat and the dancing. I got light-headed but . . . I'm better now." My mouth arranges into a feeble attempt at a smile. Irina's eyes are prodding, but the rest of her remains mute as she stands. Reluctantly I peer at Grant. "Please, you should go. Your band is probably waiting. I'm fine." I perform a slow inhale and exhale. "Respiration normal."

"No, I don't feel right leaving. They'll wait." He pushes a hand through his dark hair. "Want some more water?"

I eye the two unopened bottles at my feet. "No thanks."

The vertical blinds at the window part to reveal Seth's head. *Seth?* I shut my eyes. And now my potential *soul mate* is here? This keeps getting better.

Seth slinks out the window, crowding onto the fire escape. "Wil, what happened? Are you all right?"

So help me, if one more person asks either of those questions, I will go ballistic on all of them.

Seth glances at Grant, who's now leaning up against the building's exterior. "Ryan said he saw you half carrying a girl upstairs."

"I overheated." I crumple the bag into a ball of frustration. "Seriously, this is a whole lot of fuss over nothing."

"You almost passed out," Irina asserts.

"I did not." It was a temporary meltdown, a Pisces-induced panic attack, but I'd sooner lose consciousness than confess that bit aloud. I cock my head at Seth. "I, um, thought you had to leave or something."

"I didn't. Well . . . *obviously*." He kneels so he's level with me. "No, I was actually hoping to catch you before you left because I wanted ask you something."

I let out a nervous laugh. "As long as it isn't if I'm okay."

Seth flashes a lopsided grin before stealing a glance over his shoulder. "You doing anything Friday?"

"Unbelievable." Grant shakes his head disgustedly and pushes from the building. "You're right, Wil, I should go. It's getting crowded up here anyway."

Yes, it *is* crowded. Because any available space has been taken up by all the awkward now surrounding our four-some.

Irina shoots Grant a mutinous look before moving toward the window. "Well, no time like the present." She pauses to covertly wink in my direction. Guess she's over worrying about me, which is good. "I'll be downstairs when you're ready, Wil. Take your time."

Grant kicks his foot back and forth over the metal grates as he waits for Irina to clear out.

"Uh . . ." Okay, this situation is more uncomfortable than wearing a thong. *Backward*. "H-hold that thought," I say to Seth before standing.

Seth nods and answers his ringing cell.

"Grant?" He's already crawled back in. And I'm seized by a weird kind of panic at the thought of not saying goodbye to him. "Grant?"

His head pokes out, startling me with its abrupt nearness. "What?" The furrows in his forehead have returned.

I want to smooth them out with my fingers. I don't know why. Doesn't matter. He's completely off-limits. But . . . can't we at least be friends?

Yes. Why not? In fact, I've already made up my mind—I *want* Grant Walker to be my friend. Friendship . . . I can handle. The label alone means things will stay clean and simple.

"Listen, thanks for everything tonight. Getting me in, saving me from the Rooster"—I feel a surge of heat in my cheeks—"and the dance. I'll miss you."

Grant's eyes snap to mine.

"I mean, your *band*. I'll miss *your band* . . . tonight." *Sheesh, Wil. Why don't you peel the duct tape from his shoe and slap it over your mouth right now. I'll miss you?* I'm afraid to look at Grant. Instead, I fiddle with my glasses like they're to blame for my weirdity. I take a stabilizing breath and finally meet his eyes. "So, is there any chance of a rain check?" *Please say yes. Or no.* Now I'm not sure how I want him to answer.

His expression softens. "I'll do you one better." He reaches into the pocket of his jeans and pulls out something that glints in the streetlight. "Here." He drops the almost-weightless object in my hand.

"A key?" It's silver and half the length of my pinky finger. "You're giving me a key. I don't understand."

"It won't open any doors." Well, that clears up nothing. "Just show it to the bouncers," Grant elaborates. "That'll get you in whenever you want—no cover, no hassle. My uncle owns the club, and we get a few of these to give out at our discretion."

"I . . . wow." The key, warm from his pocket, feels scorching in my palm. "I . . ."

"Hey, G," Seth chimes in behind me. "Ryan's blowing up my cell. You're on in five. I think you better jet."

"Thanks." Although Grant's tone suggests little in the way of gratitude.

Seth cheerfully replies, "What are brothers for?"

I jolt. " 'Brothers'?" I echo, swinging my head to Seth. "You guys are *brothers*?"

Oh my God! *That's* why Seth is familiar. The bone structure, the hair, the build . . .

"Oh, you didn't realize? Yeah, Grant's my older brother—well, not much older. Only a year and some change." Seth shrugs. "And we get mistaken for each other a lot. Course . . . I like to think I'm better-looking, but that's probably because I'm jealous as hell he got all the musical talent. The bastard."

When I turn to find Grant, he's gone. The vertical blinds sway, tapping in his absence. There's a twinge of pain in my chest that stops my breath.

Exactly what are the odds that my astral match and astral downfall would not only hail from the same family tree . . . but also share the same damn branch? One in a million? A billion?

This is no cosmic coincidence.

It's a divine message. A message meant to remind me how perilously little separates the right choice in love from the wrong one. Well, unlike my departed mother,

I will choose wisely. Starting with forgetting that dance with Grant. Already it feels more dream than reality, and dreams cannot replace the wisdom of the stars.

Seth hesitantly brushes my arm. "Please tell me you're not the type to make a guy beg."

"I'm sorry?" I relax my hold on the key and pull my gaze from the sky. "What were you saying?"

"I was, uh"—he rubs the back of his neck—"asking you again about Friday? You never answered, so at the risk of totally embar—"

"I'd love to." I dig deep and produce a grin. "But do we have to wait? On Wednesday the planetarium is holding a summer night sky event. Sagittarius is rising in the southeast—your sun sign. Would you . . . be interested?" I frown. "Or maybe that's too nerdy. You're probably busy. Friday's great." I turn and inch up my skirt to avoid tearing the slit on my way back through the window.

"You really don't have a clue."

"Huh?" I stumble on my reentry, catching myself on an office chair. Seth appears at the window.

"Well"—he climbs in stealthily—"see, I've got this major weakness for hot nerds and heavenly bodies." Seth's smile is angelic, but the light from the computer monitor on the office desk shows his eyes are pure devil. "By 'hot nerds' I'm referring to you, and by 'heavenly bodies' I'm referring to the stars and planets."

I chuckle, feeling the slight flutter of butterflies. There! See? I *like* Seth. He's flirtatious and fun and apparently has a weakness for girls with nerdy tendencies. Most important of all, he is Sagittarius.

"Okay," he confesses into my silence with a boyish shrug, "I lied. I don't know jack about the planets. But I can learn. So . . . maybe I just have a weakness for you."

"What did you say his family name was?" Gram asks.

"Walker," I answer. "And he goes to Hartford, so you wouldn't know him from around here."

"So his family's well-off." Gram whistles. "As I live and breathe, so *that's* the fella who turned your head. My, my, I can certainly see why. Quite a catch from what I can see from here." She stands higher on her toes in the breakfast nook.

"Hey, get away from the window!"

She lets the curtain drop. "No need for testiness, Mena. It's natural for me to be curious. Seventeen years of age and I only recall you being interested in that one boy. What was his name? Brogan?"

"Brody Cooper," I correct, opening my purse.

"Right, *him*. He always wore"—Gram wrinkles her nose—"those saggy, ill-fitting pants." My grandmother had never warmed to Brody. There were a million reasons why. Reasons bigger than his pants—like the sheer crime of chronology.

"You didn't like Brody because he was a senior and I was a freshman." I catch my distorted reflection in the bottom of one of the pans hanging from the potrack. I wipe the lipstick at the corner of my mouth and bare my teeth, which I'm pleased to see are lipstick-free.

"Well, now, that's only partly true." She moves from the nook to take the kettle off the burner. "There was also the matter of his—"

"Gram, please! I'm nervous enough as it is without you dredging up ancient dating history."

"Yes, of course. You just forget I said a *word* about that Brogan boy." She ceremoniously clinks the teaspoon on the rim of her teacup. "Okay, then, Mena. Let's have a look at you."

With my fussing complete, I round the island countertop and brace myself for her full scrutiny. "Well?" My hands pluck at the halter dress, moving it this way and that. The A-line dress is black with little bunches of red cherries all over, a sweetheart neckline, and hem that goes all the way to my knees. Iri has assured me it's a respectable first-date dress.

Then why is Gram making that face? If she brought her hands to her neck, it would be the international sign for choking. Oh no . . .

"What?" I ask in alarm. "Too much? Is my chest getting that icky double-boob thing?" Frantic, I tug at the halter strap. There's no time to change.

The doorbell rings.

"Say something," I plead.

Gram closes the space between us in a few brisk steps and wraps her arms around me. "Absolutely stunning. The spitting image of your mama." She kisses the top of my head.

I pull back, beaming. "Really? You think so?"

Her blue eyes are steadfast, but her voice wavers as she replies, "Hand to God. Now get that door before your gentleman caller thinks you've changed your mind. Go on." Gram shoos me from the kitchen.

The bittersweet moment is fleeting. I've gotten good at fixating on the sweet and denying the bitter. Years of practice. Plus, Gram's always said living in the past can rob you blind of your tomorrows. And I want my tomorrows and all the promise they hold.

Seth Walker stands tall on my doorstep, flowers in hand, but his confident grin fades like the daylight.

I will put a pox on Irina's house. I should never have let her talk me into wearing this dress. What the hell was I thinking, relying on the opinion of someone who often wears more jewelry than clothes?

"*Wow*. You look beautiful," Seth finally utters. "I . . . I guess I should've dressed up more." He glances down at his designer jeans before fidgeting with his crisp button-down shirt. The cuffs are unbuttoned and rolled up to his elbows, revealing his tanned forearms.

"No, you look great!" As soon as I say it, relief lights his face. "Anyway, I always overdress. I have a closet full of these dresses and never enough occasions to wear them."

"Then maybe we should do something about that." He unleashes a dazzling smile. His teeth could not be straighter if I lined them up with a ruler. "Oh, I got these for you. Hope you like purple, and, um, old-school gestures."

I take the dozen roses from his hand and smile. "Look

at me, Seth, I am *all about* old-school. They're gorgeous, really, thanks." Another swell of nervousness sloshes my stomach. "Uh, come on in."

Gram's already got her eagle eye on the flowers, cataracts be damned. Of course, she's sizing up Seth as well. Her period of assessment is measured by the distinctive *ticktock, ticktock* of the grandfather clock in the hall.

"Good evening, ma'am, I'm Seth Walker. Nice to meet you." He offers his hand, which Gram takes in hers.

Ticktock.

"Yes. Genevieve Carlisle, Wilamena's grandmother." Lesser guys would surely crumble beneath Gram's steely gaze. I call it the Gram Gauntlet Gaze—the Triple G. It's the one she uses when sussing out a person's moral fiber.

"Yes, ma'am," Seth replies, smooth and not the least bit flustered. His confidence is awe-inspiring.

Gram offers a sparing nod, which means he's passed . . . I think. *Jeez!* She can be such a confounding Taurus!

She tucks back a silver tendril that's come loose from her hair clip. "Happy to put those in water if you like, Mena."

"Thank you." I give her a peck on the cheek. "We should really be going if we're going to make that exhibit before dinner." I shake my head at Seth's questioning look. Gram had been so unbelievably ecstatic over my date. It just seemed unnecessary to clarify the *exhibit* was an astronomy-related one, in light of the tower incident.

"Hmm, lavender." Gram takes the flowers, turning the bouquet. "That's a color you don't see so often in roses.

Of course"—Gram pauses to eye Seth—"you must know what that signifies since you chose them specifically for her." She grins, knowing full well Seth hadn't a clue about color connotations. For heaven's sake, he isn't a florist!

I'm about to say as much when Gram finally fills the silence. "Enchantment. It signifies enchantment."

"Then"—Seth stuffs his hands in his pockets—"I suppose it was a lucky guess, Mrs. Carlisle."

Ooh, he's good. Real good. I go back to being awed.

She chuckles. "Yes. I suppose it was." Gram shuffles toward the kitchen. And before I can feel the release of my pent-up breath, she adds, "Just be sure to keep it in your pants, son. Have a lovely evening." The kitchen door swings shut behind her.

My eyes go round as saucers and my face sizzles. "I'm sorry," I sputter. "I'm sure she didn't mean . . . well, no, actually, she *did* mean it, but—"

"Hey." He nudges my arm. "Come on, it's all good." He raises his hand. "And I, Seth Walker, solemnly swear to keep it in my pants. Even if you're as enchanting as . . ."

I stifle a laugh, shaking my head. "I used to babysit a Boy Scout, and I can tell you the solemn oath only uses three fingers."

He drops his hand. Now I can't decide which is sexier— his crooked smirk or the dangerous glint in his eye. "I never said I was a Boy Scout."

"No, you didn't." The butterflies have returned. They are overcaffeinated and pumped full of steroids as they declare war on my insides.

"Are you ready?"

"Yes," I answer automatically, grabbing my purse.

Am I ready? The question feels momentous, though of course, it isn't meant to be. Still, it won't stop taunting me with its implications. Am I ready for tonight? Am I ready for what might follow? What I have been hoping would follow since concocting this plan?

Truth? *I don't know.*

However, the planets have unanimously agreed—there has never been a better time for me to find out.

chapter 6

"See it?"

Seth leans closer; his hair tickles my neck. "No, show me again."

"There." I circle the red laser pointer. The planetarium has cleared with the end of the presentation. Meaning the two other people besides us have left. "See, it's sorta shaped like a teapot? That's Sagittarius; the constellation represents Chiron, the centaur. He sacrificed himself in place of Prometheus, who was being punished by the gods for giving fire to man."

"What was his punishment?" Seth shifts in his seat. His leg lightly presses against mine. Is he doing that on purpose? The dark room seems to amplify every touch and word, giving them odd significance.

I push up my glasses and feign oblivion to the casual

way his jeans rub against my bare skin. Otherwise, my thoughts get too cloudy. To think days ago I was concerned about asexuality! "Prometheus was chained to a rock, and every day an eagle would come and feast on his liver. And every night the liver would magically grow back. Yeah"—I note Seth's scrunched face—"the gods didn't mess around. So Chiron offered up his immortality in return for Prometheus's freedom. Zeus rewarded the act of kindness by placing him among the stars. Ergo, Chiron is Sagittarius. I guess he sorta maintained his immortality after all."

Seth lets out a low whistle. "How do you know all this?"

"Reading mostly. I've always found the constellations and astrology to be especially . . . Oh, um, never mind."

"What? Tell me more."

My heart trips over its own rhythm as Seth leans closer again. I smell the faint cologne he wore at Absinthe. I like it. *A lot.* "You . . . you want to hear more about the mythology behind the constellations?" I ask, dubious.

"Why wouldn't I? The stories make the stars more interesting. It's pretty impressive how much you know." He gives me a sidelong glance. "I bet your dates are totally into you at this point, aren't they?"

I let out a nervous chuckle and intertwine my fingers in my lap.

Seth gives me a gentle nudge. *"Oh, please.* Don't tell me I'm the first guy to dig this about you."

"Well . . . it's not like I routinely bring guys here." I

twist the onyx ring on my finger. "And, um, I couldn't say what my dates thought of me since most ended in disaster." I sigh. Honest to Aquarius, outing myself as a former dating weapon of mass destruction had *not* been how I wanted to christen the night.

But that's all in the past. It will be different with Seth.

His eyes crinkle at the corners. "I bet you're exaggerating, Wil. It can't have been that bad."

Uh, yes, in fact, it *was* that bad. But I don't want to do a postmortem on all the whys.

"Okay," Seth says uncertainly in the wake of my silence, "what's the worst thing that's happened during one of your disaster dates?"

Drawing my gaze from the man-made dots of light, I can tell Seth is anticipating something trivial like a trail of toilet paper stuck to my shoe, or spinach wedged in my teeth, or some such nonsense. *If only.* "Well . . . I once broke a guy's nose."

"Seriously?"

I blow out a breath. "Yep. Well, technically, I'm not sure it even classifies as a true date. It was just a guy I danced with at homecoming. I guess he liked me. That is until . . ." This is so mortifying.

"What?" Seth urges.

"He caught me completely off guard! I mean, one second we're dancing and the next he's telling me he likes me. Which was insane because he'd never said more than four words to me. So when I reared back to see if he was kidding, he must've been lowering his head and . . . I headbutted his nose. Broke it in not one, but *two* places." I sink deeper into my chair. "God, there was so much blood."

Seth covers his mouth, smothering the smile beneath.

I cross my arms over my chest and scowl. "It wasn't funny, it was traumatic . . . *for everyone* involved. I felt terrible. Sometimes I think I should come with a warning label."

He stifles another laugh and I knock his elbow from the armrest. "I'm sorry," he says, his leg pressing more firmly against mine. I forget I'm supposed to be scowling. "Hey, accidents happen. It was unfortunate, sure, but not the end of the world."

"You think? Because they call me the black widow at school."

Seth has the decency to look horrified on my behalf. "No shit?"

I smile wryly. "No, not really. But in the spirit of fairness, it's your turn to spill." I twist toward him, eager to hear his most mortifying account. "Okay, so what's the worst thing that has happened to *you*?"

"Hmm." Seth runs his hand thoughtfully along his jaw.

"Pressure's off. We already know you can't hold a candle to the blood and carnage of mine."

"All right. Well . . . there was this time I ripped my pants on a skateboarding jump. It was eighth grade and I was trying to impress this girl, right? So I was soaring high, and when I bent to grip my board . . . *rrrip!* Right up the middle of the seam—total blowout. She laughed her ass off."

Oh Lord. History is repeating; my own ass is in serious jeopardy. I can't stop laughing, and it comes back doubly loud in the quiet of the circular room.

Seth chuckles and with a rueful eye adds, "All I could think was *thank God* I didn't go commando. I'd never live it down. Wow, I can't believe I just told you that story." He hunches forward, resting his elbows on his knees, head hanging low.

My laughter fades with my smile.

He could be on a date with any one of the pretty girls salivating over him at Absinthe. Girls who don't require warning labels. Or have grandmothers who warned him to *keep it in your pants.*

Then a paralyzing thought occurs to me. *What if he regrets asking me out?* My stomach descends to the planetarium floor as the theory begins to sound more plausible.

I clear my throat. "Look, I know you're probably used to girls who are a lot cooler—nonplanetarium types. Let's be real, how many dates are going to ramble on about constellations and magic livers and noses they've broken?" It's a rhetorical question. Because we both know the answer is a big, fat zero. I lift a shoulder. "But this is me. And I don't know how else to be, so if I'm not what you exp—"

He silences me with his fingertip. "Stop. Just stop. You're killing me, Wil." Seth's eyes fall to my lips, where his finger hasn't moved. He exhales, dropping his hand. "Look, the more you try to talk me *out* of liking you, the more I like you. And you're not like other girls I've dated, because you're a million times cooler."

My smile stretches from one ear to the other. "So . . . you *like* me?" My Sagittarius likes me. Hope balloons in my chest. *Likes* me, likes me. Here I thought I was blowing it with my moronic babbling.

"Do you really think I'd be here if I didn't?"

"I don't know. Maybe you just couldn't think of a nice way to ditch me. I was trying to give you an—"

Seth pulls me toward him.

"What are you doing?" I ask in surprise. One of my hands lands at his shoulder as I brace myself above him.

I can tell he's on the muscular side, just like Grant. No, don't think about Grant. But now that I know they're related, I can't help but home in on the similarities. Little pieces of Grant are scattered all over. So I focus on the parts that are different. Seth's nose is just a little smaller, and his jaw is just a little less square, and . . . and his shoes don't have duct tape on them.

Seth's eyes—like mine—openly stare back. They wander my face before he crooks an index finger under my chin. My heart pounds inside my chest. "What am I doing?" he repeats at a near whisper. "Trying really hard not to kiss you." His full lips rise in a smirk. "Mainly, because I like my nose the way it is—*unbroken*."

Has he noticed I'm holding my breath? I exhale in a jittery laugh. Now my right boob is completely squashed against him. He *has* to notice that. Seth relaxes his head against the worn burgundy fabric of the seat, but doesn't break our gaze.

It's my move. Right? Wait, what's my move? "Seth, I—"

At that moment, the door bangs and the house lights come on, bleaching away our summer sky.

I push myself upright.

A janitor wheels in a trash bin and a vacuum cleaner larger than Gram's Buick. Unaware of our presence, he plugs in the extension cord while whistling an off-key rendition of "Hello, Dolly!"

The machine fires up and I can no longer hear my own jumbled thoughts. Seth grabs my hand and we laugh, racing out of the planetarium.

Seth has picked an adorable French place—La Petite Plat—on the east side for dinner. It's a gorgeous evening, so we dine outside under twinkle lights and umbrellas. I can't pronounce a thing on the menu. And I almost lose my appetite when I see the prices. Good thing, given the minuscule portions.

Do the French just have really small stomachs? Uh-oh. I might've said that last part aloud, because suddenly Seth is laughing. He then goes on to explain La Petite Plat means "little plate." Oh.

At least my starvation will be entertaining.

We talk about things that matter and things that don't. I learn that Seth loves to travel and, at the ripe age of seventeen, has seen more places than Gram has flavors of cupcakes. Which is really saying something. He also has a killer comic-book collection, and as a kid dressed as Batman for Halloween. Four years in a row.

He, in turn, is curious about my fixation on vintage

clothes and hairstyles. I'm used to this question. I try to explain the timeless allure of forties fashion. How people were forced to do more with less because of war rationing. It's why so many incredible hairstyles were born from the era, because hair was the one thing they had that was changeable.

I don't mention that many of the forties-style dresses I wear are from my mother's collection.

When I return from the restroom, I find Seth doodling on the back of his receipt.

"What are you drawing?" I ask, peering over his shoulder. But I don't get to see.

"Oh, it's nothing." He quickly crumples up the paper. "Just . . . scribbles. Stupid really. You ready to go?"

"Sure."

We decide to take a stroll along the boardwalk. It's June, so the Opal River has yet to take up the sweltering stink of August.

"You do that a lot," Seth says, with a squeeze of my hand.

I drag my gaze from above and back to the boy at my side. "What?"

He points up to the glittering sky.

"Oh, sorry. Habit, I guess." We veer around a tree branch jutting into our path.

"This would be a habit you got from . . ." He pushes his free hand through his hair. "Give me something at least. You barely told me anything about yourself the whole night."

I draw in a breath to argue.

"*Besides* the planetarium narration and love of retro fashion."

"My mother," I supply, forcing a grin. The wind rustles my dark hair—black as the gaps between the stars, she used to say. "Astrology, stargazing, it's something we always shared."

"Cool." When my speech stalls, Seth offers an encouraging grin. "Anything else?"

Happy memories bubble to the surface of my mind. I catch one, careful not to break it, careful to extract every exquisite detail. "Well, when I was little she'd wake me up—often in the middle of the night—and we'd sneak out to the backyard. *God*, I loved that. Just us and the sky rolled out like a huge movie screen."

My face splits into a smile as I relive the memory. How the smell of cut grass mingled with the sweetness of Gram's blossoming moonflowers. How my heart beat a little quicker at the prospect of doing something a bit forbidden. And getting away with it.

"So we'd lie there in our pajamas on this old peach-colored blanket that smelled like cedar while my mom pointed out all the planets and constellations we could see. Then I'd usually fall asleep to the sound of her voice, like she was telling me a bedtime story. Those were my first lessons in the *language of the sky*—that's what she called it."

"And that's why the sign thing is so important, huh?" His brow furrows. He plucks a leaf from a shrub. "I get it. Astrology is your Batman."

"My Batman?"

"Yeah, that magical thing you believe in, even if other people don't."

I chuckle. "Mm-hmm." We pause and stare out at the water rippling like black satin over river rock.

Seth leans against the wooden rail, etched with promises of love and forever, then tosses the leaf into the current. "Well, your mom sounds great. I'd love to meet her sometime. Assuming you're game for another date?"

My bubble of happiness pops. "No."

"Oh," he chokes. "Um, I thought you were having fun tonight, but if you wanna leave, I'll take you back—"

"No! Jeez, I meant . . ." I seize his hands; they're so soft and warm. "Let me try again. I would love to go on another date with you."

His relief is palpable.

"But I can't introduce you to my mom. She . . ." Instinctively my head tips to the stars; I force it down. *Just get it over with, Wil. Say it and be done.* "When I was six, my mom left to get syrup for pancakes and never made it home. Another car swerved into her lane going pretty fast—ended up hitting her head-on, so . . ."

So she died within minutes. The accident was fatal for both drivers. And even though I've repeated this story countless times with dry eyes, *this* time—it's a little too raw. Too real. As if I feel the crushing impact of the collision, my own heart rate dropping, my own body shutting down. I close my eyes, willing myself not to go there. Because the destination is pointless and changes nothing.

Seth's thumbs glide back and forth over the backs of my hands. The silence stretches. "So now she's up there," he finishes softly, tilting his face up before gazing back to me. "I'm sorry, Wil. I didn't know—"

"Hey," I cut in, giving his hands a final squeeze and then letting go. "It was a long time ago, Seth. I mean, I miss her—of course I miss her. But I always know where to find her, you know?"

He folds his arms in a quiet contemplation that I suspect won't last. Because in my experience, once you've answered one question, it opens the floodgates to a whole lot more. "Still, must've been hell on your dad and—"

"I wouldn't know. Never met him." My fingers trace the groove of a heart carved in the wood rail. "And please don't do that, Seth. Don't look at me with pity. Gram is more than most people will get in a lifetime."

Seth stands there, mute and unmoving. Can I blame him? What could he really say after I dropped a bomb like that?

Bending to scoop up a handful of pebbles, I sigh. "I think this is what is referred to as a buzzkill. I've officially killed this date. At least your nose is intact." I chuck the pebbles one by one in the river. They break the surface with faint *bloops*.

"You didn't kill anything," Seth murmurs, coming to stand beside me. "And I can't argue about your grandma, cause . . . well, I have a feeling she'd whoop my ass for talking back anyway."

I sniff. "She would." My lips form a shadow of a grin.

"You gonna hog all those?" He nods at the pebbles.

And just like that, his simple boyish gesture . . . makes me feel like a simple girl again.

I tilt my head as I regard him. "I like you, too, Seth Walker." I offer my handful of pebbles. My face warms and my heart thumps in double time as the atmosphere charges with my admission. Suddenly I can't meet his gaze anymore and become absurdly fascinated with the Snickers wrapper on the ground.

Seth's hand curls around my wrist, reeling me toward him. He bends until our lips almost touch. "I really want to kiss you, Wil Carlisle."

"O-okay." I lick my lips. "So, you don't want the pebbles, then?"

"No," he whispers. "I'd rather have you." And Seth presses his lips to mine.

The heat slowly creeps through my body.

I welcome it. No more cold, or fear, or isolation. This is meant to be. I have never been so sure of anything.

Somewhere I register the clatter of those little stones. But I'm just so damn elated by the feel of his lips, I don't recall how my hand finds its way to his neck, or how it knows to go there in the first place.

My back presses against the wooden rail as he presses his body to mine. Seth's mouth is even softer than his hands, and has the lingering flavor of chocolate and custard from the éclair we shared. I taste France and fantasize—it is not the Opal, it is the River Seine that rushes along the bank. And before I can imagine the drab yellow streetlights of Carlisle as ornate Parisian gaslit ones . . . the kiss is over.

He pulls back, but doesn't let me move away. "You know what I'm thinking?"

"I . . . I taste like éclairs?" I ask. Which is quite possibly the world's dumbest question. I blame it wholly on France.

He laughs. "No. *Better.*" I shiver at his uneven breath at my ear, shivering more when he kisses the hollow beneath it. "But I'm stopping." He takes a step back.

I close my eyes. If I'm better than dessert, why doesn't he kiss me a little longer? It's me. It must be me.

When I reopen my eyes, he's frowning.

"You think I stopped because I wanted to, don't you?"

My lips still tingle. "Well, I thought maybe it was . . ."

Seth shakes his head, placing his hands on either side of my face. "I stopped because I wanted *more,* Wil. Too much more." The last words are emphasized in a way I can't mistake.

My mouth goes slack, forming an O, but no sound comes out.

"But I wanna do this right with you." His hands slide away, much to my disappointment. "Come on." He drapes his arm over my bare shoulders. "You feel cold." He briskly rubs my arm to work up the circulation. "You should definitely bring a sweater on Friday."

"Why, what are we doing?"

"It's a surprise." He glances at me, then does a double take. "Hey, no pouting or I might say to hell with taking it slow."

I grin. "Not even a hint?"

"It'll be unforgettable."

Later that night, I fall asleep replaying my kiss with Seth. I dissect the details—the softness of his lips, the scent of his skin, the husky way he said he wanted much more. I loop it over and over. And wonder what Friday will bring.

chapter 7

One perk of astrological know-how is that you never have to wonder for very long. The generosity of Jupiter lingers for the month of June—assuring me that my happily-ever-after is all but a planetary promise.

Which makes the ambiguity of Friday's horoscope extra annoying.

Expect the unexpected. Today will bring a curious turn of events.

So, basically, I can expect . . . anything to happen tonight. "Anything" seems broad, even by horoscope standards. My eyes catch on the wall calendar, where bold Sharpie *X*s count down to June's end. I am seventeen days ahead of schedule. I should be jumping for joy, right?

"Hey, quit blinking or I'll poke out your eyes," Irina scolds, poising the eyelash curler. She crashed here last night and conveniently packed her extensive makeup collection so we could get ready for our dates together.

"Look down," she commands. "No, too far. There! Whatever you're looking at, keep your eyes *there*."

I train my stare on the dermal piercing at the center of her chest. The tiny silver disk must have hurt like hell, although Irina assures me it didn't. But I'm not sure I trust the pain assessment abilities of anyone who regularly punctures their own skin for sport.

"I still can't believe you're dating an eastsider," Iri grumbles. "I mean, take away the money, good looks, and charisma—what's even left?"

"Yeah, Seth's an absolute *loser*. I should be setting my sights a lot higher." I roll my eyes.

My night out with Seth was *the* topic of conversation over Gram's famous meat loaf and mashed potatoes last night. Gram seemed pleased enough with my recap. Iri, however, has remained skeptical. But that's a Leo thing— it's in her nature to constantly challenge.

Just like it's in my nature to see this truth and not take it personally.

Irina shakes her head before pumping the mascara wand in the tube. "But how do you even know he's the Sagittarius you're looking for?"

"Because he told me his birthday is December fifth. The *exact* date on Mr. Right's chart. If that's coincidence, then it's extraordinary."

"Look up," Iri instructs, putting a coat on my lower lashes. "So, what's the plan again for tonight?"

"Dinner at . . . um, well, he didn't say. Followed by something I'll find 'mind-blowingly awesome and unforgettable.' "

"Huh. So, you know *nothing* about what you're doing." Disapproval overshadows the sarcasm in her tone. Now she's making the face I normally reserve for choking down her *tetya*'s borscht.

"As a matter of fact I do, KGB operative. Grant's band is playing at Absinthe, and since I missed them last Sunday, I asked Seth if he'd be up for going. Want to meet up with us? You and . . ." I make a suggestive waggle of my eyebrows.

"Not sure. I'll text if we do." Iri's been tight-lipped about the mysterious suit-wearing cactus guy—Jordan Lockwood. The more I ask, the less she says. Also true to her word, she pokes my eye.

"Ow! Okay, okay, enough mascara." I wrench away to change the playlist and turn up the volume.

"So, what're you wearing on your date with He-Who-Must-Not-Be-Named?" I ask, before disappearing into my closet, flicking through the hangers.

"His name is Jordan, not what's-his-name—*Valdyvort*."

"Voldemort," I correct.

"Whatever. I'm wearing snakeskin pants and a silver tube top." She winks. "Maximum shock value."

I giggle. "What, is he a mutual-fund salesman? An Amish wood whittler? Ooh, is he a manager at that fancy mattress store at the mall with those adjustable beds?

"Iri, I can do this all night," I warn. I pull out a dress that feels all wrong and shove it back.

"Mmm. Not telling till I know if it's anything worth telling. *Dorogaya,* wear the blue dress with the belt," she hollers over the music and screeching hangers. "It'll be perfect with your eyes."

"Oh, I forgot about that one." I find the belted, off-the-shoulder dress and slip off my robe. "Hey, Iri?"

"Yeah?"

I pause for several beats. "What's the rumor about Grant Walker?"

"Grant . . . what?" She chuckles. "Oh, I think the more pressing question is why are you still so obsessed with knowing?"

I venture out of the closet, dress half on. "Will you zip me?" I turn my back to her. "The only reason I'm curious is because you won't tell me."

Irina jiggles the old zipper to get it working as she releases a long, theatrical sigh. "Okay, *fine*. I'll put you out of your misery. Here it is: Grant Walker's said to have mad skills in the sack, like the kind that spawn urban legends. Maybe it's because he's got that sensitive-musician thing happening, or could be his dexterity that makes him so—"

I cough.

She gives my back a few hearty slaps. "Hey, you were the one who *had* to know."

I clear my throat. "So, does he have a girlfriend, then?"

She fastens the pearl button above the zipper. "How would I know?"

"W-well, what do you think makes someone skilled? Is it sheer numbers or the size of—"

"Oh no!" Irina cries. I turn to find her scrounging through her bag. "I forgot shoes. How could I forget shoes?"

"You can borrow a pair of mine. You might feel sorta geisha-like since they're a size smaller, but you're welcome to—"

"Excellent!" She pops up to forage my closet. "An accomplished lover isn't really about size or experience, well, maybe a *little* about that. Mainly, it boils down to whether or not he's a 'ladies first' kind of guy."

"Ladies first?" I echo.

"Yeah, meaning the girl's pleasure is primary. If he's concerned about her satisfaction in bed, stands to reason he'll be tuned in to the other stuff." She chuckles. "And believe me, any guy who unlocks another woman's passion will *forever* be legendary." Irina struts out. "These good?"

My head bobs, but I've totally checked out. Images of Grant mingle with the words "pleasure" and "legendary," until there's no room for anything else.

She fans my face. "Whoa, you're burning up, Wil. Hey"—she lifts my chin—"is it possible that it's more than curiosity? Maybe you feel something for Grant and that's what's really behind the questions?"

"No! That's crazy. I mean"—I shake my head vehemently—"he's completely wrong. Good God, he's a *Pisces*! It doesn't get *more* wrong. And anyway, why would I want Grant when Seth is my ideal?" I cinch the belt, ignoring the junkie-like tremor of my hands.

Iri shrugs. "You tell me." She shucks off her jeans and

shirt, and lays her "shock factor" outfit on the bed. "Look, I wasn't going to say anything." She chews the inside of her cheek before continuing. "But I saw you and Grant together that night when you danced." Iri lets out a low whistle. "Serious chemistry, Wil."

Irina's standing there in her bra and see-through undies, so why am I the one who feels naked? I go to my dresser and open the jewelry box, rummaging through my accessories. "It was nothing."

"Yeah. Well, the Land of Denial can be fun to visit, but you shouldn't build a house there."

"Crap! Tell me I haven't lost one of my favorites!" I scoop up a handful of earrings and dig for the missing two-tier, faux sapphire clip-on. They had been a fourteenth-birthday present from Gram. She'd gone to several antique flea markets to find them. If I lost one, I'd be—*Aha!*

"*Hello?* Still talking here. Wil, you guys were totally into each other. The way you moved together on the dance floor . . . Let's just say I could feel the heat from across the club."

"Which ones?" I hold up two pairs—one set is the vintage birthday earrings, the other small and simple.

She taps the dangly sapphire pair and puffs out a breath. "Honestly, I thought this chart thing might be the push you needed into the dating world. Something that would get you past this hang-up you have about being romantically cursed. But now . . . I don't know. Maybe it was a mistake."

"Mistake? You're *waaaay* overreacting. And I think you

worry more than Gram. Which means the earth might've started spinning in reverse."

"And I don't think you're worrying enough. I know why you cling to this, *dorogaya,* I do."

I flash a look of warning. "Let it go."

She plows on undeterred. "Astrology won't bring her back, Wil. Neither will living your life in perfect accordance with some *ridiculous* planetary chart."

My anger flares like a struck match as I toss the extra earrings onto my dresser. "You think I don't know that?" I bark. "My mom is gone, Iri, and how I choose to honor her is *my* business—*mine.*"

How dare she dismiss my charts and twist this completely into a mother issue! After all, I don't bring up *her* mother!

"Okay," Iri replies more calmly, "then why do you hide it from Gram? Why all the secrecy when it comes to astrology?"

"You *know* why." My jaw clenches and unclenches.

Gram has strong opinions when it comes to astrology, or as she refers to it—*that cosmological hooey.* But hell, Gram has strong opinions about everything. And while she tolerates my occasional wearing of a star-themed T-shirt, I have an inkling every one of her atoms would split if she knew how deep my preoccupation really went.

"Wil, would you listen to . . ." Irina reaches for my arm and I pull away. Frustrated, she thrusts her hands to the ceiling. "You can't force yourself to fall in love with someone! It doesn't work that way! Love can't be measured or quantified like stars. It's messy and unpredictable. Hell, sometimes it's even wrong. And sometimes wrong *is* right."

I square my shoulders and fold my arms. *"Really?* Because *wrong* worked out so well for my mother? My dad *abandoned* her before I was born, remember?" Iri casts away my reasoning with a shake of her head, which only stokes my inner fire. "Well, what makes *you* the sudden authority on love? Because having your share of partners doesn't make you any more of an expert."

Iri's lips part; her hand drifts to her stomach. And there's no anger in her gray eyes, only pain. She turns her back to me and slowly tugs on her pants.

I've crossed a line.

Oh no. I can't believe I just said that. I want to yank all those words back. I want to crush them, grind them, burn them, so they never hurt her again. "Iri," I croak, "I'm so sorry. I didn't mean to say . . ."

"That I'm a slut?" Her voice is small, but oh God—I am infinitely smaller. She unhooks her bra, letting the lace drop to the floor. My heart drops with it. "I know what people say when my back is turned." She pulls on the silver tube top before turning around. "I just didn't think you were one of them."

"I'm not!" I place my hands on both sides of her face, forcing her gaze on me. "I'm not, Iri! I—I was . . . upset; I wasn't thinking. Which is a crappy excuse for saying something so horrible and *not at all* true." I brush my thumbs over her pale skin. "Listen to me; you're the most courageous, beautiful, intelligent girl I know. And I'm honored—do you hear me—*honored* to have you as my best friend. Please . . . can you forgive me?"

Maybe I'll never understand why Iri makes the choices she does. Maybe I'm not meant to. All I know is this: Irina Dmitriyev just . . . *is*. She transcends labels. She loves who she loves, and hates who she hates, with little that falls in the cracks between.

"Shit." Her eyes glisten. "When you say it like that . . ." I wind my arms tight around her. She lets out a quiet sniffle and my heart breaks a little more. "But you're more than my best friend, Wil. You're my sister, too," the indestructible girl whispers.

"Forever sisters," I murmur. Squeezing her harder, I swallow. Which isn't easy. My throat has shrunk to an eighth of its normal size. "Hey"—I stroke her hair—"I swear on Aquarius, I didn't mean it. I was being a complete idiot."

"S'okay." We separate. "That wasn't really about me." Her glassy eyes search mine. "Was it?"

"No. It was about . . ." I struggle to pinpoint exactly what *had* set me off. "I guess I'm . . . scared. *God!* I was fine ten minutes ago!" I slump to my bed. "And it's not like I'm afraid of the things I thought I'd be. The feelings, the desires I worried about? Well . . . they're there."

Irina sits beside me. "That's great, Wil. See? I told you if you found the right gu—"

"No, it isn't. Because yesterday I had this dream, and when I woke up, I was saying his name." I grab a pillow to smother my flaming face as the vivid memories resurface.

"Must've been one helluva goodnight kiss." She bumps my shoulder. "Careful, another one of those from Seth and you might spontaneously combust in your sleep."

I release a frustrated groan, tossing the pillow and flopping on my back. I stare at my stucco ceiling, peaked like meringue. "Yeah, except I was saying Grant's name. *Not* Seth."

With the wind no longer in her sails, she deflates at my side. "Oh. That's . . ."

"Exactly." I push the heels of my hands to my eyes.

"Ah, ah, makeup," she admonishes, pulling my hands down. "You know what? Doesn't matter. People put way too much stock in dreams anyway."

I prop up on my elbows. "Do you think I'm ridiculous?"

"Yes." Iri pats my cheek. "Why do you think we get along so well?" We both laugh. "Hey, would you do something different with my hair tonight? I was thinking your specialty—old Hollywood glam." She nestles on the floor at my feet. "What are those big rolls you sometimes do?"

"Victory rolls? No, those have to set overnight." I slide my fingers through her silky platinum hair. "How about some waves? Large rolling ones like Veronica Lake?"

"Sounds fabulous. Yes, do it." She stills my hand and peers up over her shoulder. "Everything will work out, Wil. You'll see."

I nod, dispelling the dark clouds of doubt. Seth will

be here within the hour. *Tonight will be perfect,* I assure myself.

Because billions of stars cannot be wrong.

There was probably a time when the paper lanterns in Korean Seoul Restaurant didn't have tears or a fine coat of dust. And I bet there were real plants before the silk ones came along. Even the booths are broken in like old saddles that mold to your butt.

The divide between the fancy French place and this hole-in-the-wall is as massive as the distance separating Western Europe from Asia. Am I surprised? Not really. Not when I'm supposed to expect the unexpected.

I get a whiff of the dish in front of me and wrinkle my nose. "Okay, how can I say this diplomatically?"

"Just say it," Seth replies.

"It reeks."

His brown eyes crinkle. "Well, yeah, it's fermented cabbage."

"I know. I mean, I've had kimchi before. I've just never acquired a taste for it."

He slides over a bowl with neon-yellow slices. "Kimchi is seasoned a lot of different ways. Maybe you'll like this one better—it's sweeter than the others."

"Sounds promising." Balancing the glowing vegetable on my chopsticks, I pop it in my mouth before it has a chance to fly across the table. "Mmm, now *that* one's actually decent."

Seth cocks his head. "Actually?" he repeats with mock indignation. "Don't you have *any* faith in me?"

I glance to the take-out counter on the other side of the restaurant, where a colorful dragon suspends like an Asian piñata. The cobwebs at the creature's mouth look a lot like smoke. I bite back a smile.

"All right, I'll grant you, this place isn't much to look at—"

"Oh, on the contrary," I say with a smirk, marveling at the awesomely tacky velvet tiger pictures on the wall, "I think it's *a lot* to look at."

Seth chuckles before picking at a bit of kimchi that resembles compost. "Wait till you try their bibimbap. They make some of the best I've had stateside." He pops the yard waste in his mouth, chewing slowly.

"It's been forever since I had good—"

"I thought I hear Seth. Seth, that you?" With her heavy accent, the *h* is silent, so it sounds like *Set*. A tiny Korean woman—voice bigger than her five-foot stature—appears at our table and sets down two more dishes. "More kimchi. Ah"—her dark eyes widen—"and you bring pretty girlfriend?"

Now my eyes widen. "Oh, I'm not . . . I mean . . . we're . . . well, I'm just sort of . . ." You would never know English is my first language. Because it seems I'm suddenly fluent in gibberish.

Seth's swallow threatens to pull a U-turn before he's able to jump in. "Um, Soo-Jin, this is my date, Wil. Wil, Soo-Jin. She owns the restaurant."

Soo-Jin shifts her adoring smile from Seth to me. "He never bring girl here. You must be *very* special."

"I love your dragon," I blurt. Because nothing creates a diversion like a mythical rainbow beast. But my comment doesn't faze her.

Soo-Jin leans in conspiratorially and lowers her voice. "For how long he been going in you? Hmm?"

My eyes almost explode from their sockets. "I . . . what?"

"Uh, she means how long have you been going *with me*," Seth hastily translates. "Not long, Soo-Jin. Thank you." He bows his head. "I think we're all good here."

Soo-Jin's cheeks plump more with her smile. "He even more handsome when his face go red, isn't he?"

I choke back a laugh and nod. Which is lost on Seth because he's preoccupied with feng shui-ing all the dishes on the table.

When Soo-Jin finally leaves, he shudders. "Well, that was only half as mortifying as it could've been."

"True. You could've split your pants."

He smirks, lifting the dented metal teapot and topping off our cups. "Give it time, the night's still young."

I take my cup, wrapping my hand around the warm porcelain. "Hey, I like that you took me somewhere that means something to you."

"It does." Seth raises his teacup. "So what should we toast to?"

"Fermented cabbage? Or . . . or maybe reinforced seams?" We laugh.

"What, and ignore the incredible velvet art on the wall?" He ponders for another second. "We could just toast to adventure. In food or . . . otherwise?"

I like the sound of that. "To adventure."

Our cups clink.

"Mmm"—I swallow—"speaking of adventure, what are you doing after graduation next year?" My chopsticks fling apart, rolling across the table. "Oops. Jeez, you'd think I'd have a better command of these by now."

He grins. "We just gotta tweak your technique. Here, hold the top one like this." I feel a mini jolt as his hands slip around mine. He patiently curls my fingers around the sticks in a way that stabilizes them. "Long term? Not a clue. How about you? I could use some ideas."

"I don't know either," I confess. "It's not like I can make a viable career out of astrology. Plus, Gram would have a coronary. I've considered astronomy, but frankly, math isn't my forte and the field is pretty saturated anyway. I guess what I'd really love is to travel." I frown. "Not that that's any more realistic."

"Where would you go? If you could go anywhere."

"Florence," I gush, without hesitation. "You know it's the cradle of the Renaissance." Using my dipping sauce dribbles, I draw little clouds on my plate with the end of my chopstick. "Italy's just so rich in culture and history— not to mention gelato. It'd be a dream come true for me."

"Funny you say that. I'm toying with the idea of bumming around Europe for a few months after graduation. Italy would definitely be one of the stops."

"Hold on." I abandon the chopsticks, splaying my hands on the table. "I need a second to explode with jealousy."

He lifts a shoulder. "Maybe you should come." His grin is sly. "You know, if you haven't broken my nose or anything by then."

"Ha-ha, funny. That would involve some very steep odds that require winning the lotto. Seriously, Seth, wouldn't your parents pitch a fit?"

He finishes chewing. "Nah, won't matter, really. I'll be eighteen and have access to my trust fund." He catches my raised brow. "Damn. Did that just sound as obnoxious as I think it did?"

"Yup. On a scale of one to ten on the Obnoxious Meter, I'd give it an eight."

"Yeah, well, my grandpa Walker was a pretty heavy hitter in the stock market. Everything—I mean *everything*—the man touched turned to gold. My family inherited a pretty sizeable chunk of his fortune."

That explains the spanking new Lexus. And expensive clothes. And Euro-bumming. I smirk. "Okay, ten, I give it a ten. Maybe even an eleven."

He nudges my foot under the table.

Curiosity commandeers my tongue. "So, Grant'll start college this fall? Or will he travel like you?"

"College. He's headed out of state—University of Michigan. Guess they've got a good business program."

"Business?" I croak. The dumpling plops to my plate shy of its destination. I pick it up again. "I . . . I would've thought music."

Seth wipes his mouth. "Well, Grant's a genius with numbers, just like Grandpa and Dad. And Mom has this thing about not living up to your potential, so she'd probably string Grant up by his nuts if he didn't carry on Dad's CPA firm."

I snort.

"Yeah, and you thought the Greeks were bad."

"She sounds terrifying."

"I'm kidding. She's actually pretty cool—when she's not in overprotective-Mom mode. I swear, sometimes she still thinks I'm a little kid. I keep waiting for her to bust out a wet rag to scrub off my juice 'stache or something."

I giggle. "Pretty sure they *all* do that. It's a parental thing. Gram would've probably frozen me at ten if it weren't for the sea-monkey incident."

"You had a *sea-monkey* incident?"

"Doesn't everyone?" I maintain my straight face for all of three seconds before Seth's grin causes me to crumble.

"Uhhh . . . no. Guess some of us have led deprived childhoods. But enough about that, let's go back to talking about the future." He peers up from his dark lashes. My heartbeat zigs and zags, unclear where this is going. "Wanna be my date to a party next Saturday? Tristan— lead singer from Grant's band—always has this giant start-of-summer bash the week his parents leave town. DJ, caterers, keg—the works."

I stop spearing the innocent dumpling and drop my hands to my lap. There isn't a reason in the world to say no. Yet my vocal cords seem paralyzed by yes. *Snap out of it!*

"Come on, it'll be fun. Some of the guys have even been known to wear loincloths and Viking helmets."

I smile at this; my vocal cords loosen a smidge. "Are you one of them?"

"I prefer not to incriminate myself. Unless that'll score me a yes?" Hope wavers in his expression. He runs a hand through his dark hair. "Look, no pressure—come, don't come—I just thought you might have a good time."

Deep down I know the true reason I hesitate. It's the same reason I'm now shredding the napkin on my lap. What if Irina is right? What if I *feel* something for Grant? A big something?

Once again, I'm on the verge of screwing up the cornucopia of awesome the universe has generously placed before me. "I'll come," I say resolutely. "I want to come."

"Yeah? Cool." But the way he tugs at his earlobe, there's something else I'm missing.

I start to reach across the table for his hand, but feel pushy and lose my nerve. Instead, I redirect my fingers to the side of the battered teapot. "Was there something else?"

"Maybe." He rests his fingers on mine. They're as warm and soft as I remember them from our walk along the river. "That night at Absinthe, when you agreed to go out with me. What would've happened if I hadn't been—"

"Two bibimbap?" The server halts at our tableside. His tray is loaded with two heavy stone bowls of sizzling rice with meat and vegetables. A sunny-side-up egg tops the dish.

"That's us. Thanks," Seth says, relaxing back in the booth. He nods at me. "Better dig in, next stop is a good forty-minute drive."

Taking my cue from Seth, I relax, too. "Can't you give me one teensy clue?" I plead.

Steam rises from his bowl as he pokes at the mounded egg yolk, stirring it with the other ingredients. "Oh, I don't know." He leans forward, and lowers his voice. "I kinda like you breathless with anticipation."

Chapter 8

Seth's right. I never would have guessed this in a million, trillion years. And . . . *I love it.* Even Iri won't be able to dismiss the epicness of this surprise.

He runs his warm hands up and down my bare arms, making my skin seem chilled by contrast. We're almost halfway into June, but it isn't unusual for evening temperatures to have a touch of seasonal dyslexia. Tonight it feels more spring than summer.

"Warm enough?" Seth asks.

The pilot opens a valve. "Hold on, I'm taking us higher," he calls out.

Propane burners roar overhead, raising our altitude. The city grows steadily smaller. Even the Opal River has shrunk to a thin vein of squiggling greenish blue.

"Who cares? I'm in a hot-air balloon!" I squeal. "This

totally puts the view from the water tower to shame. I can see *everything*."

My greedy eyes gobble up Carlisle from afar as we ascend through wisps of cloud cover. When the burners stop firing, we lapse into silence, floating like a dandelion tuft caught in a gentle breeze. Gripping the edge of the basket, I barely register the goose bumps prickling my skin as I take in the patchwork landscape below.

"See? *This* is why I said bring a sweater." Seth opens his jacket, wrapping me inside of it. "Although . . . keeping you warm definitely has its advantages."

"It does." I snuggle closer, relishing the heat and the feel of his body at my back. "I still can't *believe* you set this up. I think this ranks as one of the best surprises I've ever had. Exactly how many girls have been completely swept off their feet by this gesture?" I pause. "By the way, that was an accidental pun."

Seth laughs. "None. This is my first time in a hot-air balloon, too."

"Really?" I reply with a note of surprise. Given Seth's resources and sense of adventure, I wouldn't have guessed that he was a virgin ballooner. "So, where'd you get the idea?"

I feel his shrug at my back. "You. Listening to you talk. You belong up here, Wil."

My head rests against his chest while I gaze at the setting sun. And it's so quiet, I swear I hear the moment that great orb hits the curve of the earth, unfurling into a thousand ribbons of yellows, oranges, and reds. "Amazing, isn't it?" Silence. "Seth?" I tip my head up to see he's not at all looking at the spectacular horizon.

He's watching me.

I swallow. "This must've cost a small fortune. And you're missing it."

"You're happy?" he asks. "I mean, really happy?" His heart is racing, prodding mine to do the same.

"*More* than happy," I breathe.

He lowers his head, brushing a featherlight kiss on my lips. My eyes flutter open when Seth draws back. "Then I'm not missing anything. Because from right here"—he purposefully gazes down at me—"the view is perfect."

We arrive at Absinthe just as the opening act leaves the stage. Seth and I are inching our way through the packed crowd.

The air is thick with warring body sprays and pheromones. Nomadic eyes flit from person to person in split-second dismissals or appraisals; the judgments are instantaneous and binding.

Seth shouts or nods or lifts his chin to a number of people as we pass. Never once does he let go of my hand, not until we reach our destination in front of the stage.

"Thanks, man." Seth claps the back of a beefy guy holding a spot for us.

"No sweat. Nice to get out from behind the bar and into the action." It's Nico. I'd recognize those prolific sideburns anywhere. "You see Tessa? Girl is on the prowl tonight." He whistles through his teeth. "Jesus H, wait'll you see what she's wear—"

"Uh, Nico," Seth coughs. "You remember Wil, right?" He reaches back, pulling me in front of him through the crowd.

"Hello again," I say.

Nico blinks and quickly recovers with a predatory grin. "Please, Seth, I never forget a pretty face." He grins a little wider. "Sugar, you sure you're with the right Walker?"

And . . . I'm so stunned I can't articulate a response.

Seth slugs his arm.

Nico chuckles, rubbing his bicep. "Ow, hey, I'm just yanking your chain. Besides, Grant was the one who gave the green light to give her whatever she wanted at the bar. When I saw 'em dancing, I figured they were together. It's not like he makes the rounds like he use—"

"Don't you have somewhere to be?" Seth's tone is arctic.

Nico's grin holds, but his eyes have gone flat and hard. "Yeah, I do. But lemme give you a little advice, friend. *Ease up.* You don't do jealous; don't start now."

Seth's posture remains ramrod even after Nico's disappeared into the throng of bodies around us. And it's ridiculously trivial, but my mind's tripping over the fact that Grant bought the ginger ale, which means . . . Could Seth's sudden departure last Sunday have been provoked . . . *by Grant*?

The silence hangs between us. It's gotten louder in the club, but somehow our silence is all I hear. I need to get us back on track.

Banishing Nico's idiotic words, I lace my fingers in Seth's and pull him closer. "I thought we were having a great time. Is my company boring you already?"

Seth's mouth twitches.

Bingo.

He motions me closer. Blood thrums in my veins as his lips hover at my ear. "You and boring don't share space in the same universe."

I'm about to object. As a matter of fact, I can be *quite* boring. Like when I get sucked into a special on the Discovery Channel, and sit catatonic on the couch with a bag of potato chips that disappear faster than a falling star from the sky.

The emcee's voice cuts through the crowd's dull roar. "So, how bad do you want them?" Cheers erupt. The emcee grins. "I don't know if that's bad enough. You're gonna have to try a little *haaaarder.*" He thrusts the mic toward the crowd and their deafening cries. "Ah, that's better. Now let's give some love for tonight's headliner, Absinthe's very own . . . *Wanderlust!*"

Wanderlust? It's the band from the flyer at Inkporium.

The stage explodes with bright, glittering lights. And the crowd goes . . . absolutely nuts.

Manny raises his drumsticks, clicking them in quick succession. *"Three, two, one!"* he shouts. The beat grabs everyone's attention and doesn't let go. Manny thrives under the spotlight during the opening drum solo. He wields two sticks, but the fast blur of motion makes them look like hundreds.

The keyboard and guitar come in next. Each instrumental layer compounds the musical spell. There are whistles and cheers. People bounce and move to the fast rhythm.

The blond, shaggy-haired lead singer leaps to center stage. So this is Tristan. Whoa, his jeans are snug. I can count the change in his pockets from the front row—all two dollars and seventy-five cents in compressed coins. But my awareness of his shrink-wrapped lower half instantly disappears when he begins to sing.

Tristan's pitch-perfect voice has just the right amount of grit—smooth with rough edges—as he pours raw emotion into the lyrics.

The keyboardist hammers the keys in tempo with the drums. His newsboy cap is slightly cocked as he nods to the music.

Finally, after my eyes have explored *every* band member, I give myself permission to look at Grant.

Grant's probably the least flashy of them all in his plain gray T-shirt, frayed jeans, and duct-taped shoe. Under the bright lights, I see I was right. The tattoos on his arm are music notes.

And I'm mesmerized by the way his fingers work the guitar strings. The tendons in his forearms pop and release as he plays. Grant is dreamily lost in the music. He rocks to the beat, a euphoric almost-smile touching his lips. And I want to go to that place. Blindly follow wherever it is he's gone. Even if just for one solitary song.

As if hearing my thoughts, Grant chooses *that* moment to look up from his guitar. Gazing directly at me.

I suck in a breath. Look away. Look away. Look anywhere . . . just not . . . at Grant. But even Tristan's gyrations and throaty lyrics don't break my trance. Because everything else has fallen away—faded into nothingness. But not Grant, he is real. As real and true and bright as the North Star herself.

Then he lifts his chin at me.

And . . . I think I might come undone.

This is awful.

By the time we head backstage, I've pulled myself together. Grant is nothing more than pollen. An allergen. It's a simple matter of desensitization. Expose myself in small doses and, eventually, I won't have any reaction at all.

And Seth deserves someone worthy of his generosity and kindness. Someone equally enamored of him. For the love of Venus, I vow that girl will be me.

"Wait." I catch the hem of Seth's shirt, stopping him short of the door, where postperformance festivities are going strong. I stand on my tiptoes, pressing my lips to his, sealing my renewed silent promise with a kiss.

"Mmm." Seth raises an eyebrow. "What was that for?"

I lower back down. "Because. Just . . . because."

His mouth hikes up at the side as he curls a finger around my belt, drawing me closer. "Good enough reason for me. You know"—he peeks covertly left, then right— "Absinthe is full of dark corners. Say the word and I'll offer a personal tour."

I'm grateful for the dim light because I'm sure my cheeks are glowing. Seth's breath is hot on my skin as his lips graze my shoulder. My knees forget they're supposed to be supporting me. Which complicates standing. "Sounds like you're speaking from experience," I murmur.

"Well, of course. Can you keep a secret?"

"Yeah," I reply uneasily.

Seth drops his voice to a low whisper. "This is where I store the Batmobile. There's this elaborate underground cave system where I hide the—" He laughs when I slap his chest, and pulls me closer. Then his expression sobers. "Listen, Wil, there's something else I should . . ." Seth bites his lower lip uncertainly.

Uncertainty? *How un-Sagittarius of him.*

The backstage door flies open. A girl with a wild mane of curls halts in her stilettos. Her miniskirt is . . . let's say I've seen flexible Band-Aids with more coverage. "Well, well, if it isn't Seth Walker." Her tone is as lethal as the spikes of her heels. "Didn't take you long, did it?"

Seth lets go of me and folds his arms. "We broke it off months ago. What do you want, Tessa?"

"What do I *want*?" She lets out an evil laugh. "I want someone to run that worthless heart of yours through a meat grinder—see how *you* like it! I want to never look at your stupid face again! Or catch you feeling up some ska—"

"Then maybe you shouldn't come to a club my family owns," he replies coolly. "Just a suggestion."

Tessa's jaw clacks shut; her nostrils flare. "Mark my words, Seth. One day some girl's gonna bring you to your knees. And nothing, not even that perfect little smile, will save you." She mumbles a few more colorful phrases before stalking away.

"Yeah, nice to see you, too, Tess. And, uh . . . real creative use of the f-bomb. Seriously."

She doesn't turn around. Instead, her middle finger has the final say.

"She wants to study acting, so"—he offers an apologetic look—"drama's kinda her thing."

"I'd say she has a solid future ahead of her," I reply. "Seems very in touch with her emotions."

Seth chuckles with evident relief. "You're not mad?"

"Well, drama's not generally my thing."

"God, I'm so in like with you." He pushes open the door. "All right, we'll just make an appearance. Long enough for the guys to drool over how hot and drama-free you are, and then I want you to myself." He grins, leading me into the testosterone lair.

Backstage has none of the fanciness I envisioned. In fact, it's one step above a garage. There are crates and boxes for seating, and a brown plaid couch that looks donated by someone's great-grandmother. The place is cluttered with people and other random things—like a garden gnome with sunglasses and a cigar stuck in his mouth. In the back corner there's a skeleton with a sideways baseball hat guarding a popcorn machine. It's a mishmash of weird. So of course I love it.

I process all this in less time than it takes for the keyboardist to use a lighter to pop the cap off his bottle.

"Dude," he says as he fist-bumps Seth.

"Wil, this is Ryan. Master of the keyboard and brother from another mother."

I smile. "You guys were amazing tonight."

"Thanks." He adjusts his hat, flashing a set of dimples. "And we've sorta met already."

"You have?" Seth glances between us.

I'm as perplexed as Seth. "I'm sorry, I don't remember—"

"Oh, you wouldn't. I was the guy on the ground. You know, the one instructing you *not* to jump from the water tower."

"Oh God, that was *you*?"

"In the flesh." He chuckles at my obvious mortification. "Yeah, one minute we're cruising to the music store to get some new amps—finally got Grant to admit it was time to trade in those relics." Ryan shakes his head. "And the next, Grant's running the wagon off-road and ranting about some girl about to jump. Totally wigged out, which I guess makes sense because of . . ."

"The heights thing?" I ask, smiling helpfully.

Ryan's dimples fade as he gives Seth a peculiar glance. Seth responds with a subtle shake of his head. Well, seems I'm odd man out of the unspoken conversation. "Uh, something like that," Ryan finishes vaguely. "Anyway, you guys survived, so"—he holds up the bottle—"cheers to that."

I chuckle, part embarrassment and part resignation. "I'd love to say stuff like that is atypical. But . . ." I shrug.

"It's true. You should have seen her today in the hot-air balloon," Seth adds, snaking his arm along my shoulders.

"Managed to con the pilot into teaching her Ballooning 101, right before she almost landed us in a tree."

I elbow his ribs. "Hey, there's no crime against being inquisitive. Besides, what if the pilot became incapacitated?"

Ryan's green eyes glimmer. "Why would he be incapacitated?"

"I don't know. Hostile takeover by . . . sky . . . *pirates*," I finish lamely.

Seth squeezes me, tickling my side. "Sky pirates, huh?"

"The balloon's not going to land itself! And I was *at least* twenty feet from that tree. *Stop!*" I giggle, doubling over. "You should be grateful I was prepared."

"Oh, I'm grateful." His voice rasps in my ear only loud enough for me to hear. "And I promise to prove it later."

I shiver.

Ryan pulls out his cell. "All right, you two are gonna make me hurl. I gotta track down Ginger. I swear that girl's a damn beacon for disaster. But then, look who I'm talking to," he says to me with a wink. "Be back."

Seth carries on with the informal introductions. "Where was I? Oh, that heathen over there is Tristan. He's the one having the party next Saturday. Hey, Tris," Seth calls, "this is Wil."

Tristan pauses his conversation with a couple of fans and flicks the blond hair from his eyes. "Hey there," he projects in a swoon-worthy voice.

"Hi." I wave back.

"And the spaz next to the fridge is—"

"Succulent Wil!" Manny shouts across the room. "You bring the secret recipe or just the sexy tonight?"

"You did not just say that." I laugh.

Seth's eyebrows bounce up. "I take it you've met."

"Sure have." I'm still grinning as Manny joins us. "Ill-mannered Manny. You were fairly awesome tonight."

He bear-hugs me like we've been friends for ages. And for some reason, it feels like we have. Of course, it's partly because of his charming exuberance as a Libra. "*Fairly? Chica*, please, I lit those drums on fire, and speakin' of fire . . ." We part. "Dig the dress." He lets out a low wolf whistle.

"I was going to say the same thing about your shirt." Which boasts: LESS CALORIES! TASTES GREAT!

Manny smirks, then looks up at Seth. "Sorry, *vato*, but I'm stealing her. We've got some classified matters to discuss."

Before Seth can voice an objection, Ryan returns. "Hey, man, you got any jumper cables? Ginger's POS car won't start and she's stranded at work."

Seth hesitates, briefly scanning the backstage scene. "Manny, you seen Grant?"

"Not my turn to watch him," Manny quips. "Last I saw, he was with Lila."

Ryan fusses with his hat impatiently. "So, Seth, you got cables or not? I had to loan my car to my sister, so I'm kinda up shit creek here."

"Uh . . . yeah." Seth turns to me. "I'm sorry, Wil. You cool with hanging here for a few while I help them out?"

"Sure, no problem."

Seth reels me in by my belt loop once more. "Good, because this night isn't over. Not by a long shot." His eyes are full of promises that his lips will deliver later.

"I'm holding you to that."

"Music to my ears. I'll hurry, okay?" My Sagittarius lets go, pausing before ducking out the door. "And, Manny, I'm coming back for her, so don't get any dumb ideas."

"Whatever," Manny mutters, hooking his arm in mine. "Thirsty, Wil?"

"Bottle of water if you've got it."

He opens the refrigerator, graffitied with so many indie-band stickers I couldn't tell you the appliance's original color. He hands me a water bottle before snagging a Red Bull for himself. Yeah, he needs the extra energy boost like a jackrabbit needs amphetamines.

Manny motions toward a stack of boxes. "Have a seat."

I sit down. "Thanks. So, uh, what's this classified matter all about?"

"I'm trying to think of a tactful way to say it." Manny scratches the back of his head. His eyes divert to the door.

"Okay, that's ominous. What if I said I'd try not to be offended?"

"It's a start." He cracks open the can and takes a swallow. Then levels me with his brown eyes. "What are you doing with Seth?"

My stomach capsizes like a vessel caught in a violent squall. I right my innards, which really have no reason to be affected by the question. "It's called dating."

He takes a seat beside me. "Yeah, I figured. What I can't figure out is why."

"Well, it isn't exactly a great mystery of the universe. He asked me out and I said yes. Not that I owe *you* an explanation." I'm joking. But I do find his keen interest in my dating habits bizarre.

"You don't," he agrees. "Except I think things would've played out different if Seth hadn't barged in like he did. Kinda dickish, if you ask me."

I frown.

He nudges me. "All right, I know you *didn't* ask me. Look, I've known Grant a long time."

"From school?" I take a drink of water.

"Come on, do I look like preppy Hartford material? Hell no. My dad has a landscaping company. We service most of the houses in his neighborhood, which is how I met Grant." Manny takes another swig of the energy drink. "Turns out I wasn't much for landscaping." He flashes an impish grin. "But I *could* tell you the color and pattern of every single bikini on the east side."

I knock his shoulder. "You're terrible. Why are you telling me all this?"

"Because Grant is like a brother to me. And here's the thing . . . he won't make a move if he thinks you and Seth are a thing. He's pretty black-and-white that way."

"And why in the world would you think I'd want Grant to make a move?"

Manny eyes me like I'm denser than moon rock. "Oh, *chica*." He breaks into laughter.

I tuck a dark wave behind my ear. "Manny, we're friends. *Just* friends. Why is that so hard for you to believe? Grant's wonderful but we don't mesh—astrologically speaking. It'll never happen. Ever."

Manny stops chuckling and drapes his arm around my shoulders, speaking low in my ear. "Whatever you say, Wil. But all I know is Grant hasn't danced with a girl like that in over two years."

My brows draw together. "Really? Why?"

"That's his story to tell. And he just walked in, so I'm shutting up."

Lo and behold, there's Grant.

With a blond bombshell in tow.

chapter 9

Backstage is shrinking. The clutter and chatter and bodies, it suddenly feels too stifling.

The blonde murmurs something in Grant's ear; one of her hands clings to his shoulder. The other hand moves to his chest, her finger tapping as she speaks. He nods. *Nods?* What is he nodding for? My mind flips through a gazillion scandalous scenarios Grant has just consented to. I feel like I've been punched in the gut. When the girl moves over to Tristan, I experience a weird wave of relief, until she gives Grant a suggestive wink when she looks back.

"Is that girl with Grant?" I eye the pretty blonde's form-fitting tank dress. Her body is long and svelte—a dancer's body—like Irina's. Which is something mine could never aspire to be.

"Ha! She wishes. That's Tristan's sister, Lila." Manny

snaps his fingers in front of my face. "And, news flash, you and Grant don't look at each other like friends. You should definitely ditch Seth." He hops down.

"You have an awful lot of opinions. What's that saying about opinions?"

He takes my hand and kisses the back. "I just call it how I see it. Later, *chica*." Manny fake-punches Grant in the stomach as he passes.

"Hey," I say as Grant approaches. "That performance was . . . *wow*. Really. I was all prepared for some mediocre garage band, but you guys blew me away." I stand and suddenly don't know what to do with my arms. They hang at my sides like limp spaghetti. I cross and then uncross them. Do I hug him? I hugged Manny. Would it be more suspicious if I didn't? This is dumb. I'll hug him.

"Thanks," Grant replies, but doesn't move to embrace or touch me in any way.

Okay, that's settled. So we are friends who don't hug. Good to know. I sit back down.

"Walker, what the hell happened to you during the second set?" Tristan asks as he flops on the plaid couch, pulling an adorable brunette with a pixie cut onto his lap. It's asking a lot of the stitches in his pants, but he looks every bit the part of rock and roller.

The girl giggles and slaps his chest.

"Sorry, man, guess I was a little off tonight," Grant says.

Wait . . . did he just look at me? No, he's turned and is grabbing a bottle from the fridge. I'm hallucinating. *Grant is pollen,* I remind myself.

"Where's Seth?" Grant asks.

Pollen. Pollen. Pollen . . .

"Huh? Oh, he went to get jumper cables for someone named Ginger, I think."

Grant smirks. "Then I'll say a prayer and make an offering to the gnome on behalf of the car. Seth's got about as much mechanical skill as Manny. Probably less."

"I heard that!" An empty Red Bull can whizzes through the air.

Grant ducks and it misses him by inches. "Want company?" he asks me.

"Um, sure. You know, if you were off tonight, it takes a more critical ear than mine to detect it. I was impressed."

He takes a swig. "You're sweet, but I screwed up." Grant gives me a sidelong glance. "You look really pretty tonight."

I tell myself he's just being nice. That's what he does. But my rejoicing heart doesn't care. "So do you," I gush, then realize the stupidity of my words. I blush furiously as the comment dangles uncomfortably between us. "I mean—I don't know why I said that."

Grant leans forward and bats his eyelashes. "Because—*duh*—I'm pretty." He primps his messy hair, and we both laugh; the moment miraculously goes from awkward to perfect.

"Well, I'm drawing the line at letting you borrow my lipstick. It's not cool. I don't care how avant-garde your artsy musician friends think it is. You can't pull off Parisian Pout—your skin tone is all wrong."

"Damn." He grins. "And here I thought things were about to get interesting."

I chuckle, feeling more at ease. My desensitization is working! I squint at the back wall. "Dartboard? Seems kinda dangerous given the tight quarters here."

"Nah." Grant places his bottle on the floor. "Not as long as you're up-to-date on all your shots."

Someone turns up the music. My ears perk at the sound of a remix of the vintage Dinah Washington "Is You Is Or Is You Ain't My Baby?"

There's a loud whistle. "Grant!" Lila shouts as she sways her hips. "Dance with me?" She rotates for everyone to view her perfectly sculpted, spandex-hugged dancer's ass.

It's a miracle my eyes don't stick in the back of my head, given the velocity of their roll.

"Sorry, Lila, this one"—Grant thumbs in my direction—"already challenged me to a game of darts." The guys watching Lila salivate enough to raise Carlisle's water table.

"Aah!" one of the droolers yelps when Tristan opens a can and sprays him.

"Cool off, asswipe. That's my little sister."

Grant turns and motions not so subtly to the back of the room.

Oh, that's my cue. "Darts, yes!" I hop down and follow him to the small open space in front of the dartboard. "Grant, I have to confess I'm not really up-to-date on my inoculations."

He yanks the red and blue feather-tipped darts from the

board. "Don't worry. I'm a good shot. Question is"—he hands me the red ones—"are you?"

I draw back my shoulders. It doesn't matter that I'll likely be destroyed. I will go out in style. I will get my ass kicked with panache . . . and bluff every step of the way. "Good enough to destroy you."

He grins crookedly. "Oh, prepare to be slaughtered, little lamb."

"*Hmph,*" I snort. My first dart flies, hitting the bull's-eye. No one is more surprised than me. I compose myself, camouflaging my shock before turning around.

"Beginner's luck," Grant grumbles, adding a slanted tick mark to the chalkboard. "Two more throws. Do you even know how to play Cricket?"

Cricket? I'm aiming for the center and hoping for the best. Doesn't that pretty much sum up the game of darts? I lower my arm. "I just need to hit the bull's-eye, right?"

He shakes his head, stifling a laugh. "That's what I thought."

Grant then goes on to explain the specifics of the game—the rules, the numbers I need to hit, the scoring, etc. Sheesh. My version of Cricket is so much easier.

"So be the first to close out all your numbers and bull's-eye—and you win," he concludes.

"What do you win?"

Grant shrugs. "Bragging rights. Indentured servitude." He blows off a piece of cork from the tip of his dart. "Or . . . whatever."

"Whatever? That leaves a lot open to interpretation,

doesn't it?" I check my two remaining dart tips, finding them debris-free.

"Then I guess you better not lose." His crooked smile makes the blood speed faster in my veins. But I don't let my reaction show.

"Game on, Walker." My eyes narrow and I throw. It sinks in the eighteen spot. I will count that as lucky and hope to hell the luck will carry me through the remainder of the game.

A half hour passes and I've managed to close out almost all my numbers. I only need a seventeen and twenty to win. Grant still needs a nineteen.

He's taking out his darts from his last throw and catches me checking out his butt. *Oh my God, when did I start looking at his butt? And since when am I a butt ogler?!*

Panicked, I lob a conversational grenade. "S-so, why didn't you want to dance with Lila?" I glance over to see her head thrown back in laughter. She shimmies next to one of her girlfriends. "She's very pretty and"—I rack my brain for something else nice to say—"she seems to really enjoy music."

"And attention, and she's not my type. Your play," he says.

"Then"—I take aim—"what *is* your type?" I throw and whoop when it hits the seventeen, performing a premature victory dance.

"Well, not Lila. Do you know your tongue sticks out of the corner of your mouth whenever you focus? You've been doing it the entire game."

Of course I know that, but I can't change a seventeen-year habit right now. "Gets me in the zone. Why, does it bother you?" I line up my shot, zeroing in on the twenty spot.

"Let me think." I see Grant cross his arms in my periphery. "Does your tongue bother me? Hmm . . ."

I release my dart as Grant ponders my tongue. The dart veers off, sinking in the outer ring of the six. He botched my throw! And, adding insult to injury, he's smirking and all self-satisfied over it.

My nostrils flare. "You did that on purpose!"

He bursts out laughing. "Your face is so red right now. Hey, I don't need to cheat to beat you, so we'll call that last one a do-over. Fair enough?"

I lift my chin. "Fine, but *no* talking during my turn. It messes with my concentration."

"I promise to stand quietly and make a mental list of all the things you'll have to do during your servitude. Beginning with washing and waxing my car, and there's that dry cleaning I've been meaning to pick up . . ."

I yank the wayward dart from the board. When I spin around, I see Grant's eyes guiltily flick up from my backside. His face flushes the way it did at the top of the tower. I could point out how red *his* face is now, but that would acknowledge something other than friendship. Which I *won't* do. I pretend it didn't happen, and line my toes up with the peeling black-and-yellow caution tape on the floor.

Sucking in my breath, I close one eye and fire the dart.

Direct hit. No. Way. No freaking way!

"No way," Grant echoes my thoughts. His light-brown eyes are round and wide.

"I won? I won! I won!" I squeal and clap before shaking his arm. "I destroyed you! I win!"

His jaw twitches. "Destroy is an exaggeration; you eked out a win. You won't be so lucky in a rematch."

"So *you* say. I just hope your delicate male ego can handle getting crushed twice in one night." I fish my cell from my purse while Grant erases the board. Iri's texted that she and the Suit won't be coming and that I shouldn't do anything she wouldn't do. I smirk, trying to wrap my gray matter around what that might be.

I notice there's also a voice mail from a number I don't recognize. Plugging my finger in my other ear, I try to block out the commotion and home in on the garbled voice. My smile falters.

"Wil? What is it?" Grant asks.

"Uh . . ." I distractedly hang up. "It's my grandma. Mrs. Kessler—one of the ladies from her bridge club— was just letting me know she had a dizzy spell tonight. Almost fell." Grant's thick brows draw together in concern. "She's fine," I add quickly, as much to Grant as to myself. "I think Mrs. Kessler just assumed Gram wouldn't tell me. Which is . . . probably true."

I frown. *What if there's more Gram isn't telling me? What if there's something else wro—*

"Do you need to leave?"

I consult the rusted Coca-Cola clock on the wall. *Yikes!*

I didn't realize it was approaching my curfew, too. "Yeah. I should probably check in on her. I'm sure she's fine but . . ." The seed of doubt has already been planted and will likely blossom into full-blown anxiety if I don't go now.

I stand on my toes, surveying backstage. "I wonder what's keeping Seth so long?"

Grant pulls his phone from his pocket. "I'll call him and make sure he hasn't blown anything up." Seth's phone rings. Unfortunately, I can hear it because he's left it in the pocket of his jacket, which was tossed on the gangster skeleton's shoulder.

Grant stows his phone and takes out his keys. "Seth'll understand." He tilts his head in the direction of the door. "Let's get out of here."

"I'm sorry, Grant. If this were anything else but my gran—"

His hand rests at my low back, stirring up memories of our time on the dance floor. "You don't have to apologize or explain, Wil. Let's just get you home." Grant nudges me ahead.

"Hey, where you two going?" Tristan asks, twisting open another beer. "Party's just getting started. Besides"—he points at me with his bottle—"I thought that was Seth's girl."

His sister, Lila, has stopped dancing. Her bottom lip puffs out in disappointment at Grant's early departure. The pout rapidly transforms into a snarl as she processes that Grant's not just leaving—he's leaving with me. I want to tell her she's wasting a perfectly good snarl, because my only objective is getting home. I don't care who takes me.

"Yeah, well, Seth's still off helping Ryan and Ginger, and Wil's gotta leave now. I'll catch you guys later."

"Bye," I say to anyone listening.

Tristan does the hair flick again. "You *are* coming to my party next weekend, aren't you, Cinderella?" His voice manages to pierce through the noise.

Cinderella? I turn back. "Sure, sounds fun."

"Great." Tristan's mouth tips up in a sly grin. "That'll give you a week to come up with a way to stay out past midnight. Everyone knows that's when all the fun happens."

"Right," I reply, wondering how on earth I'll convince Gram to ease up on her curfew manifesto.

Manny shoves the drumsticks he's spinning into his back pocket. "See you soon, Wil." He squeezes me goodbye. "And think about what I said earlier. Deal?"

I shake my head. "Sorry, no deals." Explaining the cosmos and how much it influences our lives was often an uphill battle, a battle I had little time for tonight. "Bye, Manny."

I follow Grant's brisk pace through Absinthe's underbelly, passing ancient boilers and water heaters along the way. My heels bang extra loudly with my haste, echoing against the concrete. The red glow of an exit sign lies ahead.

"You're central, right? Historic district?" he asks, twirling his keys around his finger.

"Uh-huh, Turner Street."

Pushing through the heavy back door, we emerge in the parking lot. It's still packed with cars, but I don't spot Seth's among them.

"Should be able to skate through town no problem. Not much traffic at this hour. This one's mine," Grant says as we come to the last car in a line of reserved parking spots. He unlocks the door.

It's the station wagon from the water tower. Now, I have never been one to care what a person drives. Cars to me have always been simply a way to get from point A to point B. I mean, jeez, I should be so lucky to have a vehicle of any kind, even if it's the color of pickles. Still, I'm surprised.

Grant stretches across the front seat to manually unlock the passenger side.

I slide in. The interior is pretty clean, except for the guitar picks I find scattered about the floor, and sheet music and a couple of amps that look like they've seen better days littering the back. Those must be the relic amps that were supposed to be replaced.

"I know. Not a fancy Lexus like Seth's." He cranks the engine. "But she's my first and I bought her with my own money. Took a whole summer of bagging at World of Food."

"That's a lot of groceries. You *should* be proud."

We turn onto the main road. "Music?" Grant's hand hovers at a metal spoke once covered by a plastic knob.

"Quiet might be nice. Unless you'd rather—"

"No! No. Quiet is good."

Our arms rest side by side on the seat. We aren't touching, but it feels like his skin is on mine. Like invisible fingers tickle my flesh. I glance down and see the solid ten-inch gap between us.

I decide to play it safe anyway, tucking my arm back into my lap. "Thanks again for the lift. I worry I'm becoming the needy friend you keep bailing out."

My attention's drawn to the jangling key chain as we bounce over a series of potholes. The key chain is a military-style dog tag with a stamped message that I'm able to read once it stops wildly swinging from the ignition. It says: HAPPY BIRTHDAY, G! With the date FEBRUARY 23 inscribed beneath it. Which is proof positive of what I always knew.

Grant is unequivocally a Pisces.

I experience a strange wave of melancholy. Like a microscopic part of me had hoped I was wrong. Had thought that maybe—

"Well, don't." His eyes veer from the road. "Worry, I mean. I don't do things unless I want to, and I'm sure if you had a sweet green ride like mine, you'd have done the same."

"In a heartbeat."

He flashes a crooked grin. "You have fun tonight? I mean, other than the sudden end."

"Yeah, it's been great. And, hey, now I officially know how to play Cricket so . . ." I glance out the passenger window as we pass an SUV full of kids. Five of them are wedged in the backseat, singing at the top of their lungs. "I loved hearing you guys play. You're really talented, you know. I'm a sucker for music genre mash-ups—a little rock, a little folk, a little punk."

I hesitate to say anything about my *actual* date, because I don't know how much of my time with his brother I should share. There's an undercurrent of awkward when it comes to that.

"Glad you enjoyed it." The soft glow of the dash lights Grant's features. His brow is wrinkled, jaw muscles tensed, as his fingers tap the side of the steering wheel. "You know, I think Seth likes you—a lot."

I can feel his eyes on me as I occupy my restless hands with the string hanging from my hem. I'm shallow-breathing, and the longer I'm quiet, the more it spotlights my nervousness. Which again, I have *no* reason to be. "He . . . he's been really sweet. Even tolerated me bogarting the dumplings at dinner."

"Now I *know* he really likes you."

"He, um, also surprised me with a hot-air balloon ride. It was pretty amazing."

Grant chuckles to himself, making the tension hold less tightly on my body. "Yeah, Seth's a fan of grand gestures, always has been. Classic example, when he was in fifth grade, he was desperately crushing on this seventh grader—Morgan Mitchell."

"Pretty big age gap for then."

"Oh, for sure, it was scandalous. So Valentine's Day rolls around—"

"Wait, wait, let me guess. He got her an industrial pallet of those candy hearts?"

"Close. He had a dozen roses delivered to her classroom."

"Aw, that's so cute!"

"Every hour on the hour." Grant stops at a light and laughs at my bug-eyed expression. "I know, that's, like, five dozen, and each delivery had a single-word message. Until it pieced together the question: Will-you-be-my-Valentine?" He shakes his head. "Course she said yes."

"Whoa," I breathe, "and that was only fifth grade?" Although, knowing Seth, it wasn't as far-fetched as it sounded. "But how does a ten-year-old get that kind of coin?"

Grant makes a hammering motion with his fist. "Slaughtered his piggy bank. He'd been saving up for a rare comic or something. Guess they cost a pretty penny."

"That's devotion," I marvel. "Okay, so what about you, how did you win over your Valentine?"

"Huh. I don't remember that year. But I remember in fourth grade, I had some pretty wicked skills on the jungle gym. I was the tallest kid in class, and my playground prowess was second to none. And red rover? Forget it. I was an unstoppable force."

"Oh man," I giggle, "I can see it now, you wooing the girls on the monkey bars."

"In the end, it was probably my pocket full of warm gummy worms that won Amanda over."

"Warm? Oh, ick." I shake my head. "Gummy anything

is bad enough, but warmed to a balmy ninety-eight point six?"

He grins. "Hey, they were in a bag. It's not like they were covered with pocket fuzz or anything."

"Don't care. My position on gummy is absolute." The message alert chimes on my phone as we take the downtown exit off the highway. I quickly read it. "Seth and Ryan just got back to Absinthe."

"What took them so long?"

"Uh-oh . . . They reversed the jumper cables. Ended up frying Ginger's battery *and* her alternator. Plus Seth's onboard computer is toast. So they had to wait for two tow trucks."

He laughs. "Yeah, I'm psychic."

No kidding. He's a Pisces. That alone warrants extrasensory perceptions. I reply to Seth, explaining my hasty departure and suggesting a movie tomorrow night. My phone chirps. "Bummer," I mutter.

"What?"

"Oh, just, Seth has inventory in the morning and will be out of town the rest of the weekend." I slouch in my seat. "Now I feel really bad about having to leave."

"That's right." Grant nods. "I think he's ca-brewing with our cousin Jonah and some buddies up north in Lannister."

"Ca-brewing?"

He chuckles. "I take it you've never been?" I shake my head. "Ca-brewing is canoeing—plus a lot of beer."

"Ah. Got it." My cell chimes again. Seth's last text perks

135

me up. And it's definitely *not* one I can share with Grant. Because it involves a lot of—

"He's disappointed he didn't get to take you home, huh?" Grant's tone is teasing, at odds with the tightness that's resumed in the set of his mouth.

"Yeah, how'd you know?"

"Because I would've been." He quickly averts his eyes. "I mean, in general, as far as dates go. That's when you usually . . ." Grant clears his throat. "You know."

My heart thuds in my chest. I *do* know. And so does Seth, which is why he's extra disappointed we didn't get any time alone before I left. No goodnight kiss. And now Grant knows it, and we're all thinking about the kiss that wasn't.

We turn onto my tree-lined street. Old Victorians sit shoulder to shoulder on narrow lots disproportionate to their girth. "Which house?"

My blood feels fizzy as if carbonated. Relentless bubbles bounce around my veins. "Five fifty-two. The . . . the second to the last on the right." Gram hasn't left the porch light on. Maybe it's a sign she's still not feeling well. Or maybe she feels just fine and is wearing night-vision goggles.

Grant pulls into our driveway, and before he puts the car in park, I'm frantically unbuckling my belt. I have to get out of here. *Now.* I can't be having thoughts of kissing while alone in a dark car with Grant. In my rush, I knock my purse to the floor—keys, lipstick, some cash— everything spills across the floor.

"Shoot!" I hiss, blindly feeling around the scratchy

floor mats for my things. When I find the most embarrassing of my whatnots, I breathe a teensy bit easier. Tucking the tampon back in my purse, I continue my search.

"Here, lemme help." Grant leans, groping around the floor. "I'd turn on the interior light, but something's wrong with the wiring. It's been on my list of things to—"

Our hands touch in the darkness. The shock of the contact ripples through me. We are both stock-still. I can hear him breathing. I shouldn't be aware of Grant's breath or the subtle way I imagine it's accelerating. But I am. God help me, I am.

"Interesting necklace," Grant says softly. "Isn't that the key I gave you?"

I look down and notice the silver key dangling alongside my amethyst. The stream of light filtering in from the streetlamp catches and reflects on its metallic surface. My pulse rate quadruples.

I sit up and shove the key back under the neckline of my dress, pressing a hand hard against my racing heart. "I . . . I lose things sometimes." It's true. It's totally true. This would be the very sort of thing I would misplace. And it is my golden ticket into Absinthe.

"Well"—he moves slowly back to his seat—"I guess as long as you don't go losing your heart, you'll always know where to find it."

Seconds span what feels like hours. Oh God, this is worse than flashing my thong. The key has betrayed me, hinting at things that it shouldn't, posing as something illicit and meaningful. So it will be removed from the necklace tonight.

But if it weren't for the fact I was dating Seth, or that the constellations had arranged themselves in such a dangerous way on the day of Grant's birth—this might have been *our* date. I find myself wondering what we would have done. Definitely not the hot-air ballooning. But we would have had fun. We would have laughed. I bet he would have kissed me right here in the green station wagon with the crescent of moon as our only witness. And I would've asked him the meaning behind the tattoos on his arm.

Because secretly, I am dying to know.

While I feel the loss of what could've been, there's the certainty of what is. What is meant to be. *Seth.*

Grant's hands curl around the steering wheel, ten and two. He stares at our blue three-story Victorian with its loose shingles in dire need of replacement. "I hope your grandma's feeling better. Goodnight, Wil."

The dismissal brings me back. I fumble with the handle, recalling my desperation to get out. "Yes. I . . . g'night, Grant."

I race up the porch steps without a backward glance. I don't want him to see how shaken I am. Once inside, I lock the door and slump against it, tossing my clutch to the bench.

The house comforts me with the sugar and vanilla baked into its walls. Walking down the hall to Gram's bedroom, I find her snoring softly beneath the patchwork quilt made by her mother's hand. The quilt rises and falls, marking the steadiness of her breath, the certainty of another.

I release a ragged breath of my own before bending to kiss her temple. "You're okay," I whisper. But it took seeing it with my own eyes to truly feel it.

Returning to the entryway, I realize I still haven't checked to make sure I got everything back in my purse. So I do a quick inventory.

That's when I see it.

Right there, nestled in among my keys, cell, and Parisian Pout.

A guitar pick.

It glows, like a little piece of Grant, lost and waiting to be found. I count seven *ticktock*s of the clock before I'm mobilized again.

"This has to stop." I gaze to the ceiling and visualize the starry sky that stretches beyond layers of plaster and wood. "I won't let you down."

Then I shut off the light and head upstairs.

chapter 10

The message alert chimes on my phone—my daily horoscope. Excellent.

> State your intentions in current relationships and discover happy revelations.

Talk about divine timing. This is precisely the affirmation I want for what I'm about to do. The traffic light turns green as I chuck my phone back in my bag.

It's Saturday morning and I'm the only animated thing in the warehouse district. Downtown is buzzing with activity as people set up for tomorrow's farmers' market and artisan fair—but here, it's a graveyard. Building after building, dilapidated cement structures hunker like rows of headstones made drearier under the blanket of gray. I flick on the wipers to clear the sheen of mist.

Absinthe stands at the end of the street, a little taller and prouder than the other warehouses, as if sensing a grander purpose than housing surplus tires or cheap textiles.

I creep over the speed bump and steady the coffees on the passenger seat. I want to catch Seth before he leaves for his camping adventure to apologize in person for my disappearance last night. And nothing says *I'm in like with you* like one of Gram's humongous cinnamon rolls washed down with a large coffee.

Coffee with a splash of guilt.

Capricorn's beard, *nothing happened*! Grant's fingers touched mine. Big whoop. So his guitar pick is a screaming banshee in my bag. Once I've exorcised that, I'm totally in the clear.

Today I will state my intentions to Seth. My horoscope's dead-on with that prediction.

As I pull up to the front of the building, the clouds go from misting the city to pelting it with chubby raindrops. While I'd had the sense to pull on my favorite red galoshes, I've forgotten the umbrella to go with them. Fabulous.

I make a mad dash to the cover of the awning. The striped cotton dress sticks to my skin; my hair hangs damp and drooping. Balancing my bag, the goodies, and our coffees, I hook a free finger in the door handle, relieved to find it unlocked.

"Hello?" My voice echoes down the tunnel entry, rubber boots squeaking loudly. "Helloooo?" The magic of

Absinthe has totally transformed. Without the music and fairies and mysterious green lights, it seems so . . . *ordinary.* "Is anyone he—"

"Wil?" Grant appears at the end of the hall, pencil tucked behind one ear and a stack of file folders in his arms. "What . . . what are you doing here?"

I trip over my own feet and nearly dump the coffees.

"Whoa!" He tosses the folders on a nearby table and rushes over. "Why don't I handle the precious cargo, okay?"

Bewildered, I stare through my rain-splattered lenses. "The, uh, front door was unlocked. Isn't . . . is Seth here?" The question edges on desperate. But I am desperate. I have to state my intentions and Grant was *not* part of the morning's equation.

Thunder rumbles. That's the universe belly-laughing at my expense.

"He was on the schedule, but—shocker—he overslept. Packed up and headed straight to Lannister." He checks his watch. "He's been on the road a couple of hours now. Probably about halfway there."

I numbly follow Grant past the hodgepodge of chairs and couches, and over to the bar, where he sets the coffee carrier down. He holds out a towel he's taken from behind the counter. "You look a little soggy. Did he say he'd meet you here or something?"

Great. I'm drenched *and* my mission is a giant fail. I set the pastry box on a stool and take the towel. "Thanks. No." I frown, patting myself dry. "I was going to surprise him."

"Oh. Then sorry to break it to you but your trip's a bust—just me here." Grant brushes the dust from his flannel shirt before pushing up a sleeve. Once again I find myself wanting to decode the musical tattoo. "So, what's in the box, or is it for Seth's eyes only?"

"The box?" I stare at the cube like geometry is the most intriguing thing on the planet. "Uh, cinnamon rolls. Gram had some extras from a batch she made this morning."

"She's better, then?"

"Yep. Fit as a fiddle, according to her."

"That's great." Grant's eyes continue to devour the package.

"Did you want one?"

He wipes his chin. "My drool give me away?"

I chuckle. The tension in my shoulders softens, because Grant has the uncanny ability to put me in a tranquil state of nervousness. "Only a little. Well, the drool, and the fact that you were undressing the pastry box with your eyes."

"I skipped breakfast and surpassed starving about an hour ago. Seriously, I think my stomach has started eating itself." He settles himself up on a barstool. But my galoshes remain hammered to the floor. Why can't I move? "Wil, I won't bite. Unless you morph into a cinnamon roll, then no guarantees."

He takes one of the coffees. I envy his steady hand and repartee. It's the sort of easiness that comes from not liking someone *that way*.

And as Grant continues his effortless chatter, I begin to wonder if he's developed amnesia in the last ten hours, or if somehow his attraction to me has withered and died overnight.

Which is for the best—a bullet dodged, actually. My Fifth House is complicated enough—what with the planet Uranus giving rise to sudden infatuations that tend to fizzle out as abruptly as they start.

Yeah. I bet that's *all* this was, a silly little infatuation—because of what—a dance? A ride home? A stupid key?

"So, not to come off as a complete ingrate, but are these froufrou? I know Seth likes those macchiato mocha something." things."

Get over yourself, Wil. My mind continues reeling over its own idiocy.

I blow out a breath and scooch onto the stool beside him. "Nope. They're black, but I grabbed cream and sugar just in case."

After a hearty slug of coffee, Grant rests his arms on the counter, leaning closer as I open the pastry box. "Between you and me, I'm gonna feel no remorse over eating Seth's cinnamon roll. None." He grins when I pass him a fork wrapped in a napkin. "Is there anything you haven't thought of, Carlisle?"

I catch his gaze and quickly look away. *Uh-huh. How to be alone with you and not think things that will make me feel guilty later.* But I can't say that. Obviously.

I shake my head, dispersing the unwelcome thoughts. "Consider it payment for taxi services rendered."

He sticks a fork in the warm roll and takes a bite. "Man, these are . . . holy . . . *unbelievable.*"

I break off a chunk and swirl it in a pool of icing. "Oh, I know. Some things are worth a four-figure caloric intake."

He swallows, his eyes rolling back to a neutral position. "Please tell me you're not actually counting. Because you don't have to worry about any of that bullsh—"

"Mmm, mmm, definitely not." I finish chewing. "And even if I were calorie-obsessed, I'd never be a twig. Which is fine." I add, "I'd rather be happy. And this"—I point my fork at the ooey-gooey roll—"is pure deliciousness."

Grant is sucking icing off the side of his thumb. I forget to blink or breathe or do any of those other supposedly involuntary actions.

He wipes his mouth on a napkin. And then says something I think I'll remember for all of eternity. "Wil, you're way better than twigs."

The morning downpour lessens to a light pitter-patter. I've lingered at Absinthe too long. Hanging out with Grant has just been so fun that I've lost track of the time.

When I return from the restroom, I'm struck by an irresistible melody drifting from the back of the club. And there's Grant plucking away at his guitar, long legs dangling over the side of the raised stage. A single light forms a diffused circle that cuts one side of his body, leaving the other in shadow.

His eyes lift from the guitar. Entering a room undetected in rubber boots is an impossible feat. It's as bad as trying to sneak up on someone in snow pants.

"Um, sorry, I didn't mean to interrupt. I was just about to head out." But the music continues to lure me with its vibrational pull. I find myself squeaking my way closer. "That's my favorite Beatles song. You play it so well."

"Yeah?" There's a flash of his slightly crooked front teeth. My stomach flips like a coin. " 'Blackbird' is the first *real* song I learned—not counting 'Hot Cross Bells' or 'Jingle Buns.' Er . . ." I giggle and he smiles. "You know what I mean. Anyway, I locked myself in my bedroom when I was twelve. Played it over and over until I could get through without messing up." His hand hovers at the strings. "Do you play?"

"Guitar? No. I'm afraid my fingers aren't that coordinated."

"Another instrument?"

"In sixth grade I played a mean recorder. Got a solo part and everything."

Grant snorts and scrubs a hand back and forth through his hair. "You're aware that's a half step above the tambourine."

I place my hands on my hips. "All right, I'll see you one recorder, and raise you two years of choir in junior high." I drop my hands. "Which, now that I mention it, is the extent of my short-lived music career."

"Well, voice we can work with." He slaps a hand on the floor next to him. Dust motes dance like flecks of fine glitter beneath the spotlight. "Come on up."

I eye the raised stage, trying to decide the best method for getting up without looking like one of those sea lions

I once saw on Pier 39 in San Francisco. Thank God for the stairs I notice to my right.

Once I've settled down beside him, I smooth my dress over my legs. "Okay, maestro, now what?"

He resumes his strumming. "Now we sing. You know the lyrics to 'Blackbird,' don't you?"

"Sing? As in . . . right now?"

"Unless you have a rule against singing on Saturdays?" Grant asks with an amused twist of his mouth.

"No, it's just I might have a strong aptitude for sucking." I push back one of my limp waves. "What if I make your ears bleed?"

"My ears won't bleed. And you won't suck," he assures me.

But I'm not nearly as certain. My throat feels packed with wood shavings that absorb all moisture. "Can I . . ." I point to his water bottle, which he passes over. I take several generous gulps.

However, I reason if I can sing for the Crotch—Mrs. Crotchler, my evil junior high choir teacher—I can sing for Grant. Because no one could be more heinous than the Crotch.

He counts off, tapping the guitar—*thump, thump, thump*. The melody follows and the sureness of his fingers captivates me once more. The way they slide up and down the neck of the guitar and don't get lost along the way. Mine would. My fingers would trip all over each other.

He nods his head, indicating the start of the duet.

And we sing. Grant's voice is magnificent, like a boy

147

version of the fabled sirens. I would totally splinter my boat against rocks just to follow that sound.

"Louder, Wil."

Oh but I'd rather not. I'd rather close my eyes and let this quiet song and his smooth and gentle voice wash over me. The occasional squeak of the guitar strings lulls me, too. And so, because I want to capture it, I have to close my eyes, and hope the lyrics find their way past my lips.

Our voices overlap in pleasant harmony. Just as he made me seem a better dancer, I think he's gone and done it again with his singing.

And when the song ends, I savor the last chord before opening my eyes.

Grant's staring at me. He smirks. "Yeah, you suck."

I shove his arm. "And *you* just talked yourself out of future cinnamon rolls, my friend."

"I'm kidding!" He laughs. "That was great—no joke. You've got an awesome voice."

"Thanks. Even if you're only saying it to make me feel better."

"I mean it, Wil." He glances down at the guitar. "Hey, uh, I could teach you to play . . . if you want. Seems a shame to appreciate music the way you do and not play something."

Did I say yes? I must've, because he pushes the guitar with unbridled enthusiasm into my lap. The instrument is warm against my stomach and thighs.

"Check you out, you're a natural," he says, beaming. "Okay, but you want to hold it like . . ." He springs to his feet, crouching behind me. His arms cage either side of me. "Here, like this. Bring your elbow down. Good. Now relax your grip. *Relax, Wil,*" he murmurs at my ear. His upper body brushes against my back as he arranges me in the right position.

Relax? He's lucky I haven't splintered the poor guitar. I feel every place Grant is near, whether he touches me or not. I want to lean back and melt into him. And my heart doesn't thump; it makes sonic booms. His voice is close at my ear as he guides my hands into position.

"Let your hands get used to the feel of the instrument. Don't worry about how it sounds. Just play around with it. See how the tension varies in the strings?" Grant carries on with his impromptu lesson, gushing about sound holes and bridges and headstorks. Er, *headstocks.*

Meanwhile, goose bumps have declared a Million Man March across my skin. And I'm freaked he'll know. He'll know *he's* the reason—him and his damn Pisces allure! I need to strengthen my defenses. Ignore the way he smells. The way he speaks. Focus only on the acoustic guitar. See? I'm paying attention; I know what kind of guitar it is.

"Like this?" I ask. The instrument *plink-plonk*s with none of the audible beauty it had in Grant's skilled hands.

"Yep, that's it." His words blister my shoulder. Does he *have* to do that? Be all . . . all blistery?!

I bristle, and zero in on the feel of the strings. How the thicker ones are rougher, and the thin ones slip more easily past my fingers. But . . . it's not working. Not with Grant wrapped around me like night on a star. Just when I'm about to run like a screaming nut job off the stage, my cell rings.

There is a God in heaven! Thank you!

I release the breath I've held hostage. "I should get that," I say, shoving the guitar to his lap and rocketing to my feet.

"Could be Seth," Grant says with a hint of annoyance before turning away.

I retrieve my phone from my bag, near the stairs. "Nope, it's Gram. Hello?"

Grant busies himself packing up the guitar.

"No. No, I can be there. Half hour." My pause is immediately followed by my grandmother's breathless run-on stream of hysteria. "Gram, calm down. We'll get it done. *We will*. Okay, bye."

"Everything all right?"

"Well, it's not a health crisis, just a baking one. Sisters of Society put in a last-minute order for twelve dozen cupcakes for an event tomorrow. Gram's been trying to slowly cut back on the workload, but the money's good, so we can't really refuse—"

"A hundred forty-four cupcakes, huh? We better get rolling." He jumps down from the stage.

"We?"

"Sounds like a perfect time to call in one of your favors from the Cricket win, Songbird." Grant holds out a callused hand.

I take it in mine, making the four-foot leap to the floor. "Um, that's a pretty huge favor. I wasn't aware you baked." And Songbird? Is he giving me a nickname?

"I don't." He goes to a wall panel and begins flicking

switches. The club gets progressively darker. "But I'm done here and you seem desperate enough to go for it."

"Grant"—I sway my head—"you don't have to do this. You're under no obligation to help my grandmother and me make cupcakes. I release you from your servitude."

"Look, the guys stayed out late last night. No one will be vertical until about three in the afternoon. Might as well be of use somewhere."

"Okay," I reply uncertainly as we head to the front door. "But Gram's going to insist on paying you for your time."

"Luckily, I accept most pastries and major credit cards." He pushes the door open to the late-morning drizzle.

"You're positive? You'll be giving up an entire Saturday. I mean, I'm sure you can fill your day a thousand other—"

"*Wil.* I'm positive. Now, I'm gonna lock up and set the alarm. Meet you around front."

I stare into his brown eyes, which also possess a fine web of gold. That must be why they always look so warm. So arresting and—

"Wil? This would be a great time to say thank you, Grant, and hop in your car."

"Um, right . . . thank you," I breathe, and race into the rain.

chapter 11

Dean Martin's velvety voice sings of booze and love lost as we jog up the sagging front steps of my house.

"So Gram's got this thing for Dean when she's on a tight deadline—her version of Red Bull. He recorded over five hundred songs, so, you know . . . prepare to get Dean-faced," I say to Grant as I slide my key in the lock. I peer up over my shoulder. "It's not too late. You could still turn back."

Grant is smiling. "What, afraid I might possess a secret black belt in baking?" He shakes the rain from his hair.

"No," I laugh, assured of my cupcake superiority. "Just don't say I didn't warn you."

We step inside. Grant follows my lead as I tug off my red galoshes and set them on the mat under the bench. His beat-up Chucks tuck in beside them, looking perfectly at home.

He peeks around the hall into the living room, where two overstuffed chairs and a large green sectional sit—just as they have since the Reagan administration. Antique plates hang on the wall, along with a large framed collage of sketches, watercolors, and finger paintings I made during various stages of development. The grandfather clock bongs. His eyes wander the detailed woodwork from the baseboards to the coffered ceiling. "This place has so much character, so much history. It's like it's got its own soul." Grant's expression turns sheepish. "Sounds crazy, huh?"

"Not at all. The soul, the character, I think that's what makes it home. What's your house like?" I ask, hanging my bag on a hook.

"Different. Not like this."

"Oh. Well, kitchen's this way." I push through the door. "Gram? I'm here! And I brought reinforcements!" I turn down Dean's crooning several decibels.

"Angel of mercy! Reinforcements, you say?" Gram's head is partly in the oven as she puts in another tray of cupcakes. Closing the door, she wipes her hands on her violet-covered apron.

"Gram, this is my friend Grant."

A look of confusion flickers over her face. "Have we met?"

"No, ma'am. You're probably thinking of my younger brother, Seth. There's a strong family resemblance."

"Ah." Gram's spectacled gaze takes in his rumpled flannel shirt, frayed jeans, and bare feet. Her blue eyes twinkle. "And I'd venture that's where the similarity ends."

He flashes his cutely crooked front teeth. "You'd venture correctly, Mrs. Carlisle."

"Please, call me Eve."

My head snaps up; I stare at Gram. Excuse me, has Grant suddenly become a bridge club member? What the . . . And where in Orion's belt is the Triple G—*the Gram Gauntlet Gaze*? She wields that on *everyone* she meets the first time. Is it because Grant's being sweet and helpful that he automatically skips to the informal exchanges? Or is it because he's not Seth? I fret, considering the latter.

"Well, don't just stand there, Mena, we've got plenty of work to do. Get this dear boy an apron."

I go to the wall and select the least flowery apron from the bunch. I settle on the one with dancing strawberries and bananas shaking maracas.

Gram swivels back to Grant, who is unbuttoning and shedding his flannel layer, his trademark gray T-shirt lurking beneath. "Now, son, I want your word that what you're about to witness today"—her voice turns ominous—"*will not* go beyond these walls."

His forehead wrinkles into a very serious my-word-is-my-bond expression. "I swear it, Eve."

"You're positive? Because that old crone Rima Bazinski has been dyin' to get her liver-spotted mitts on my Caramel Turtle recipe, and if she knew how I get the caramel to—"

"Gram," I interrupt, donning my own poppy-covered apron, "he's got it."

"Then what am I blustering on about?" She claps. "Let's

get to baking! And, Mena, turn ole Deano back up. I can barely hear him."

I exchange glances with Grant, who is fighting back a laugh.

"Warned you," I mouth.

The afternoon passes in a flurry of flour and frosting. Six dozen completed. The only cupcakes left on the order are the Toasted Coconut and Hubba Hubba Hazelnut. I've just put the last batch of Key Limalicious in the oven and set the timer.

Unfortunately, Gram has to run back to the store since Grant—in lieu of lightly toasting—blackened the coconut. He stared at the stinky, tar-colored curls like he'd committed a cardinal sin. Which, I guess, for the coconut it was—death by Black and Decker toaster oven.

We're also famished, so Gram offers to pick up sandwiches from Valentine's Deli on her way back from the grocery store, following a pit stop at the bank. Generally, these are the kinds of errands that could be accomplished in less than sixty minutes, but Gram's speedometer rarely sees anything over thirty-five. I expect to see her next Tuesday.

And I'm alone with Grant. *Again.* It's beginning to feel like a damn cosmic conspiracy.

"I don't get your T-shirt," Grant says, passing the baking tin for me to dry. "What does it mean?"

I changed out of my dress after the burning incident,

hanging it on the back porch to air out. Now I'm wearing jeans (a travesty) and a navy T-shirt that depicts a stick figure carrying an overflowing pitcher. Underneath it reads: AQUARIANS ALWAYS GRIN AND BEAR IT.

"Well, I'm an Aquarius. Aquarius is the sign of the Water Bearer, not to be confused with an actual water sign—which is what you are. I'm air."

"How do you know what I am?" Grant asks, handing me another pan.

"*Very* educated guess. My mom was sort of an expert on the subject, so I guess you could say I was born with an affinity for the stars. Even after she di—" I press my lips together. I didn't mean to let that slip. I power on with my T-shirt explanation before he questions it. "Anyway, the T-shirt . . . the water inside the pitcher represents truth, which Aquarians give freely to the world. The 'grin' part is in reference to our most likeable trait—friendliness." My eyes flick to Grant as he rinses a baking sheet. "Yours is compassion, if you were wondering." Not that he should, because it's his compassion that has him scrubbing dishes in my grandmother's kitchen.

"Interesting." His lips tilt up. "So, you never lie? Ever?"

"Grant, I'm still human. Sure, there've been some white lies, and I did sort of allude to writing an astrology book at Absinthe, but, by and large, *yes,* I tell the truth. Even when it's difficult."

"Okay, so let's have it. Give me a hard truth." He turns to the counter and grabs a stack of dirty mixing bowls.

Oh, jeez, there are innumerable hard truths I could tell.

And none of them are ones I should. I take a bowl from the rack, wiping it dry.

He misunderstands my apprehension. "Look, don't sweat it, I can handle it."

"Um, all right," I say carefully. "But you should get a chance to do the same—offer me a hard truth. I've got a moon in Libra that demands balance."

Grant clamps his lips to mask the emerging grin. "Okay, Wil, I followed about half of what you said. But yeah, I'll swap you—truth for truth."

I put away more dishes, buying myself time to come up with something that doesn't feel dangerous. "You're a brilliant musician," I say, turning back around.

"That's your *hard* truth?" He chuckles. "I'm disappointed in you, Songbird."

"I'm not done, Captain Antsy Pants. Now, as I was saying"—I walk back to the sink, assessing his tall form—"you have this *incredible* musical gift. And you practically lit up like the aurora borealis when you were teaching me this morning. So"—I plant my feet—"it's positively criminal you're going to U of M in the fall to study business. *Business, Grant?*"

"It's what I have to do." He scrubs a little harder, sloshing dirty water on his torso. It doesn't bother him. Course, neither did fishing the eggshells from the trash for Gram's compost. I try to envision Seth doing either of those things and the image won't come into focus.

"What you have to do?" I repeat skeptically. "You know, Seth's talking about having all these European adventures after graduation next year. Meanwhile, *you're* pursuing an uninspired career that will bind you to the family empire. You're doing what's expected." I touch his arm; he flinches a little. "Grant, you're doing what's safe, and that's not embracing life. That's not living. Hard truth: The guy I saw on stage, *he* embraces life. He squeezes out every last drop."

"That's all very poetic, Wil, but you've only got half the picture." His jaw clenches, then relaxes. "I owe them . . . my parents."

"Why?" I find myself staring at the tattoo again.

"Let's just say I wasn't always a model son. And let's just say, if it weren't for their unconditional support . . . my life would've turned out very different." He closes his eyes. "So I owe them everything. They believed in me when no one else would." Several moments pass before he returns, eyes slowly reopening.

I want to ask questions but I don't. Because I know if our roles were reversed, I wouldn't care to satisfy his curiosity by dredging up my own past.

His mood shifts, becoming lighter. "And really, it makes sense for me to eventually take over the firm. I'm the oldest, and *way* more responsible. That, and Seth couldn't calculate his way out of a paper bag."

I laugh. "True, but he'd probably fold the bag into a really cool airplane or something."

Grant nods. "Okay, my turn." He pulls the plug; the drain gurgles. "Are you ready?"

I feel light-headed. Must be low blood sugar. I dip my

finger in a bowl of leftover buttercream frosting. "Go ahead," I say, licking my finger.

"I like you in jeans."

I whip my towel at him. He catches the towel's corner and yanks it from my grip, using it to mop the wet spot at his stomach. "That's not a hard truth," I say, using his words against him.

"Honey, I'm not done," he mocks. Somehow his use of the word "honey," even in jest, warms me more than liking me in jeans. "You're fearless. And . . . wondrously . . . *strange*." I meet his gaze. "That last part was a compliment."

"Uh-huh, I sense a giant 'but' coming on." I cross my arms. People's opinions have never mattered much to me, but right now, I'm terrified to know what Grant thinks. Actually his "but" has me sweating bullets.

"*But* I think you use this astrology stuff as a crutch."

Is that it? My body feels solid again. I shake my head and smile. Because I could rebut this in my sleep. "And why *wouldn't* I use a system backed by thousands of years of exhaustive research and study? It's a navigational aid, Grant, a tool for making sense of the world around us." I move to the island and begin putting cupcake liners in the clean tins. "Astrology gives us a broader sense of purpose and insight into what we're doing here."

His brows knit as he edges next to me. "I just don't agree with basing important life decisions on the *randomness* of star patterns. It takes away all accountability."

I hand Grant a stack of liners. "Well, I disagree. It's

called making *informed* decisions. And it isn't random—it's science."

"So science dictates everything? Right down to who you go out with? *Pssh*." The dismissive noise is the icing on his smug tone.

I freeze. "Just what are you insinuating, Walker?"

"Look, all I'm saying is I'm not the one who showed up in a club with a blueprint for who I can and can't date. Wil . . ." His eyes bore into me. I refuse to engage, but my blood does. Oh, it boils. "Can't you see how much power you give this? Hard truth: You need to *own* your choices."

The injustice of his oversimplification sparks flames in my cheeks. I take my prepped tin, letting it clatter on the counter beside the stove. "Well, if your whole faith-in-people system's so superior, then why don't you have a girlfriend? Hmm? Or will that be arranged by your parents, too?"

He drops in the last liner before facing me. His eyes dance with the flames from my face, or perhaps they're of his own making. "Maybe I don't *want* a girlfriend. Maybe I *like* playing the field."

"Funny, you don't strike me as a player," I blurt, despite the inclination to sling another insult. But it's the truth. He doesn't strike me as the type who preys on the innocent. Or uses cheeseball lines to get in a girl's pants. Nothing about him says love 'em and leave 'em. But then there's that stupid rumor Iri told me knocking around my head.

"Plenty of girls who would argue otherwise, Wil."

Our eyes meet. I steady a hand on the counter because the room has gone all topsy-turvy. "Then . . . they don't know the Grant Walker I do."

The timer buzzes. The Key Limalicious are done.

So is this conversation.

I push past Grant, stopping the timer and pulling out the cupcakes. In my distracted and irritable haste, my forearm grazes the top rack.

"Aaah!" I yelp, barely getting the cupcakes to safety. "Shi—" I shake my arm; the burn feels like it has a mini heartbeat that *tha-thump*s down my entire limb.

Grant rushes over and turns on the tap. "Lemme see." Before I can say anything, he grabs me by the waist and plunks me on the counter. And now my waist burns where his hands were. I will have to bathe in a vat of burn ointment by the day's end.

"It's nothing," I mutter as he stretches my arm under the cold rush of water. The inch-long burn is furiously red. "Grant, seriously, I've got a boatload of those marks on the other arm." I hold it up. Thin white lines scatter here and there across my skin. "See? Cupcake battle wounds. That's why Gram keeps that monster aloe plant in the garden window."

"I'm sorry, Mena." My breath catches. He continues cradling my arm under the cool stream. But I don't really register the cold. How can I, with him touching me and calling me Mena? *Mena,* it feels like its own caress. Is it wrong I want to hear him say it again and again?

I swallow. "You . . . you called me Mena."

"I did?" With me on the counter, our faces are level. I nod. "Well"—he shuts off the water and grabs a clean dish towel—"must be from hearing your gram say it over and over."

Drying off, I risk another glance. "And why are you apologizing? It isn't your fault I was careless."

He rubs his neck. "It is. I upset you. What I said was . . . harsh. Obviously, you have your reasons for believing the things you do."

I shrug. "Well, likewise. I mean, you've got your reasons, too . . . for wanting to make your parents happy. They sound like good people."

"They are."

I stare down at my bare feet. The red polish is chipped, and completely missing on my pinkie toe. "Hey, and for the record, that 'hard truth' thing was your idea."

He cringes. "God, it was, wasn't it?" Grant rests against the counter and stares at his own feet. He has nice feet, no hammertoes or other foot deformities. "I'm full of bad ideas. Well, except for the one about us being friends. That was one of my better ones."

The lightbulb clicks. Suddenly my horoscope is startlingly clear. Stating my intentions was never about Seth—*it's about Grant*. Because relationships can include friendships, too!

"Friends," I echo, and offer my hand.

Grant's hand slips into mine, and we're both grinning. And then we're not. Am I making up how he squeezes my hand? How I can feel all of him even though only our hands have made contact? I can't figure out if he's leaning closer or if the kitchen's leaning.

I lick my lips and swear to Venus his mouth is calling mine.

Come closer. Closer.

The doorbell rings and we lurch apart. "I . . . uh, Gram must have her hands full." I leap from the counter, racing to the hall. My heart threatens to crack my ribs from its overzealous pumping.

Yanking open the door, I gasp. And just like that, my heart stops. *Stops.*

"Seth?" I croak.

He grins crookedly. "Surprise."

chapter 12

"We got rained out," Seth says, stepping into my house. "I tried calling but you didn't answer so I took a chance."

I unstick my mouth from its fly-catching position. "Um, sorry, my battery's probably dead. I'm terrible about charging it." Inside I'm reeling; my head can't seem to catch up to the fact that Seth is standing right here, right now.

He shrugs. "Like I said, I took a chance and came by. Your grandma gone? I didn't see her car."

"Yeah, she . . ."

Seth arches an expectant brow. "So, it's just you and me? Alone?" His smile mirrors his mischievous thoughts.

"Well—" But I'm cut off as he lifts me up in his arms and squeezes me, his face nuzzling my hair.

"Mmm, you smell yummy." He sets me back on my feet, but his arms stay tethered around me.

I lay a hand on his chest. "Seth, we're not actually—"

"Shh." He presses a finger lightly to my lips. "Don't leave me hanging here, Wil. I'm dying to know if you taste as good as you smell." He closes his eyes, lowering his head. His breath heats my lips.

"*Ahem.*" And if *ahem*s could be lethal, then Grant's is a poison-tipped dart that sinks smack between my shoulder blades.

Seth straightens, letting go of me to stare at his brother, who leans casually against the kitchen doorframe, his feet crossed at his ankles. "*Grant?*" Seth's eyes narrow into suspicious slivers. "What the hell are *you* doing here?"

"That's what I was trying to tell you," I say.

"Tell me what?" Seth eyes me, then shifts to Grant. "You give her one ride home and suddenly you're trying to be her BFF? Or are you workin' a different angle?"

Grant smirks and gives his head a shake. "Grow up, little brother."

Seth continues glowering, burning holes in the kitchen door, where his brother has just disappeared.

"Hey." I jostle his arm. "Look, Grant is here because he offered to help with a last-minute baking order. I went to Absinthe this morning to, ironically, surprise *you,* and Grant just happened to be there when I got Gram's freaked-out plea for help. So whatever you're thinking, you've got it wrong. We've been making cupcakes, Seth. *Cupcakes.*"

Seth gnaws at his lip. "I thought because it was just the two of you—"

"And Gram"—I try to dial back my annoyance—"she

165

was here, too. She just went to run some errands and pick up a late lunch for us." I watch as all the information sinks in, waiting for Seth to realize the situation isn't at all sketchy.

"Oh." Seth rubs his hand over his face, groaning. "God, I'm a total ass, aren't I?"

"Yes." I unfold my arms and sigh. Seth's decked out in cargo pants and a snug orange T-shirt speckled with rain. "But you're a cute ass, so you've got that going for you."

He drops his hand. "It's not you I'm worried about, it's *him*," he says, casting another venomous glare toward the kitchen. "Still don't trust him."

"Grant hasn't done anything wrong," I repeat.

Seth mumbles something like "yet" under his breath. Which I won't dignify. "It'd just be nice if you called *me* when you needed something. Give me the chance to help out, you know?"

I stop rolling my amethyst necklace between my thumb and forefinger. "But, Seth, you weren't even in town. How would you have helped?"

"I know I was gone, but . . . Look, I'm sorry. I didn't mean to imply that anything was . . ." He tucks my hair behind my ear. "I'm sorry, okay? I swear I've evolved past primate."

My shoulders drop. "It's all right."

"Yeah?" He smiles with a playful glint in his eye. Suddenly he's beating his chest and making ape noises. I giggle. "Me *like* pretty girl." He resumes the chest beating, and lumbers toward me.

"Wha . . . hey, what are you doing? Seth!" I squeal, diving for the living room and hiding behind a stuffed chair. He squares off across from me. I point at Ape Seth. *"Behave."* But it's clear behaving is the last thing on his mind.

His nostrils flare as he sniffs the air. "Me *want* pretty girl who smells of cupcakes. Must have pretty girl." He lurches around the chair to grab me.

"Aah!" My feet slap the hardwood as I race into the hall. Where I promptly collide with Grant. *"Oof!"*

Grant's hands are wrapped around my arms, holding me up; his mouth is tight. My smile evaporates as he quickly lets go, like I'm toxic.

Seth lunges, grabbing me by the waist and dragging me backward. And I'm giggling once more. *Not* because it's funny. *Nothing* is funny about the granite lines on Grant's face. But my tickle tolerance is low, so all the while I'm laughing, inside . . . I'm . . . destroyed.

Finally relenting, Seth slings a proprietary arm over my shoulders. I stiffen. "Leaving so soon?" he asks Grant.

"Yup." Grant tugs on his flannel shirt. "Manny wants to practice some new stuff we've been working on. Tell your gram I'm sorry I had to take off. You'll be good with the last batches, right?" He avoids my eyes as he bends to slip on his Chucks.

I duck from Seth's arm and move toward Grant. "Sure. But . . . you're not going to stay for lunch? Valentine's has the best prosciutto and provolone sandwiches. The olive oil alone is . . ."

"Nah. Besides"—he slaps a hand to his hard stomach—"I think I killed my appetite on that fifth cupcake."

"Oh." I wilt like a flower without water.

"Well, my appetite's alive and well," Seth adds, slapping his own hard stomach. "And prosciutto and provolone sounds pretty mouthwatering. That is, if it's all right I stick around? I don't mind if you put me to work."

Grant holds my gaze for the briefest moment. In that flash, I see disappointment, a disappointment that has nothing to do with deli sandwiches. I blink, and the emotion has evaporated, leaving me to question whether I'd really seen it to begin with.

"Of course," I say to Seth. I swallow. "Well . . . goodbye, Grant. Thanks again."

"Bye." His reply is flat. He turns and pushes roughly past his brother, knocking back Seth's shoulder.

"Watch yourself," Seth growls, despite having blocked Grant's exit and not budging an inch to let him pass.

I don't like this storm that's brewing between them. Nor do I know how to go about quelling it.

But I do know this.

I won't spend another minute alone with Grant.

"Ready, set . . . *go*!" I leap from the changing room. My eyes round and so do Irina's. I point a finger and double over in hysteria. I wheeze, "Dear God, you look like a carpet!"

Iri laughs so hard she snorts. "No," she gasps. "I look like a *couch*!" She holds out her arms so I can take in the

Oh my God, don't say Spawn of Satan. Don't say Spawn of Satan. I am totally going to say Spawn of Satan.

"Brittany," I carefully enunciate. Yes! I deserve an award.

She props a French-manicured hand on her slender hip. Her eyebrows rise in dual judgment. Even her cute little sundress seems to mock me. "Please tell me this outfit is some kind of joke."

"Yeah." I pull my Fedora lower. "It's just for fun." I thumb toward the walking upholstery behind me. "You remember my friend Irina, don't you?"

Duh. I mean, yes, of course she does. Irina's one of the many reasons we aren't friends anymore.

Once upon a time, Brittany and I had been inseparable. But then high school happened, and all the things that never mattered to me suddenly mattered to her.

Now, looking at Alexander High's newest varsity head cheerleader, I see no evidence of the Brittany I knew. The girl who craved fun and star-fueled adventures. The girl who was equally curious to know what would happen if we put gummy bears in the microwave. Because that girl . . . has vanished.

Brittany twirls the blond ponytail trailing over her shoulder, smiling tightly like someone has given her a wedgie. In retrospect, maybe her smile has always had a constipated look about it. Cheerleading just perpetuated it.

"Hey," she says to Iri, succeeding in making the one syllable sound like an obscenity. Brittany shifts her handbag so that the COACH tag is more visible.

pated smile, I get the smug one. "That's what I thought."
Brittany twirls around, elbowing her way through the
clothes as she leaves.

I expel a fiery breath. I should've asked if her bacne
ever cleared up. Or if—

"She's jealous of you, *dorogaya*," Iri says from the dress-
ing room.

"Well"—I consult the dangling tag at my wrist—"for
the bargain price of eighteen dollars her jealousy can be
bought."

"That's not what I meant and you know it." Iri steps out
and faces the mirror. She wiggles and tugs at the stunning
red dress I don't at all remember handing off to her.

"Wow. It looks gorgeous on you." I move in behind her,
pulling up on the straps. "I think if we alter it a bit, it'll
be perfect for your artsy-fartsy event."

Iri looks away from her reflection. Her face pinches. "I
hate that you're being persecuted for being my friend."

I drop my hands. "Okay, *that's* dramatic."

"Wil . . ." Irina drops her voice but, unfortunately, not
the subject. "That plasticized bitch is always looking for
ways to tear into you. All because her douchebag boyfriend made a play for me."

I groan. "How many times do we have to have this
conversation, Iri? *It's not your fault*. We stopped hanging out way before that happened. Come to think of it, it
was probably around the time her bitchmorphosis kicked
in. Anyway, Brittany and her threats can kiss my velour-
covered booty."

The repercussions of crossing Spawn of Satan and her

entourage aren't even a blip on my radar. Because honestly, I'd rather have five good friends than fifty fake ones.

And I'd still choose Iri over any of them.

I meet her brooding gaze in the mirror. "So, are you buying this fabulous dress or what? Because this synthetic nightmare is making me sweat. Not perspire—*sweat*."

She pulls in a breath and on her exhale replies, "I think I like Jordan."

"I know."

Irina swallows. "I'm scared because I might give a shit."

"I know," I repeat, giving her hand a squeeze. "But it's going to be okay."

And I pray that it will be. For both our sakes.

Avoidance is a temporary bandage on a situation in need of a tourniquet.

I'm paraphrasing, but that's the gist of Monday's horoscope.

Thanks.

My panic is now beyond the reach of modern medicine.

The thing is, *I know* Seth is the right guy for me. So then why am I still consumed by thoughts of Grant? Why can't I snuff out this silly infatuation? It isn't as clichéd as wanting what I can't have. I don't work that way. So there has to be another explanation.

Epiphany strikes in the wee hours of the morning on the heels of a terrifying dream. I bolt upright in a tangle of bed sheets with my hair knotted from thrashing and my

forehead slick with sweat. Mane of Leo! Could my nightmare be true? What if this goes light-years beyond an unlucky Fifth House? What if I am actually . . . *cursed*?

Sure, it's a long shot, probably nothing more than grasping at supernatural straws. But I have to know for certain.

Heart thumping, I free myself from the cotton restraints and immediately research signs of an occult attack. In the glow of my laptop, I'm awash in horror as I identify many of the earmarks of an otherworldly assailant.

Nightmares: Check.

Health issues: Um . . . possible check? I had some residual achiness after the tower fall. Come to think of it, my tower tumble reinforces two more signs. . . .

Bad luck: Check.

Relationship difficulties: Double check.

The more I investigate, the more the possibility has me on the verge of forming hives over every inch of my body. *And* there are only thirteen days left in June; I am officially closer to the end than the beginning. Stars above, I can almost taste the sun-ripe blueberries of July.

So—under threat of blueberries and hexes—I will take drastic measures.

chapter 13

I tug the cord for my stop and jump off the bus the moment the doors open.

Heat radiates off the cracked and littered sidewalk of Dugan Street, a mere six blocks west of Inkporium. While two days ago might've been cool and rainy, today it's hotter than blazes and the air is liquefied. Weather whiplash is but one of the many splendors of Midwest living.

Perspiration dampens the hair at my neck, a combination of nerves and the heat index. I double-check the address—*almost there*. I ignore the seedy guy chain-smoking outside Pinky's Topless Bar—he doesn't return the favor. He crams his grubby fingers in his mouth, producing an ear-splitting whistle. The words that follow are fouler than whatever's decomposing on the sewer grate. If Gram were here, she'd have half a mind to break those

fingers just to teach the man some respect. And normally, I'd have choice words of my own, but I steel myself to stay focused on the important task at hand.

I stop in front of 729 Dugan. The shabby brownstone is taller than it is wide, with barred windows spanning all six stories. I scan the nameplates beside the buzzers until I find the one I'm searching for: LAVEAU.

I ran across the name, along with a phone number, in one of Mama's old astrology books. A book I was shocked to discover a number of years ago, buried in a pile beside the trunk that used to sit in Gram's bedroom. Inside the book's cover was my mother's large, looping writing with the word "diviner" underlined numerous times.

I took to heart that it meant Miss Laveau was the genuine article—an honest-to-goodness *real* psychic, and about now I need every branch of metaphysical help I can get.

I press the call button. Fanning my face with my clutch, I unkink the crinoline of my dress with my free hand.

"Don't take solicitors here. Includin' religion," the voice crackles over the ancient intercom.

Second thoughts have bombarded me since before I even stepped off the bus, and I'm sure as the North Star Gram wouldn't approve of my coming. But I need clarity on this situation. Bad. And if I *do* have a curse on my hands, well, then it'll take more than knowing the language of the sky to lift it.

I lean in to the speaker. "I, um . . . I called earlier this morning. I have an appointment with Miss Laveau."

"You got a name?"

"Wil Carlisle."

Caustic laughter echoes from the speaker. "Oh yeah, she been expectin' you."

I'm buzzed in and follow the zigzag of narrow stairs leading to apartment 8F. My trepidation rises with each floor. Will Miss Laveau be able to tell by looking at me whether I've been a victim of occult activity?

When I reach the top floor, the fluorescent hall lights flicker, and the door to 8F opens. A cloud of incense ambushes me, sweeter than any sage my mother used to burn.

A slight woman stands in the doorway. Her coal eyes probe, possessing both an age and a wisdom that are at odds with her dark, unlined skin. She scratches the silk scarf wrapped around her head. "I'm Angeline, Miss Laveau's . . . *liaison,* so to speak. You bring what I told you, Wil Carlisle?"

I nod, opening my clutch and digging out the single wooden matchstick and a clove cigarette. I add, "I have the money, too."

"All right, all right." Angeline impatiently waves me inside. "Put all of it over there." She points to a bronze bowl sitting on a stack of boxes adjacent to the door in the entryway. As I place the cigarette, match, and fifty dollars in the dish, she elaborates. "Can't touch what's not made in offer to me, you see? Muddles the energy of the exchange."

"Okay," I reply uncertainly, swallowing the knot of fear

in my throat. I still don't understand what one match and an herbal cigarette have to do with anything. But I didn't come here to judge the process. I came to know, once and for all, if incorporeal entities are working against me from the otherworld.

Angeline moves over to the cramped kitchen, placing a kettle on the range. The gas pilot *tick-tick-tick*s before igniting. "There's some rules you must abide, 'fore I can let ya pass through that curtain." The swathe of purple velvet hanging to my left ripples from the sudden rush of air from the AC unit.

Since Angeline hasn't invited me to join her at the chipped, gold-speckled Formica table, I don't move from my spot next to the boxes and offering bowl.

"Rule Number One: Don't speak unless spoken to. Got that?"

"Yes, ma'am." Staying silent is easy, especially when I'm scared out of my gourd.

"Rule Number Two: No touching. She might ask you for your hand, but you never reach first. *Ever.* That goes for looking, too, she don't like for people to watch her. Ya hear?"

My head bobs. I will be a mute statue who sees nothing.

"And Rule Number Three: No guarantees on what gets told, so don't go thinkin' you can roll in here demanding answers. What gets said is the spirit's choosing. And it could take five minutes"—the woman lifts a bony shoulder—"could take sixty, but you'll know what you know when they want you to know it. Understand?"

Umm . . .

"Can she tell me if I've been cursed?"

Angeline rolls up her newspaper, giving it a hard whack on the table. She flicks away the squashed fly. "Girl, did any of Rule Three sink in that head of yours?"

I jump at the sudden scream of the kettle. Angeline rises, smirking at how easily spooked I was. "Well, go on, Wil Carlisle. Miss Laveau's ready for you."

Slowly I cross the room until I reach the curtain. My hand trembles as it clutches the soft velvet, and my heart hammers a Morse code warning me of imminent danger. I give my amethyst stone a squeeze.

Please don't let this be a mistake.

Then I force myself over the threshold and to the other side.

I enter what looks to be a sparse living room made crowded by the curling wisps of burning incense. Votive candles in glass holders are on the floor along the perimeter. Stifling a cough, I immediately spot Miss Laveau in an upholstered rocking chair facing a barren wall. But I can't really *see* her, only the top of her wiry black hair threaded with streaks of silver.

I remind myself I can trust this woman. After all, my mother wouldn't have written her name in one of her books if she were some conjurer of evil. Those books were Mama's bibles.

"Sit." Miss Laveau's deep voice slithers like smoke through the icy air.

I take wobbly steps to the lone chair, stationed at the

back of her rocking chair, and dutifully sit, staring at the threadbare fabric smack in front of me. Then I can't help staring at the top of her head, curious about the body attached to it.

"Child of Grace Carlisle, you've come for insight, just as your mother before you. Are you prepared today to receive it?"

"Y-yes, ma'am." Even with the chilly air, I'm damp with nervous sweat.

And a strange hum begins. At first I think it's the old AC unit, but soon discover it comes from Miss Laveau. Her head has tipped forward and she shakes something in her lap. A bunch of somethings. Whatever she's holding makes a clicking sound like dice being shaken. The continuous hum in her throat joins the clicking in a mystical melody. The rhythm of her shaking speeds up faster and faster and her chair rattles and rocks in time.

My heart races as I slide to the edge of my chair, afraid to stay but more frightened to leave.

Then Miss Laveau freezes, and all sound and movement in the tiny room ceases instantly. Her weathered hand slowly stretches out from the chair and drops an object on the black cloth covering the table at her side. It tumbles across the surface.

Chewing my thumbnail, I lean in closer to see. A rune of some kind? It's roughly the size of a domino and is etched with black markings—it must be a rune. The clairvoyant pauses, drawing her arm back to her lap. She then drops a second and, finally, a third tile on the cloth.

"Chaos," she murmurs, without close inspection of the runes. "And temptation—I see two suitors." A shiver runs the length of my spine at her prophetic accuracy. "But one brings suffering, devastation . . . you have been warned of this before."

Startled, I draw a breath to speak.

"You needn't answer, girl, I can feel its truth." Her hand hovers above the ivory tiles, flat and still. "Love . . . trust . . . forgiveness . . . that is the crux of your solution. But fear warps your perceptions, child of Grace. If you ignore the voice—that wisdom inside you—then eventually it will stop speaking."

My mind spins as I bite my nail, trying to piece together Miss Laveau's perplexing reading. "So . . . the solution is . . . *inside me*? Is that what you're telling me?" If so, then I'm totally screwed. "Wh-what about a hex? Do you see any of those? Any curses, I don't know, *plaguing me*?"

The old woman bristles. "The only curse you have is the one you've placed upon your own head. Now give me your hand," she demands. "The spirits will do the asking now."

Not wanting to piss off Miss Laveau *and* the spirits more than I already have, I lean forward, stretching out my shaky hand.

The diviner's chapped hand grips onto mine. I tense, squeezing my eyes shut, waiting for whatever happens next. Will there be voices in my head? A bolt of psychic lightning that will strike my third eye, causing it to flutter open? Oh my God, I haven't even considered the

possibility of soul invasion! How would I explain a soul possession to Gram and—

Miss Laveau's body begins to shudder. She's . . . *laughing*? She releases my hand and her alto laughter reverberates in the room. *What the hell?* The old psychic shakes her head. "You amuse the spirits, girl."

"Peachy," I grumble under my breath, my angst and fear now transformed into spiritual annoyance. Without a care for speaking out of turn, I ask, "Can you at the very least see the outcome?" Regardless of the metaphysical medium, there's usually *some* sort of outcome. Please tell me fifty bucks would—at a minimum—buy me that.

She turns, although not enough to glimpse her face, and nudges the little table with the runes toward me. "See with your own eyes."

I lean forward. "What about that one?" I point to the blank ivory tile on the left. "It doesn't have anything on it. Is it turned over or something?"

"No," Miss Laveau sighs, the air of humor dissipating. "That's the symbol of the Fates, girl. A precursor to an end . . . or a beginning—a birth or possibly a death. It means the outcome is so fixed nothing can change the course of things to come. It is inevitable."

My outcome is . . . *inevitable*? And involves possible death? Could there *be* a worse fortune? Obviously, this has to be a mistake! Some sort of astrophysical lines of communication that got crossed. Or misread.

Her wrinkled hand floats over the runes momentarily before pulling away. "You won't wait long for your

outcome. All will come to pass before the seventh month." The psychic's chair begins to softly creak with her rocking. "Go now. The spirits have said all they will say on this matter."

"What? You must be kidding!" I exclaim. "But that can't be *it*?"

Miss Laveau stops rocking and stiffens in her chair. The air charges with her displeasure, causing all the little hairs on the back of my neck to rise on end. Suddenly I'm recalling Angeline's Rule Number Three, about knowing what I know when the spirits want me to know it. I was given three rules to follow, and I've broken two.

Somehow knowing that doesn't make me any less pissed.

I snatch my purse from the floor and stand. But the good manners Gram's instilled come involuntarily, whether I feel them or not. "Thank you, Miss Laveau." *For nothing.* "You've given me a lot to think about." *Assuming I can make sense of* any *of it.* "Goodbye." *To you and my cash.*

I pass through the velvet curtain. Angeline doesn't so much as glance up from her newspaper crossword, engrossed in her land of puzzles.

So I mumble my farewell and show myself the door.

Walking back out into the blistering heat of Dugan Street does little to distract me from the irritation brought on by the fruitless session with Miss Laveau. No. It's the scuffle outside of Pinky's Topless Bar that plunges me back to reality.

And I run. As fast as my high-heeled feet will carry me, believing the image ahead *must* be a mirage.

It isn't.

It really is Grant. And he has the foul-mouthed creep who yelled at me earlier pinned against a brick wall.

The creep wheezes, lips stretched tight over his nicotine-stained teeth, scrabbling at Grant's iron grip at his collar. *"Let me . . . go . . ."*

"Stop!" I shriek. "What are you doing?" But Grant doesn't respond.

"If I *ever* hear you talking like that to a girl again, you piece of shit," Grant snarls, "I'll knock every last tooth from your worthless head."

My gaze catches on what I presume to be the girl in question, hurrying in the opposite direction much as I'd done.

Grant's hold manages to tighten. "And I swear to God, that isn't a threat . . . *it's a promise.*"

The creep's blotchy face bounces up and down. *"N'kay."* His voice comes out a strangulated whisper.

"He hears you!" I grab Grant's arm, attempting to pry him away. "Let go," I say firmly when he doesn't budge. Wedging myself between the pair, I place a hand on Grant's flushed cheek, directing his wild stare to me. "Grant, you need to let him go now." I shake my head. "He's not worth it. Do you hear me? He's not worth it."

Somewhere my words must reach him, because Grant drops the guy and slowly backs away.

"Come on," I say, slipping my hand in the crook of his elbow. He doesn't resist as I pull us in the opposite direction. Tremors of rage continue rippling through him, making his skin hotter than the sidewalk.

"Are you okay?" My voice sounds foreign to my ears, almost as foreign as the boy beside me.

"Yeah, I just need a few minutes to . . . calm down."

I start to let go of his arm. "Alone or . . ."

He stills my hand, holding it in place, making my adrenaline spike even more. "Stay with me?" It comes out more plea than question.

I nod. Already I'm breaking my decree against being alone with Grant. It lasted less than forty-eight hours. But how can I tell him no?

We walk two blocks without speaking. Grant inhales and blows out slow, steady breaths.

"Any better?" I ask, squinting up at him.

"Yeah." He gently disengages me from his elbow. "Um, thanks for being my anchor. I don't invite trouble, but disrespect is sort of a hot button. Always has been, but it got worse after A—" He clamps his mouth, and his jaw muscle twitches. "It just bothers me."

I am learning when it comes to Grant, the simpler the response, the more likely a complicated story lies behind it. He has shut down, exactly as he did Saturday in my kitchen. Maybe one day he'll trust me enough to tell me the real reason disrespect sent him into a blind fury. Maybe one day I'll tell him all about my mom, and then he'll understand why astrology means so much to me.

Someday.

But not today.

"Sorry if I freaked you out back there," he says.

"No, you didn't. I mean, I was a little thrown but . . ."

full effect of the paisley jacket and skirt—circa 1968. "And it's corduroy!"

I wipe the tears from my eyes. "I don't know. This one might be a coin toss." Then I turn to check out my own reflection. Or not. The velour jumpsuit *is* a fairly nauseating shade of green. Adding to the heinousness, I've paired it with a purple fedora—complete with feather.

Iri works to compose herself. "Okay, you win the Butt Ugly Award. Paisley can't beat out pimp. Lunch is on me. Now"—she unbuttons her jacket—"it's time to get serious and find me a sexy something for that art-gallery thingy." Irina pulls an outfit that's covered in flowers from a nearby rack. Wrinkling her nose, she adds, "Why I said yes to Jordan and an evening of self-important blowholes is a mystery."

Now I'm positive. Irina *likes* Jordan. But she'd sooner chalk up her yes to an unexplained phenomenon than admit she likes the guy.

"What's that?" Iri asks of my mumbling.

"Oh, you know, I just find it incredibly ironic that two days ago you were lecturing *me* on denial," I reply with an innocent smile.

"And?" The word is a dare. Her expression, a double dare.

"You like Jordan," I singsong.

She tosses an orange feather boa at me. "Do not."

"Do too, Duchess of Denial." I throw back the boa. *"And* you've stopped referring to him as Suit, Stiff, or Cactus Guy." I rest my case.

Her eyes narrow. "Keep it up and I'll be prying the *full*

story of yesterday's Betty Crocker bake-off out of you. Because you, comrade"—she points with her hanger—"are withholding."

I quickly wipe the amusement from my face and drop it like it's hot. "Hey, I'm gonna dig over here." Moving to the "new arrivals" section, I start thumbing through the possibilities. Actually, I'd trade my thumbs for crowbars, considering how tightly these clothes are jammed in here.

But I'm thrilled Irina's in need of my vintage-shopping expertise. After worrying myself sick over the tense incident between Grant and Seth, distractions have become my newfound hobby. And coming to the Rusted Zipper—my favorite vintage shop—is about the best kind of distraction a girl can ask for.

Iri squeezes her way into the next aisle. The store somehow crams ten thousand square feet of clothes into one thousand—defying both physics and reason.

In an effort to limit my hunt, I ask, "So, what are you thinking? Cocktail, floor-length, or—hold the freaking phone!" I pry out the garment, holding it up to admire it. "Iri! Ooh, Iri! You have to check out the most *spectacular* red wiggle dress I just fou—"

"Wil? Wil Carlisle, is that you?" The high-pitched giggle makes my skin crawl. "What on *earth* are you wearing?"

I whirl around, coming face to face with one of the *last* people I'd like to—Brittany Milford, aka Spawn of Satan.

I stand there blinking, waiting for my brain to catch up. Finally, the neurons fire. "Oh, hi . . ."

The phrase "mortal enemies" comes to mind as I watch the two size each other up. And the tension in this already claustrophobic store makes my polyester jumpsuit feel eighty times less breathable.

I tug at my collar.

A malicious grin fixes on Irina's lips as her gaze moves up from Spawn of Satan's purse. "You should stick with insecurity. After all"—her tone sweet as honey—"it's your signature accessory." Irina then ducks into the changing-room stall, yanking the curtain shut.

Good one.

Brittany glares before shoving a hanger back on the rack. "Nothing here but used trash anyway."

"That's enough, Brittany," I warn as my blood pressure soars.

"Whatever, Wil. You made your choice. The moment you sided with that"—she lowers her voice to a growl—*"Russian tramp."*

My eyes burn with a thousand fires as my hands curl into fists. "The only *tramp* is your boyfriend—whether you want to acknowledge it or not. Because Irina wouldn't give him the time of day. Not then. Not ever." I step back, putting more space between us. "I think you should leave now."

Brittany folds her arms, holding her head high like royalty. "And I think you should be a little more careful what you say to me, Wilamena. Because I can make your senior year a living hell. *Try me.*"

Dozens of comebacks ping around my head. And not one has the decency to pass my lips. Instead of the consti-

Suddenly Grant's hand is on the small of my back. Again. And now I *am* freaking out. His touch sends a surge of electricity buzzing up my spine. I suck in a breath and look up. God, he's so beautiful—the way the sun halos his head, he could be Apollo. It takes all my strength to remind myself he's the harbinger of heartache and devastation.

"Broken glass." He motions toward the amber shards on the sidewalk. Oh . . . right, he was being nice and guiding me around it. His hand falls away. "What are you doing in this neighborhood, anyway?"

"I was . . ." Well, crud. I can't tell him I was consulting a psychic about the melee of my warring emotions for him and his brother, *or* that I temporarily believed it to be the result of an otherworldly attack. Instead, I settle on something truthful, if not complete. "I was visiting an old friend of the family."

"Cool." He stuffs a hand in his pocket.

"Um, my bus stop is the next block up, and I'm afraid I can't keep walking without these shoes chemically bonding to my feet." I fan my face again. "Are you good? Or I could catch the next—"

"I'm parked over on Chestnut"—he pauses—"and you're not taking the bus." Grant smirks at my relieved smile. "Huh, not even an argument? That's a first. Usually you put up some sort of fight when I offer to help."

My eyes widen. "Are you kidding? Do you even *know* the condition of this city's public transportation?"

He chuckles. We cut across Dugan, working our way

toward the side street where the pickle wagon awaits. "Uh-oh. What is it?"

"Hmm?"

"Well, either you're about to throw a dart at me, or you're concentrating really hard on something else. Your tongue," he clarifies.

"Oh, um, no. I just . . . the ride home. I don't want to create any more"—I fumble for the right word—"*friction* between you and Seth."

Grant sniffs. "I keep forgetting you're an only child—friction's the *norm,* Wil. And my brother and I, we tend to butt heads. A lot."

"Did you ever get along?"

"Yup." And that's the extent of his answer to that question. "Seriously, though, if Seth's getting that torqued up over a couple of car rides and some cupcakes, *he's* the one with the problem."

I'm fretting over how to respond when Grant kicks a semicrushed can in my path. I grin and kick it back. "So, what brought you to this end of town?"

He picks up the mangled aluminum and tosses it in a trash can. "Java Hole. They've got great live music. Friend of mine, Roman, often plays here, so I popped by to catch him." His eyes slide over to me. "I think you'd really like his music—he plays a killer acoustic guitar."

"Yeah?" I squint ahead. "You'll have to let me know when he plays again, then."

"Well, won't be long before you're giving Roman a run for his money."

My grin falters. "Oh right, I keep forgetting." I root around my purse. "I accidently took this the other night from your car." I hold out the guitar pick.

He shakes his head. "Keep it. You'll need it."

I stare at the pick and then Grant. "I can't." I hold it back out. *Please don't ask why.* I can't confess I don't trust myself with the sort of closeness guitar lessons would warrant. Or how I almost burst into flames last time. The pick is an extension of Grant—every time I'd hold it, I'd be holding him. So I have to let it go. I *have* to.

"Keep it anyway." He curls my fingers back over the triangular bit of plastic. "In case you change your mind."

About what?

The question hovers at the tip of my tongue until I bite down on it. I know what I must do. While Miss Laveau may not have shed much light on my future, she was right about the past.

I was warned about Grant before.

And I won't compromise the promise to my mother any longer.

When he isn't looking, I drop the pick on the pavement behind us. Where it will lie abandoned along with any shred of feeling I have for him.

Chapter 14

Rousing myself early the next day, I try yoga in hopes of attaining enlightenment. When that doesn't work, I set up a "sacred space"—complete with a "clarifying" sandalwood candle and special floor cushion—in the corner of the living room.

I didn't realize listening to the voice inside me would be so labor intensive, but I figure I should try to glean *something* from yesterday's reading. My forehead creases as I strain to receive the faint messages. Finally, the voice is speaking! And . . . it tells me my nose is itchy, I might've pulled a hamstring during downward dog, and my right foot feels all pins and needles because it's lapsed into a coma.

A short time later Gram shuffles by as I'm in the middle of a loud *"Ommmmm."* The pads of my thumb and index fingers lightly touch, because the yoga DVD says this will help open my channels of energy and awaken my kundalini. Which . . . come to think of it, sounds kind of scary and messy.

Gram backs up, pausing in the doorway. Then she shakes her head and keeps on walking.

Once again, considering my frustrating lack of results, it's now clear the problem must be that I have not properly connected with nature. I spread a blanket in the backyard, finding a flat spot beneath the crab apple tree where the moles haven't churned up the earth. The fluffy blossoms on Gram's peony bushes perfume the summer air.

Lying on my back, staring up at the softly clapping leaves, I wait. And wait.

And within five minutes . . . I am asleep.

"You hate it, don't you?" Seth whispers.

" 'Hate' is a strong word. I, um . . ." I gnaw my lower lip. "I didn't know there were so many ways to blow something up." Plus, it's downright depressing to think the only person to survive the end of the world is Vin Diesel.

"You hate it."

"Shh!" A guy with no neck wearing a football jersey shushes us. Like dialogue is a critical element of an action flick.

"It's almost over," I whisper to Seth.

He rolls his eyes and grabs my hand. "I'm not gonna

make you suffer all the way to the credits. Let's get out of here."

We exit the theater into the humid night. Since Monday offered zero insight into my current conundrum, I've decided to allow fate to have its way with me. So when Seth called, asking if I wanted to grab dinner and a movie, I didn't hesitate to say yes.

I tug off the thin sweater covering my black dress.

Seth whistles. "Oh yeah. I'd much rather look at you than Vin for another hour."

"Well, just don't ask me to flex, because my muscles don't do that."

He chuckles and grasps my hand. "I'd get a complex dating a girl who could bench-press more than me anyway."

Stray cats are hissing in a turf war near the theater's Dumpsters. Furry bodies streak through the parking lot and into a nearby field.

"Wil?" Seth pauses.

"Hmm?"

His mouth twists as he bites the inside of his cheek. "I need to say something but . . ." He stalls and frowns.

"Now you've really piqued my curiosity." I grin, giving his arm a little shake. "What? Come on, out with it."

He hits the power lock, walking me to the passenger side of the Lexus, and opens the door. The interior light shows what the darkness hides. Nervousness. His eyes flit around, refusing to land anywhere more than two seconds. His free hand tugs at his earlobe. It's rare to see Seth fidget. Anything that makes him this uncomfortable can't be good.

"I don't like the amount of time you're spending with my brother," he confesses. The light and fluffy popcorn becomes ball bearings in my stomach. He releases my hand. "*Grant* took you home after our last date, and then spent all of Saturday with you." Seth sniffs. "I think your grandma pretty much worships the ground he walks on. She couldn't say enough about him. And then I heard you guys saw each other yesterday. . . . It's like he's spending more time with you than I do."

"Well, it's not like any of it was . . . *planned*," I point out. "Seth, I would've called you but—"

"That's the thing, I *know*." He kicks at some crumbled asphalt, causing it to roll beneath the car. "Hell, listening to myself, I sound like a jealous asshat. And it's so stupid and lame, and I know we've already talked about it, but—"

"It's . . . not stupid. Unnecessary maybe, but . . ." My mind whirls. I frantically grab at the scattered thoughts to cobble together *something* that will put him at ease. "Would you really want to spend a whole Saturday making cupcakes with my grandmother?"

Seth braces his arm against the doorframe, and stares back at the ground. "I don't know, maybe. Grant was still high as a kite when I saw him Sunday. I haven't seen him like that in forever. He's happier lately, less . . . serious." Seth lifts his eyes to meet mine. "Wil, I think it's because of you."

My laugh is a little too high and borders on maniacal. "Oh, come on! He was probably still in the throes of a sugar rush. You know he ate *all* the reject cupcakes." I turn and climb into the car.

Seth closes the door. I catch a glimpse of his low-set brow and rigid posture. My words aren't enough. He's not even in the vicinity of reassured. I'm going to have to step up my actions to convince him.

He slides in and cranks the engine, adjusting the AC. He sits for a moment in silence, fingers curled at the wheel. "I'm going to ask you this only once, and then I'll drop it—for good. But I need to know." His brown eyes pull away from the windshield. "Are you absolutely positive there's nothing between you and my brother?"

It isn't until the question is posed point-blank that I realize how close I am to obliterating everything. I swallow. "Well, actually . . . there is."

He closes his eyes.

Tentatively I touch his arm. "Seth, we're friends. Just friends."

The sadness leaves his face and his lips stretch wide. His teeth belong on television—news-anchor worthy. "Really?"

"Yes." I shift closer; the leather crackles beneath me.

"Because I think you better break it to him that it's nothing but . . ." His smile wavers as I inch nearer. "What are you doing?"

"I . . ." I am flipping out. What am I doing, making the first move? My heart's ready to stage a jailbreak from my ribs. But I'm more afraid of losing him if I don't.

Miss Laveau had all but told me I was fate's marionette.

Which makes Seth Walker my destiny—my one and only. So from this moment forward, I will stop fighting and questioning what is written in the stars. And I will throw myself into this with abandon.

"I want to kiss you," I whisper. "No interruptions."

Seth leans in, meeting me partway. His cologne mixes with the scent of peppermint and leather as his hand slides along the side of my neck. "That's all I've thought about since the last time I saw you," he murmurs. "It's been driving me crazy."

My gaze drifts to his mouth, so like Grant's. My heart speeds faster. *No! No! Nothing like Grant!* I banish the unwelcome thoughts, focusing completely on Seth.

"You know, I have this history with guys."

He licks his lips. "Black widow, I remember." He moves a bit closer, until the distance between us can be measured in millimeters.

"So this could still end in disaster."

"I'll take my chances."

I hold my breath . . . and take the plunge. The moment our lips meet I feel the rush. The one that comes from what is new and undiscovered. I think of the first time I climbed the water tower and then looked down. That's how this feels. Thrilling with a side of vertigo.

As we kiss, I catalog the way he tastes—peppermint, like me—and the way his mouth feels—warm, unhesitating. It's a certainty that comes from lots of practice. Like Grant. I feel a railroad spike at my chest. I am determined to make it go away.

I deepen the kiss and push myself harder into Seth's

arms. But . . . what happened to the rush? This doesn't feel the same. Does *he* notice it doesn't feel the same? Maybe if I just . . .

Quit overanalyzing!

Burying my hands in his hair, I move against him. He likes it. I assume he likes it, anyway, because his breathing gets even faster and more erratic. We carry on like this for a long while. Then I discover the logistical nightmare of making out in the front seat. My knee bangs the shifter.

I whimper.

Seth pulls away, breathless. "What? Did I hurt you?"

"Mmm, no." I shake my head. "Just an old bruise."

"Where?"

I pull my dress several inches above my knee to reveal the yellow, discolored skin.

He lowers his head. The distant theater lights make the tips of his brown hair golden. His lips graze my knee. "Better?"

"Uh-huh." I am back to holding my breath, resting my head against the glass of the foggy passenger window.

Seth sits up, reaching out to toy with one of the waves that have fallen across my eye. "You scare me, you know that?"

My breath escapes in a shuddery exhale. "Then you have a really strange way of showing it."

He closes the space between us, softly kissing my swollen lips before moving to my ear. "I think about you more than I should," Seth whispers.

"Is that bad?"

His fingers follow the chain of my necklace. "Depends on whether or not you think about me."

"Seth." I grin. "I wouldn't be doing this with you if I didn't."

"Doing what?" he asks, voice dropping low, like his fingers that follow my necklace.

My chest rises and falls under his touch. "Fogging up your windows." The reply causes him to chuckle, even though I wasn't meaning to be funny.

His face turns serious again. "What am I going to do about you, Wil?"

Uh, I'm confused. I thought I'd been crystal clear about what I wanted. Maybe he's not so sure now. Maybe he's waffling about his feelings for me. Which definitely adds a secondary layer of WTF-ery on the situation. "I . . . can't answer that. What do you want?"

After a few skips of my heart, he stretches out his arm; his finger makes squeaky noises against the glass.

I study his intense expression, full lips pressed together as he works. More squeaks follow, until he's satisfied and drops his arm. I turn to read the message he's written in the condensation above my head:

YOU. JUST YOU.

He only wants me. More emotions than I can name go flooding through me. Weeks ago I sought to find love, love and universal synchronicity. Which has been impossible with the steady dance of doubt and uncertainty shadowing my thoughts. But tonight, with Seth . . .

I think I'm finally sure. "Just you, Seth. That's all I want, too."

He smiles, and it's as bright as the moon hanging in the inky sky. He gathers me in his arms and I feel the elation in his kiss. It makes me happy to be the one to put it there.

More minutes pass and his cell beeps. It beeps again.

And again.

I turn my head in the direction of the noise. "Seth?" He's totally oblivious. I can't fathom how. "Are you going to get that?"

"What?" he rasps.

"Your phone. Don't you hear it?"

"Wil," he chuckles, "I don't hear anything when I'm with you like this." But he groans and finally moves away.

I take the opportunity to tug my dress back into place.

Gradually I become aware of how he's gripping the phone. He curses under his breath as he taps out a response, and sends the phone clattering into the cup holder.

"What?" I ask with sudden alertness. I sit upright.

The headlights blaze and he's throwing the Lexus in reverse, barreling through the parking lot.

I scramble to fasten my seat belt. "Seth, what's going on? What's wrong?"

His sole focus is the road. And his hands are wringing the life out of the steering wheel. "You missed curfew."

Oh God. The glowing clock on the dash informs me I've *missed* curfew by over half an hour. It'll be almost an hour by the time I get home. This is bad, real bad, but doesn't explain Seth's explosive reaction. His phone lights up with another text.

Seth grabs it, scowling once more. "And my punk brother needs a lesson in boundaries."

"Your brother?" What could Grant possibly have to do with this? I thought we'd passed that obstacle. Beyond freaked, I snatch my cell—still muted from the movie—and listen to the messages. It's worse than I thought. Gram's voice is fraught with worry and desperate to know my whereabouts. And she has managed to enlist the help of the *one person* I wished she hadn't . . .

Grant.

Any assurances Seth had about the nature of our relationship seem to dissipate like his writing on the glass.

"S-Seth," I stammer, "I don't even know how Gram got his number. It must've been Saturday, when—"

"Don't." His hand pushes irritably through his hair as he stops at a light.

We ride in uncomfortable silence until we're less than a mile from my street, and finally I have to broach the question. "Are we . . . are things between us still . . . ?" Between being unnerved by Seth's reaction, and unnerved by what Gram's reaction *will* be, I can't seem to articulate the question.

But I can tell he sees what I'm driving at, despite my ineffective, floundering words. Seth rubs his fingers over his temple. "I don't know, Wil. I really hate this back-and-forth vibe. It's like I'm constantly wondering what's going on in your head. One second you're kissing me and it seems like you're into it, and the next . . . I don't know. It's like you're there, but not."

I wish I could refute that, but before tonight, my head

was in a vicious tug-of-war. I just didn't realize I've been so transparent.

Seth exhales. "Honestly, the only way I see this working between us is if you're willing to do one thing."

"Anything." And I mean it. I'd do anything to reassure him of my feelings for him. "Anything, Seth."

"Don't see Grant anymore."

Anything except that.

"But . . . we're friends," I croak. The car interior spins around me. "You can't ask—"

"I like you, Wil," Seth plows on. "I really, *really* like you. But if we're gonna have any kind of shot at this, you can't keep seeing him, even as friends. I think it just . . . *confuses* things."

I stare at my hands clutching my purse. Wait a sec, is my Sagittarius giving me an ultimatum? He can't mean it. He just *can't*. Because a true soul mate would never do that. Right?

"It's not his fault Gram called him," I deflect.

Seth pulls into my driveway, where the vehicle idles more calmly than the situation. "Wil, please . . ." He starts to reach for my hand when the porch light flicks on.

Gram appears at the screen door; her anger shifts the tectonic plates.

My mind instantly turns to the heap of trouble I'm about to face.

"Not now." I pull away, wrenching open the door. "I gotta go."

chapter 15

"Don't be nervous," I tell my reflection. I dust on some powder to dull the pink in my cheeks. "Go downstairs, say good night, and don't make unnecessary chitchat. Babbling will only give you away. Okay? Okay." I blow out a rattling breath, and grab the overnight bag stuffed with my green dress, heels, and a bottle of Downy Wrinkle Releaser.

For the first time in eleven years . . . I am out-and-out lying to my grandmother.

I mean, technically, I *will* stay the night at Irina's. But first we're going to Tristan's party on the east side. Which is the part I don't mention to Gram, the part I *won't* mention to Gram. Even under threat of torture.

It's been four days of atonement since my date with Seth, when we kissed until my lips went numb before the whole night went to crap, plunging us into a relationship no-man's-land. And if questioning our status wasn't awful enough, I also broke curfew by fifty-two minutes.

Curfew. The *one* thing Gram's an absolute stickler for. Oh, and don't think she didn't voice her disapproval of any boy who doesn't have the proper respect and courtesy to get a girl home at a reasonable hour. *Lord have mercy!* The incident had Grant rising even higher than he already was in Gram's estimation. Grant would never do this and Grant would've done that . . . I checked my ears twice for bleeding.

Overnight my grandmother flipped from trusting me completely to being convinced I'd follow in my mother's footsteps.

Seventeen and knocked up.

No amount of pleading has swayed her. The irony, of course, being you actually have to *have* sex to get pregnant.

But with only eight calendar days remaining, and June slipping like water through my fingers, I've got to do everything in my power to right things with Seth.

So I'm lying to Gram.

Irina arrives, Natasha's headlights panning across the living room, making my palms slick with sweat. I breeze over to the armchair where Gram's tucked under an afghan, reading. "I'll be home by noon. Okay?"

"All right, Mena." She kisses my cheek. "I suppose you've done more than enough chores this week to earn a relaxing movie night with Irina." Yeah, in addition to house arrest and having my phone confiscated, chores have been my other punishment. Mildew removal, dandelion genocide, and oven-scouring to name a few. "Go have fun," Gram adds with a pat on my cheek.

I avert my eyes so she doesn't see the untruth burning inside them. "Thanks, I will." I practically sprint to the hall.

"And, Mena?" I freeze at the door, positive she smells the stink of dishonesty roiling off me. "Love you, child."

My chin drops to my chest. I am pond scum, the absolute sludge of humanity. "Love you, too. G'night, Gram."

Dashing down the front steps, I yank open the passenger door, tossing my bag in the back, and myself in the front.

Irina's arched brow strains higher. "Where do you think you're going dressed like that?" She's wearing a short, form-fitting dress, with tights that remind me of black cobwebs, and her trademark neck-break heels.

I glance at my silk pajama bottoms and threadbare T-shirt featuring all the constellations. I push up my glasses. "Curio's."

She flicks the curtain of blond hair over her shoulder, resting a hand on the gearshift. "You want to go eat hamburgers in your pajamas," Iri deadpans.

Curio's is a regular haunt for much of the Inkporium crew. Everyone knows us, which meant no one would bat an eye if I hogged the bathroom for the time it took to finish getting ready.

"Look, Gram thinks we're having a girls' night in. I

haven't seen Seth or talked to him in four whole days, and there's no way she'd let me go to this party with how she's been acting." I pull down the visor and start removing the clips that held my waves as they dried. "I just need to change and slap on a little makeup. Come on, I'll even spring for the first round of fries." I add the last bit because Iri can't resist fries. They're her Achilles' heel, and Curio's has the best in the Northern Hemisphere.

"Sold." She jams Natasha in reverse.

Night's fallen; the winding torch-lit path illuminates the immaculate grounds of the three-story mansion. And the east-side grass isn't just greener; it's softer, like walking on rolling carpets of velvet.

The distant noise of the party grows louder.

"Quit fussing, it looks perfect," Iri says, prompting me to drop my hand from the hair I've been fiddling with. She sighs as I tug at my hem. "Wil, you used a gallon of that wrinkle-repellent stuff on your dress. I swear to God, that dress should be doing the walking for us. Why are you so nervous?"

"Besides the obvious conniving and lying to Gram?" I glance up at the drifting clouds. "It's . . . I'm running out of time, Iri."

"You are not." She slaps a mosquito on her arm and gives it a disdainful flick. "Just because you haven't been able to talk to Seth doesn't mean he's written you off."

"I guess," I reply, unable to break my gaze from where

Mercury was visible a couple weeks earlier. If only the planet was within my view now, I'd be telepathically sucking out all the intelligence and communication energies it's known for. "But what am I supposed to do if Grant comes? It wouldn't exactly help the situation."

Iri sniffs. "Of course Grant will be here, he's in what's-his-face's band."

"Tristan." She gives me a funny look. "What's-his-face," I add, exasperated, "the one throwing this party?"

"Well, whatever. Seth having a raging case of jealousy doesn't give him authority to pick your friends—*ever*." Iri plucks a white flower from a bush as we pass, sniffing it, then discarding it over her shoulder.

"I don't think that's how he meant it, Iri. And, anyway, if we're still a thing"—my gut twinges on the "if"—"I can't realistically avoid Grant." I release a heavy sigh. "I just wish Seth and I had the chance to sort this out— preparty—you know? So I knew where things stood."

"Where things *stood*?" She laughs. "Wasn't it obvious from your time in his car? Unless he wasn't—"

"Oh, ha-ha." I bump against her. "I'll have you know our time together was *very* satisfactory."

Irina's expression turns grave. "*Satisfactory*? Jesus, tell me that's not how you'd describe kissing him."

"No, I was—" But I don't get the chance to defend my thoughtless word choice.

Shouts ring out in the night.

Charging over the crest of the path is a pair of Vikings— literally, two guys clad in Viking helmets and faux-fur undies. So Seth wasn't exaggerating. A trio of girls race up behind the half-naked warriors, shrieking and giggling as they mercilessly hose them with Super Soakers. Tristan warned the party wouldn't be at full throttle until much later.

It is only nine-thirty.

Lights strung high above the network of patios light the raucous scene below. Nestled in the far patio is a stone fire pit large enough for a virgin sacrifice; outdoor chairs and couches cluster around it. We stand, mouths gaping, staring at the nearest patio, which serves as the dance floor and bar. An enormous pool with a slate waterfall lies between them. The waterfall is backlit with constantly changing lights that glitter on the pool's surface.

Iri lets out a low whistle. "Who are these people, the Trumps?"

"You'd think," I reply. Someone jumps in the pool, inciting screams and splashes.

"Will!" It's Seth.

Elated, I stand on my tiptoes, but the crowd obscures him. "Seth! Where are you?" My return shout turns heads in our direction.

"Here! I'll come to you!" Seth hollers from wherever he is.

One of the turned heads takes an instant shine to Irina. The muscled guy takes off his ball cap, turning it backward, before mouthing a sexy hello. Except . . . uh, I've never seen anything so *unsexy* in all my life. Then he tries to wink but his eye function is delayed, so his one eye sticks closed. Now he just looks like a deranged pirate.

"It's bad enough Jordan canceled. You owe me to infinity and back," Irina grumbles in my ear. It's the second time she's reminded me. Had it not been for my monumental desperation, I wouldn't have asked, because I'm *well aware* of her eastsider contempt.

Spotting Seth, I feel anxiety coursing through me once more. But I plaster on a smile and wave before addressing my friend. "Give it a chance. You might have fun. Everyone else here seems to be." Her squinty eyes assure me that ain't happening. "Okay, could you at least *try* to keep havoc at a minimum?" I plead.

Irina's dark red lips twist in a smirk. "Then how am I supposed to have fun, *dorogaya*?" She chuckles. "Go on, reunite with your boy. And it better be more than *satisfactory*. I'm going to mingle."

Clearly, havoc will not be at a minimum. Terms I've come to accept where my comrade's concerned.

Seth squeezes through a dancing cluster of girls who are eager to have him press against them. Is it possible he's gotten even hotter in four days' time? His shorts are slightly baggy, but fitted in all the right places, and the light blue T-shirt makes his skin look beautifully bronzed.

"Hey, gorgeous." He scoops me up in his arms. And now that I'm wrapped up in Seth, I decide I *was* probably worrying for nothing. Perhaps I'd even blown the whole conversation over Grant out of proportion. "Mmm, I missed you."

"Missed you, too." I bury my face in his warm neck, breathing in.

"I had a bad feeling you might not show. I called and texted." He sets me back on my feet. "What happened?"

"Gram confiscated my phone. I'm sorry, Seth, I didn't have a way to reach you. And she was watching me like a hawk, so . . ."

He traces his thumb over my fretful brow. "Hey, now, don't apologize. I figured your punishment was gonna be steep. I'm just psyched you came. Must've worked some magic to get here tonight."

"Gram doesn't know I'm here."

Seth cringes. "Really? Aw, hell, the woman doesn't need another reason to hate me."

"She . . . she doesn't *hate* you. And she won't find out. Let's not talk about it, okay?" Because every time I think of my scheming deception, the guilt feels like asteroids pummeling my solar plexus. Which will dampen the night like a big soggy blanket.

You know what? *Screw it!* No more angsting over what I've done to get here. In another seven months and change, I'll be eighteen and no longer subject to Gram's antiquated rules anyway. Tonight I will take full advantage of my hard-won freedom. Starting now.

Seth laces his fingers in mine, drawing the back of my hand to his lips. "Am I allowed to say how effing incredible you look tonight?" He brushes another kiss on my hand. "Ah, *now* she smiles. How about a drink?"

"Sounds perfect."

Seth gestures toward the fire pit. "Ryan's over there

with his girlfriend, Ginger, who's dying to meet you." He scans the area. "And you have to meet Brody and Jack, because they think I'm making you up."

"Brody Cooper?" I ask weakly.

"Yeah, you know him?" Seth peers back at me.

"Uh . . ." Well, it's not like I can tell him Brody was Mr. Saliva from freshman year under the bleachers. What are the odds? "Yes, we've met. It was a long time ago, so he might not remember."

A girl can hope.

"Guys, it's like I've always said." Ryan's girlfriend, Ginger, rises from the couch, adjusting the wrap dress over her petite figure. She might be small, but nature has packed adorable into every inch of the redhead, right down to the spray of freckles on her nose and cheekbones. "Seth just had to find the right girl. The *right* girl can tame even the *wildest* boy."

"Who you calling tame, woman?" Ryan challenges.

She rolls her eyes before gathering her long copper curls over her shoulder. "I'm talking about *him*." Ginger points at Seth.

She's referring to the doting and continuous displays of affection. *"Later,"* I promise Seth when he leans in nuzzling my neck and his hands begin to wander.

Of course, I've missed him, too. I just . . . don't need to prove it before an audience. It's bad enough the couple on the other side of the fire pit are going at it.

"One day, Wil," Ginger says, smirking, "promise you'll

tell me what you did to win the heart of Absinthe's serial dater."

I flash a hearty smile I don't feel. It's nothing to do with jealousy, and *everything* to do with how I'm suddenly smothering under Seth's attention. *What the hell's my problem?* He finds me mesmerizing, *enchanting* even—those sweet words should have turned me to putty, coming from my soul mate.

Why, then, do I feel like Andromeda chained to a rock?

"Ginger's exaggerating about that serial-dater thing," Seth says softly in my ear. He drapes an arm over my shoulders, caressing my skin.

Ryan pipes in, "I think that was Grant's title, actually."

The mere mention of Grant causes Seth's fingers to spasm midmotion on my arm. I hoped to skirt the subject tonight. Hoped he'd forgotten his heat-of-the-moment ultimatum. Maybe that was unrealistic. But was it too much to ask for a single night of worry-free fun?

"Yeah, *was*." Ginger frowns, taking a swig of her drink. "Has Grant even dated anyone in the past year?" If not for being shackled by Seth's arm, I would lean forward to hear the answer.

"Babe," Ryan groans, "you know he hasn't. There hasn't been anyone serious since . . . you know."

Ginger nods to herself. "Well, he's going to be my next project. I'm going to find Grant a girl. Not just any girl either. She's going to be extra, extra special. He deserves that after everything he went through."

The smothering feeling manages to worsen, as if the weight of the sky bears down on my chest.

Now the guys are in deep discussion, planning their next trip to Lannister since the last was rained out. With Seth distracted, it's a perfect opportunity to get a little breathing room. I wriggle from his arms, which have managed to replicate four times. *Because I am suddenly dating an octopus.*

"Where are you going?" Seth's brows draw together.

"Refill." I shake my empty cup and rise from the couch.

"I'll come with you." He jumps to his feet.

"No, I'm . . . going to use the bathroom, too."

Ryan gives his head a shake before standing. "Dude, give the girl some oxygen." Seth laughs and flips him off. "Sorry, Walker, you're not my type. Besides, our beer-pong title won't defend itself." Ryan cocks his head. "You in or out, man?"

Seth looks uncertainly down at me.

"Go. Defend your title," I say, pecking him on the cheek and all but shoving him into Ryan's ready arms. "I can entertain myself for a while."

Tentacle-free, I work through the partygoers to the nearest bathroom, in the pool house. With the exception of the basement level, the rest of the mansion is locked up tighter than Fort Knox. Totally understandable. I wouldn't want a quarter of this rowdy crowd in my back-yard, let alone my house. As if on cue, a girl barfs on a patch of neatly pruned bushes while her friend holds back her hair.

Ick. I quickly take care of business and return to the festivities.

I spot Manny, who's apparently appointed himself

guardian of the keg. He tops off the red plastic cups of several girls circling him. They're rapt as he sits on the long table, explaining the secret to a minimal-foam pour. I have to suppress a giggle, because you'd think he was spouting poetry.

And it doesn't matter that Manny's short by guy standards. He's got a rare charisma that makes him shine brighter than the people around him. They want to bask in his glow. And I don't blame them.

"Hey, *chica!*" Manny bursts into a smile, holding up an arm for me to tuck into. He gives me a squeeze. "Where you been hiding your fine self? Hmm?"

"Hey." I grin. "Unfortunately, I've been under house arrest." I tug the bottom of his T-shirt featuring a giant handlebar mustache packing pistols on each end. "Can I ask where you even find these?"

"My cousin has a screen-printing business. If I dream it, he can do it. *Ahem,* ladies"—he tilts his cup in my direction—"this is my girl, Wil. And by 'my girl' I mean she *would* be if the Walker boys hadn't snatched her out from under me."

The eyes all flick to me. It is a lot of eyes. They outnumber the octopus arms I just escaped. "Walker *boy,* Manny—singular, not plural. Has he been this delusional all night?" I ask the semicircle. One of them drunkenly giggles.

"Oh, cut me some grammatical slack. English *is* my second language, after all."

"You're so full of it." I turn toward the table, with its

various jugs and pitchers, and go for the safest bet. Otherwise, I'll be joining the pukefest in the bushes. I twist the spigot on the large glass container filled with lemonade and fruit slices. Consuming a week's worth of sodium from Curio's fries has made for an unquenchable thirst.

I sip my drink as Manny talks about Wanderlust's last performance, when someone threw ginormous silk panties on the stage, which I thought was only done by old ladies at Tom Jones concerts. He goes on to describe in great detail how the parachute bloomers landed at Grant's feet and Grant turned eight shades of green. We crack up.

Manny glances over my shoulder. "Ah, speak of the devil. *¿Qué pasa, mano?*"

The approaching figure makes my heart seize midpump. My legs go wobbly. The lemonade in my throat turns to fire, blazing all the way to the pit of my belly. Grant.

And he's swapped his usual gray T-shirt for a fitted black one. I can see the contours of his arms and chest. He's also gotten a haircut. He looks . . . *whoa*.

For a night so full of carefree promise, it suddenly has catastrophe written all over it.

chapter 16

Manny fist-bumps Grant. "How long you been here? Haven't had any sightings yet."

"Not that long," Grant replies.

My limbs are reduced to pure gelatin as I reach for another glass of lemonade, knocking it back in a few gulps. Grant arrived—*not that long ago*. Well, maybe that accounts for Seth's sudden smothering behavior and overzealous PDA. But can I justify being annoyed, let alone angry, with Seth when my reaction to Grant is . . . *whoa*?

Manny tosses Grant a Fresca from the ice tub next to him.

"Gracias." Grant moves in beside me.

Tristan's family compound sits on eleventy billion acres, and I hear there are even sprawling gardens that put Versailles to shame. Yet Grant has to occupy my tiny three-by-three space. Manny goes back to lavishing his attention on the girls; their sunflower faces stretch to meet him.

Grant cracks open the soda. "So, you gonna give me the silent treatment now?"

Light-headed, I spit out a perfunctory, robotic greeting.

Grant leans against the table and crosses his arms. I do not notice his biceps. "That's a very courteous hello. Which I guess is better than nothing. Look, if you're still mad about Tuesday, that wasn't by choice—your gram called *me*." He releases a frustrated sigh. "She was out of her mind with worry! What was I supposed to do, Mena?" We both catch the slip. "I mean, Wil."

I've favored the name Wil since middle school. Maybe deep down I've wanted to preserve the name Mena, just for Mama and Gram—like a treasured keepsake. But now hearing it fall from Grant's lips makes me feverish. Which is all sorts of wrong. All. Sorts.

More lemonade. I refill my cup, dribbling the yellow liquid on the tabletop. I quickly mop it up with a napkin. "I know. I'm not mad at you." I take a swallow. Then another. The lemonade feels like complete lava going down. And a flush creeps up my neck like Mount Saint Helens preparing to blow.

"Yeah?" Grant tips the Fresca to his lips, taking a slow drink. "Then why are you acting so weird? By the way, your cheeks are really red."

"What?" I sputter. "I'm not acting *weird*!"

"Uh-huh." Grant holds his fist to his mouth, covering

215

up his stupid cute teeth. "Hey"—he plucks the cup from my hand—"you're gonna dump that. What's with you tonight?"

"What are you . . . ?" And then it hits me. My gaze swings to the supposedly innocent jug of lemonade. "Oh." But the proof is right in front of me, wavering. The lemonade must be spiked. Spiked! I grab the table behind me, steadying myself. It *has* to be spiked, because why else would the patio start to fold in and out like an accordion? I stare at my jittery hands, then shake them, trying to gain control of their function. It doesn't work so well. "Oh . . . shitballs."

Grant spits out his Fresca, laughing.

"It's not funny," I reply, panicky. "I think I might be buzzed."

"Oh, really?" Grant replies in a tone laced with skepticism. He glances at the lemonade jug while I totter to a nearby cooler and sit, blowing at a dark wave that has flopped over my eye.

After a few seconds, Grant follows. He pushes a bottle of water into my hand. "Drink it. You'll be fine; I guarantee it." He crouches down and tucks back the hair I keep unsuccessfully blowing from my eye.

Manny is heckling me about being a lightweight and brainstorming all kinds of variations on my name. Wussy Wil. One-Drink-Wonder Wil—the hits keep coming.

Even if I do feel fuzzy around the edges—enough is enough. "Yeah, well, Uranus called and"—I jab a finger at Manny—"and it wants its asshole back." The group goes

silent for a moment before exploding in laughter. I give up on trying to figure out if what I've said even makes a lick of sense, and giggle.

Wiping his eyes, Manny looks to Grant. *"¡Mierda! Ya entiendo por qué la adoran."*

"¡Basta!" Grant's eyes remain crinkled in amusement. "Drink some more water, Wil."

"Fine, but not because you're the boss of me. It's because I'm quite thirsty." I take a long guzzle before placing it on ground. "And I'm not supposed to be talking to you. Seth doesn't like it." I snicker like I've said something on a par with Uranus assholes. "Actually"—I shake my head—"he's not the boss of me either."

"For his sake, I hope he figures that out sooner than later. And another thing, Wil?"

"Hmm?" I get distracted by the way Grant sways back and forth in front of me.

He smiles. "Um, that lemonade you drank? It doesn't actually have any alcohol."

My grin fades. "What?" I reply weakly. No, that's impossible. I feel tipsy, woozy—surely I'm *a little* buzzed?

"See?" Grant points to the glass container. "It's got DD written on the side."

Designated Driver. Of course. That's why I didn't detect the booze. "Oh," I mumble lamely. "My mistake." Which makes me the *Designated Dork.* So all my symptoms of intoxication were really just . . . nerves? Nervousness because of Grant?

He grows quietly aware of my mortification and changes

the subject. "Seth'll get over it." Grant clarifies, "Us talking, I mean. He's just never had a girl get under his skin before. Usually it's the other way around."

"Have you?" I blurt. "Has a girl ever gotten under your skin?"

His head lowers, and he nods at the ground. "Yeah."

"What happened?"

A smile touches his lips—a heartbreakingly sorrowful smile. "I had to let her go."

"But . . . why?"

"Because I wasn't sure I could ever be what she wanted, you know?"

"That's crazy," I murmur. An unexpected lump forms in my throat. "How could you *not* be what she wanted? You're perfect." I bite my lip and damn my tongue. Why did I say that aloud? I can't even blame the comment on drunkenness. I avert my eyes to the patio stones at my feet.

"Nobody's perfect." His insistent gaze feels like a brand on my skin.

"Wil!" Ginger wedges through the partyers, copper curls bouncing. "There you are!" She appears puzzled, her blue eyes flicking back and forth between Grant and me. "Er . . . am I interrupting something?"

I shake my head as Grant quickly rises.

Ginger continues. "Um, it's your friend, the Russian girl. She's in the game room and—"

"Ooh, Ginge," Manny pipes in, "you talking about the smokin' blonde with all the piercings?" She nods. "I saw her earlier on the balcony tormenting some *pendejo* with a number after his last name. Flicked her tongue ring right before she gave him a purple-nurple. God, he about shizzed himself." Manny roars with laughter and slaps his knee. "Priceless. Totally priceless."

"What about her?" I stand, feeling instantly alert.

"She's okay," Ginger says, reading my alarm. "It's just, the guys are still wrapped up in beer pong, and . . ."

"What?" I lightly grasp her arms, fighting the urge to shake the information out of her.

"I think maybe someone should monitor what's going on," she finishes.

And if Ginger has said anything else, I'm not there to hear it.

I crash through the French doors, weaving my way through the mansion's lower level. Shouts erupt from a room at my left, sending fear spiraling through to my toes. *"Go-go-go-go!"* the crowd chants. My anxiety dials back when I realize it's the beer-pong tournament. There's a thunderous crack of pool balls at the end of a dim hall.

I follow the telltale noise to the game room. The three pool tables are swarming with people—mostly guys—who laugh, jeer, and egg each other on. And it isn't until I spot Irina at the farthest table—unharmed and untouched—that I find my full breath again.

"Thank you, God," I whisper to myself, resting a hand to my booming heart and sagging against the wall.

"That's her, right?" Ginger asks, slightly breathless, coming up beside me.

"Yeah."

"Oh, Wil, sweetie"—Ginger rubs my arm, her expression turning worried—"I didn't mean to freak you out. I only thought someone should keep an eye on things. Your friend's just doing really well at the tables." She pauses. *Really well*. I'm not sure some of these guys'll appreciate that, so I—"

"No, no, it's okay." I squeeze her hand. "You did the right thing finding me. It's just . . . sometimes Irina has a way of finding trouble."

"Funny, that's what I've heard about you," Ginger replies.

Grant and Manny enter the game room, flanking us. "Everything good?" Grant asks, wrinkles crowding the center of his forehead.

I hate that I've put them there. *Again*. I liked it better when I thought I was tipsy and making him laugh. "Yeah, it's fine." I spot Tristan's sister, Lila, circling closer in her sparkly tank top and petal-pink shorts, her gaze locked purposefully on Grant. "Looks like you've got company," I say to Grant. "You should"—I falter before purging the rest of the words—"you should probably go."

"Ay . . . mi diosa," Manny murmurs in a trancelike tone, totally spellbound by the Russian bombshell dominating the last table. He shakes his head as if coming to. "I'm gonna need a front-row seat for this."

I follow Manny, without sparing a glance at Grant. It shouldn't matter what he does . . . or who he does it with.

Because *I* am committed to Seth.

Balls sink in quick succession, first the solid blue and then the eight ball.

"Yes!" Manny catapults from the bench while pumping his arms. *"Ha! Ha!* That's right, baby, you show those rich boys how it's done!"

Ginger squeals and whistles, nearly shattering my eardrum. She pulls me into an apologetic embrace. "Sorry, Wil. I just can't believe Irina made that last shot! She's unreal!"

"I know." My grin fades. I also know we're treading on thin ice. When it comes to pool, Iri has one goal, and one goal only—winning. Winning is everything. Sometimes she wins by a landslide and sometimes by a hair. But make no mistake; Irina Dmitriyev knows *exactly* what she's doing.

"Shut it, Rodriguez," a deep voice snaps from the sidelines.

Manny smirks as he leaps onto the bench, lifting the bottom of his T-shirt. "Why don't you pucker up and smooch this beautiful"—he gyrates—"brown"—he gyrates some more—"ass, Bradley? Second thought"—he jumps down—"I think you'd like it too much." Laughter erupts and more verbal jabs ensue.

Irina straightens, feigning confusion in the chaos. "Then . . . I win?" Someone informs her yes. "Oooh!" She claps the arm of the defeated challenger. "I *cannot* believe my luck tonight." Yeah, he doesn't look like he does either. But Irina was sneaking into pool halls when most girls were getting their first babysitting gigs.

"It's not luck, it's called hustling." The loser scowls, plucking the unlit cigarette from behind his ear.

Irina scoops up her winnings. "Hustling? My dearest *mudak,* this is nothing more than a friendly tournament. And everyone knows you should never bet what you can't afford to lose." Her Russian inflection has mysteriously returned. No doubt she's employed it to gain a competitive edge. And it's working. "Now"—Iri chalks her stick, blowing off the excess—"who's next?"

We watch as Irina's name is erased off the chalkboard and advanced to the next bracket. The game progresses, and the number of onlookers fringing the pool table grows with the stakes.

Irina's gaze narrows as she bends to line up her shot. Many of the guys are too busy checking out her ass to notice the acute level of her focus and determination. If they saw her face the way I do, they'd tuck tail and run.

She sinks the twelve in the corner pocket.

"Nice," a goateed guy praises, his eyes nowhere near the pool table.

"Like that?" Irina leans, wiggling her rear as she gets a better angle. "Then you'll love this. Fifteen, side pocket."

A stocky, red-faced guy hovering at the end of the table steps up. "No way. No freakin' way." He slaps a fifty on the edge of the table. "That's how sure I am you're gonna choke that shot, Ruski." There's a murmur of agreement.

"Who are you?" Irina squints at Big Red.

"Justin," Big Red replies. "But knowing my name isn't gonna change how this ends—*me* walking away with *your* money."

Irina's eyebrow arches higher. "Well, *Justin,* good thing I feel lucky."

The cue ball banks off the end, narrowly missing a cluster of balls, and grazes the fifteen on its way back. It grazes just enough to nudge it in. *Thunk!*

"No way," he repeats, head swaying. A collective silence follows around the table.

"Told you I felt lucky." Irina tucks the fifty away for safekeeping.

And the longer Iri plays, the more hostile the undercurrent becomes. She makes impossible shots left and right, taking bill after bill of winnings.

"Wil," Ginger murmurs, "those guys look pissed." She discreetly nods at a group formed behind Iri. "This isn't good."

I agree, as do the hairs prickling on the back of my neck. I sidle up to Irina and whisper a warning. "You need to stop."

I scan the room for Manny, who went to top off his beer during a break in the game. *Why isn't he back?* And Grant—I don't see him anywhere. It's noisy, and the other two tables are so engrossed in their games, I doubt they're aware of anything else going on.

Irina ignores me and takes her next shot.

My stomach sinks like the pool ball in the corner pocket.

Ginger's apricot cheeks turn ashy. Flicking back her curls with false confidence—the confidence we've all been instructed to fake in dangerous situations—she edges next to me.

Iri grins; the diamond above her lip glitters. "I'm just getting warmed up. They haven't seen half of what I can do."

"No." I nervously eye the closing circle of guys. "I think you should stop. *Now.*"

"I hate to say it, but she's right, Irina," Ginger whispers. "This isn't *friendly* anymore."

Alarms are clanging in my head until I hardly hear anything else. One of the guys bumps up against me.

Irina shoves him back.

"Hey, easy, Wild Cat, accidents happen." His friends laugh.

It isn't funny. It's a threat. And my mouth goes dry as the guys inch closer, trapping us against the table.

I close my hand around the bridge stick resting in front of me. I have no idea what I'm about to do. But whatever it is, I won't be empty-handed.

Cigarette smoke swirls beneath the yellow light hanging over the table. The white tendrils come from the guy Irina beat earlier. He takes a drag, rolling the cigarette between his thumb and index finger as he watches me. "There are accidents, and then there're the accidents people have coming to them." His gaze travels down my body until I feel so dirty I want to shower in bleach. When he licks his lips, my hand tightens around the stick.

"There a problem here?" Manny appears, breaking through the imposing group. I want to hug him and his mustachioed T-shirt. "I *asked* if there was a problem?"

Grant steps up behind Manny. He is livid. It's the same fury he'd had with the guy outside of Pinky's. I notice his grip on Manny's arm, and anyone watching would think he was holding Manny in check. But I know different. Manny is actually Grant's anchor.

"Yeah," the smoking guy sneers. "This Russian bitch hustled us."

Irina bares her teeth, gripping her stick harder. "Say it again and I'll show you the kind of bitch I can be. I won that money—fair and square."

Cigarette's face turns red and a vein pops in his wide forehead.

"Sounds like you owe the lady an apology," Manny says. "My advice? Say you're sorry, and leave. No reason for this to turn ugly."

A rumble of hushed gossip gains momentum as it spreads through the gathering. It's about Grant, and something about a trip to the ER, but that's all I catch. The circle begins to disband.

Seeing no other way, Cigarette jerks his chin at Irina. *"Sorry."* The word is riddled with so much disdain, I almost miss it was an apology and not another insult.

Out of the corner of my eye, I see Ginger dart from the room.

"Irina," Grant says low and measured, "take your money now."

Her nostrils flare as she snatches the remaining cash. "Perhaps next time you'll use your other head before you place a bet." She flashes an icy smile at Cigarette. "But I'd wager it isn't much smarter."

Once we're safely down the hall, I whirl around to face Irina. "Why couldn't you stop? You had to needle and goad and take them for everything. *Why?*" I demand. "And don't try and tell me it's just about the win—it's more. I know it's more."

Iri's face remains colored with anger. "Because they're so goddamn entitled! They think they can treat me like garbage because they come from money." Irina sucks in a breath. Her gray eyes are hard as concrete.

"So what, that was some kind of punishment?"

"And no less than what they deserved."

She'd get no argument from me. Still, I worry about the reckless way Irina often finds her justice. I worry what might've happened if Manny and Grant hadn't been there to intervene. Most of all, I worry that none of these thoughts would ever occur to my friend.

Manny jogs down the hall to meet us, a triumphant grin plastered on his face. "We made sure those dickwad crashers were escorted off the premises. So, how much you clear, hustler?"

Irina shoots him a withering look and folds her arms.

"Either you start talking, or I'm gonna belt out the worst rendition of 'The Gambler' you have *ever* heard. Ask Grant." Manny thumbs to his friend as he joins us. "I'm serious as a heart attack. There's a reason they don't ask me to sing backup." The dark mood begins to brighten. Because that's what Manny does. Even Grant appears more controlled.

Iri's mouth twitches, her hard shell cracking. "Four hundred and change."

Manny whistles. "So, like, enough change to take me to Denny's for some Moons Over My Hammy? I could dig some swine."

I sniff; Grant catches my eye and suddenly we're sharing a private smile. A secret little your-friend-likes-my-friend smile. He shakes his head in further amazement while Manny employs his own brand of hustling involving a scrambled egg and pig rump sandwich.

Irina peers down at Manny, a solid four-inch height differential. "You should know I eat boys like you for breakfast."

"And you should know I find that crazy hot," Manny replies, undeterred.

"You're very odd." Irina cocks her head and studies Manny like a bug she can't decide whether or not she should squash.

Seth arrives with Ryan and Ginger in tow. "Wil!" He wraps his arms around me. Hugging him back, I feel the concern in the rapid thumping of his heart.

"Everything's fine, Seth. We're okay."

He lets go. "No, I should've been there, but I was trying to give you some space because of how I was earlier. And look, I've been thinking about what I said the other night. . . ." Seth becomes aware of our small audience, and I become aware Grant's disappeared like an apparition. "Can we maybe finish this in private?"

Irina touches my shoulder. "I'm sorry, *dorogaya,* I know you want to stay longer. But I'm done here."

"Um, of course . . . yeah. We should go." Disappointment crashes like a meteor at my feet.

"No, take this." Irina pushes fifty bucks into my hand. "Stay. That's more than enough to cab it back to my place if you need to."

"Iri—"

"*Shh, shh.*" She kisses both my cheeks. "No arguing. Have *fun* tonight. That was the point, remember?"

"That wasn't entirely the point." And she knows it.

"Well, then, it's the new point." She glances over my shoulder at Seth. "You're *sure* this is what you want?"

"Positive."

"Then talk to him and hash out whatever's got him looking so damn pitiful. Smiling faces by night's end. Hear me?"

"Yes." I hug her. "Thank you, Iri. And I'm sorry you had such a crappy time. Those guys were—"

"Hey, it wasn't a total waste." She grins as we separate. "Least I cleared a nice chunk of change tonight."

I tilt my head. "Since when are you an optimist?"

"Since my bra runneth over with cash. Manny"— Irina spins on her heel—"you're coming with me. And so there's no confusion, Denny's is the only thing on the menu."

"*¡Carajo!* Really?"

"Yes, really. All this talk of swine has whet my appetite."

Manny takes her hand and gallantly kisses it. "You won't regret it."

Irina laughs. "I already do." Slinging her arm over his shoulder, the most unlikely pair of the century take their leave.

A loud and mournful sound echoes from outside. It pauses, then resumes its low, primitive hum.

"Tristan's battle horn." Ryan gleefully rubs his palms together. "Means the game's about to start."

"Well, c'mon!" Ginger tugs Ryan's hand. "Labyrinth Marco Polo is my *favorite*."

"Oh, you just want to have your way with me in the foliage," he teases.

She giggles before turning back to us. "You guys are coming, too, aren't you?"

Seth waits for me to answer, nervously shuffling his feet. He wants us to be okay. So do I. The fact that he recognizes his earlier behavior was off-putting renews my faith in him, and by extension, in us.

"Absolutely," I say to Ginger.

Seth beams at my response, clasping my hand and squeezing it. "Thanks for staying."

I grin. "It's a gorgeous night and this party is unbelievable—Irina's right, we *should* be having fun."

"Your good time will be my personal mission." He kisses my temple. And you know? It doesn't feel at all smothering. It's . . . nice.

The battle horn hums a second mournful call.

Joining Ginger and Ryan, we head for a set of doors on the north end of the house, which is a shortcut to the gardens. Happiness unfurls inside me. This night is going to be salvaged after all. But as suddenly as my joy has blossomed, I feel it shrivel and blacken.

Because I see them.

Stabbing pains pierce my heart—it's Grant and Lila. *Together.* Lila leads him by the hand into a dark room as we pass. Her silhouette begins kissing his neck as the door shuts. Seth is talking to Ryan, so he doesn't see how my eyes instantly gloss with unshed tears.

I blink, willing the moisture away, and gaze at where my hand joins Seth's. *This* is what I choose, a partner molded and blessed by the heavens.

I press a hand to my chest. Really, it's a suitable punishment for my traitorous heart, this overpowering ache that ravages it, threatening to split it apart.

But maybe this is what I needed—to see Grant in the arms of someone else—so once and for all, I'd be free of him.

chapter 17

"Marco!" Tristan booms in his stage voice.

"Polo!" Voices answer from all over the twisting gardens. The labyrinth's high, sculpted hedges have nooks and crannies perfect for hiding.

As I move deeper and deeper into the labyrinth, my green dress helps me fade into my surroundings; even the pain in my chest has miraculously faded. Bare feet thump over grass, scampering in all directions.

Someone's coming up fast behind me. I dive off the main path into one of the heavily shadowed nooks. The person passes. It wasn't Tristan, who's "it," but I breathe a sigh of relief anyway as I step out from my hiding place.

The large moon, bold in the cloudless sky, illuminates the crystalline beads of dew forming on the grass. Like everyone else, I've kicked off my heels, adding them to the shoe pile at the garden's entrance.

"Gotcha!" Tristan shouts, tackling someone one hedge over, grunting with the fall. "Ha, you're it, Bree!" Tristan takes off from the newly tagged girl. The horn wails again, signaling the start of a new round. "Marco!" Bree shouts.

"Polo!" We call out in chorus. I tear around another bend, seeing flashes of people running every which way. The darkness charges the air with veiled expectancy.

"Marco!"

Oh God, she's super close. I shout my "Polo" and dodge into another bushy alcove. I peer through a gap in the branches.

Bree slows. She wears a sleeping mask with realistic eyes painted on, so it appears she sees even in her blindness. *Creepy.*

I hold my breath, afraid my racing heart will tip off my whereabouts. I'm crouched several feet away in a dead end of foliage.

A twig snaps. Bree's eerie eyes move from my direction, and she fumbles her way ahead.

I exhale just as a familiar silhouette creeps by. *"Psst!"* I hiss.

Seth stops, glancing back. With a quiet giggle, I grab his arm, pulling him into my shadowed hideout.

We tumble to the ground. Before he can outmaneuver me, I seize the front of his shirt, pulling him downward until his lips crush mine.

He draws a sharp breath, mouth tensing. But . . . isn't

this what he's been waiting for? Why does he seem frozen by my lips? Surely, he can't still be worried about us? Tilting my head, I reposition my mouth over his, deepening the kiss. I'll make damn certain my actions will dispel his doubt.

And they do.

Oh. My. God. Seth has been holding back. I gasp as the frenzy of his passion makes every single nerve ending scream for more. He shifts his weight so I'm not crushed into the damp grass. His hand slips under to cradle my head, pulling me closer. Winding my arms around his torso, I lose myself.

I feel tossed into the strongest current of the Opal River, held captive in a whirling eddy. I want to stay in this spinning place forever. No moment compares to the feel of his weight, his mouth, his skin. . . . And if time were really measured in grains of sand, I would take this grain and flatten it. Stretch it as far as physics allowed, let myself bask in this feeling. Forever and ever and ever.

Kissing Seth has always been nice. But this, *this* speaks to the truth of what we are. *We are soul mates. We belong.*

The game continues unfolding around us. Laughter rings out. "All right, you a-holes, who depantsed me?" a deep voice snaps. But the shouts and laughter sound light-years away, in another solar system, another dimension.

I hover outside myself, watching the barefoot girl sprawled on her back in the dewy grass, and the boy who kisses her like he's fulfilling a dying wish. If the moonlight could reach them, it would draw sparkling lines over his broad shoulders and her pale skin, painting them with silvery magic.

Strange, for the first time I don't notice Seth's cologne—not that it's ever been overwhelming, just something I've come to expect. Maybe it's because I'm overwhelmed by the smell of the green around me—pungent, earthy, and sweet.

The rhythm of our breaths makes the goose bumps rise, causing my body to tremble. And it isn't until his hand cups the side of my neck, and his thumb travels the distance from my chin to just beneath my ear, that I realize why everything is amplified. It's nothing to do with the moon or grass or dark muted colors. . . .

I'm not kissing Seth.

I am kissing Grant Walker.

I gasp, scrambling back on my elbows from under him. My heart hammers and I'm overcome with so much dizziness that the Earth feels wobbly on her axis.

Grant rocks back to his knees, breathless and stunned. "I—I . . . I wouldn't have . . . but then you grabbed me. And . . ." He rubs a shaky hand over his face.

My lips are still throbbing with the memory of his. I clap a hand over my mouth to keep them from betraying me any more than they already have. More than they already do.

"Jesus," he whispers. There's a subtle collapse of his shoulders. "You thought I was Seth."

I slowly nod, afraid to unclap my hand from my mouth, afraid of the words that might spill out: *I'm glad you weren't*. The thought makes me ill and brings with it other thoughts I want to banish and leave hidden deep in this labyrinth.

Grant braces his hands on his thighs, surveying the matted grass around us. "No. No, I don't believe you."

My hand falls from my face. "What?" I whisper.

"Maybe at first, but then you *had* to have known—"

"No," I say in a rush, "I didn't! You said yourself people mistake you all the time. And it was dark and you're the same height and . . . you were inside with Lila! She was kissing you! Why aren't you with Lila?" My argument loses steam when the truth crashes in—I *did* know. Maybe not consciously at first, but at every level the kiss felt different. It felt . . . *more*.

"Nothing happened with Lila, Wil. I couldn't go through with it. She's not who I want to be with. Not when all I think about is—"

"This was an accident." I rise on unreliable legs. "We can't tell anyone, especially Seth. He . . . wouldn't take it well."

Seth and I are barely back on solid ground, and this would break us. I am positive. I can wave goodbye to my perfect match, and hello to a decade plus of loneliness. Of cold.

Grant stands. "So, what, you want this to be our dirty little secret?"

"It wasn't dirty," I lash out.

"Oh?" He takes a step closer. I can't believe moments ago I was totally wrapped up in those strong arms, never wanting to let go. "Then what was it?"

I stumble back against the bushes.

235

"Because I'd love to know." He continues leveling me with his eyes. The battle horn echoes. The game is still going on, but the players are changing. Now it feels like a game between only Grant and me.

I square my shoulders and step closer, until we almost touch. "It was a mistake, Grant. A mistake that will never, *ever* happen again." I feel the tears build as I say it, but I must end this between us. Sever the invisible cord that binds us . . . for the *last* time.

The anger churning in Grant mixes with a sad sort of resignation. "The way you kissed me back wasn't a mistake. The only mistake is—"

"*Shh!*" I cup my hand over his mouth. Padding footfalls rush by. I peer through the branches until the coast is clear. I yank back my hand with the sudden awareness of how his breath feels like licks of flames against my palm.

Floodlights blaze, saturating the labyrinth and backyard with yellow light. The shadows are harder to find now. There is nowhere to hide. Nowhere is safe.

The game is over.

"Please," I whisper, "promise me you won't breathe a word of this. I'll . . ." I squeeze my eyes shut. "I'll tell him. I'll explain. *Somehow* I'll make him understand." But staring at Grant, I realize the likelihood of that is minuscule.

"Fine, I won't *breathe a word,*" Grant replies, anger edging back in his voice. "But I want you to answer one question." He grits his teeth before pressing on. "Would your feelings for Seth change if he were any other sign? If he weren't whatever your astrology mandated, would you still have chosen him?"

My lips part, only the words don't come. But . . . the question's unfair; it's a vast generalization.

"I know what you're thinking, and you're making this too hard. Because the answer's so damn easy, Wil." His lips tilt in a rueful grin. "It shouldn't matter. If you had truly fallen for him . . . it *wouldn't* matter."

I open my mouth to argue. To tell him it *would* matter. He doesn't understand the high price of recklessly following my heart's desires. It would mean dishonoring the wishes of my mother. Obliterating my promise—the very thing that kept her closest to me.

Grant holds up a hand. "No more. I don't want to hear you." He slowly backs out from the alcove. "I don't want to see you. I don't even want to *think* about you."

"Wil?" Seth calls in the distance. "Wil? Where are you?"

My breath feels strangled. And the world won't stop its incessant wobbling. I stagger outside the nook and sink back to the ground, burying my face in my hands. I want it to stop. I want everything to just . . . *stop*. How did things become so twisted?

Before Grant crash-landed in my life, my path was always sure, my footsteps certain. With astrology as my guide, I've always had my map to life. I never had to question.

But now, no matter how I flip or turn my map, there's no denying . . .

I. Am. Lost.

Hopelessly pulled in every cardinal direction.

"There you are! What are you doing on the ground?" Seth grins widely, but then his eyes narrow. "Hey . . . you've been cheating, haven't you?"

"Huh?" I croak, my stomach capsizing. Panicked, I look around for Grant. He's gone, having disappeared into the thickets of the garden.

"I said you've been cheating. I don't think I heard you shout 'Polo' for the last four rounds." He reaches down, hoisting me up to my feet.

"Oh, um, guilty." The most honest statement I've made all night, and I can't meet his eyes when I say it.

Seth smiles. "Aw, come here, my little rule breaker. I won't tell." He twines his arms around my waist and bends to kiss me.

I duck, pressing my cheek to his chest. "I—I'm sorry. I feel a little nauseous all of a sudden." Without a doubt, I do feel sick. I hold a hand to my roiling gut.

"Why do you have wood chips in your hair?" He chuckles, pulling out a few and tossing them to the hedges. "And grass? You're all damp, Wil." His hands brush over my back. "No wonder you never got tagged, you were staked out in the bushes."

"Seth, I really don't feel well." Bile bubbles up my throat.

"Oh?" He studies me as he places a palm at my cheek. "Huh. You do feel warm. Maybe we should call it a night. Let you rest up so you can feel better for tomorrow."

"What's tomorrow?" My vocal cords sound braided.

"Family dinner." He grins and takes my hands in his. "I think it's time I introduced you to my parents, don't you? I mean, my mom's on the verge of disowning me if I don't bring you home so she can meet you." Seth laughs. "Which is bananas because she's never been that amped to meet anyone I've ever dated. So"—he squeezes my hands—"what do you say, sweetheart?"

Say? There is nothing I *can* say. The monumental guilt of passionately making out with his brother not five minutes earlier has left me utterly gagged.

It takes five, okay, six wardrobe changes before I deem myself fit to meet the parents. Let's call a spade a spade and say three of those changes were because of Grant—who, if I recall, doesn't want to hear, see, or think about me.

My guilt has *got* to be detectable from the edges of the tristate area. I expected Gram to pick up on the stench of my lies the second I stepped foot in the house this morning. Just like I expected her to tell me I couldn't go to Seth's for dinner. She surprised me on both counts.

My secrets corrode my insides like a coating of acid. If I keep this up, I'll need organ transplants by the end of next week. And I barely slept last night. Not even after waking Iri from a dead sleep to unload my sins.

She imparted two coherent words of wisdom before tumbling back to her dreams. "End it." End it with Seth, she meant.

Thing is . . . I can't.

I've rehearsed out loud. In the shower. In the car. In my bed. But I can't seem to find the right words to tell the person who is so perfectly compatible and wholly wonderful that—as it turns out—my heart may not agree.

I don't know what to do.

It's this indecision that lands me on the Walkers' doorstep, pushing the doorbell and praying to God I don't collapse in a gooey heap on the porch next to the Tuscan urns and topiaries.

I smooth my dress and let out a slow, purposeful breath, clutching the pastry box Gram has sent with me. My eyes track the sprawling house. The exterior is a sort of off-white plaster, with three arches at the front. The roof has those rounded clay tiles that I've seen in pictures of Italy. I frown at the arrangement of pale purple irises and greenery I threw together. This house is too nice for my plain-Jane arrangement. I should have hit a flower shop or . . .

The door opens. Seth is dressed to impress in a button-down shirt and khakis. "What are you doing here?"

"Y-you invited me for dinner." I catch the twinkle in his eye.

He wags his finger, "Oh, you're *that* girl. Didn't I pick you up at some club? Um, what was it . . . Abstain, Altruistic . . ."

"Absinthe." I hear the nervousness in my laugh, but find little I can do about it.

"You look beautiful. I love this dress on you," he says, running a finger beneath the strap of the polka-dot garment before kissing my shoulder. "And Mom's gonna love that you brought flowers. Purple—now *that's* interesting. What did your grandma say about that? Purple signifies . . . enchantment, right?" He sweeps me in his arms, dipping me back in a grand Hollywood gesture. "Well, consider me enchanted, Wil Carlisle."

My body goes into rigor mortis as he moves in for a kiss. I turn my face so his lips are deflected to my cheek. He pulls back in clear disappointment.

"Baby, what's wrong? Oh . . . you're nervous. That's it, isn't it?" Seth rights me on my feet. "You're nervous about meeting my parents. Well, don't be. They'll love you; I know they will."

I swallow. "How are you so sure? They might not. I could be an acquired taste. I could be kimchi."

His gaze lingers on my lips before traveling down the rest of me. "Uh-uh, I've tasted you. *Definitely* not acquired. More like addictive."

My cheeks sizzle. "Let's not open with that, all right?"

Seth smiles and takes my hand, guiding me into the large house. "I have a surprise for you." He takes the flowers and cupcakes, setting them on a table in the large foyer.

"You're really Batman?"

He chuckles. "Sadly, no. Not that cool."

There's a huge slab of stone affixed to the wall; water runs down it, collecting in a copper base. I gaze up to the atrium window, where what's left of the late-afternoon sun is passing through its panes to the plants below.

My heels echo across the tile floor. "Wow, your house is . . . nothing like mine."

He grins. "I'll give you the nickel tour and then I want to show you the surprise. It's upstairs in my room." He takes my other hand and walks backward as he leads me. "It's not a ploy for seduction, so you can stop looking worried. But if you wanted to seduce me, I doubt I'd put up much of a fight." He laughs as I push him away. "No? Well, let me know if you change your mind."

Walking down the hall, Seth points out a large sunken room with a stone fireplace and the guest bath adjacent. There's a study, door partially shut, but I catch a glimpse of a wall full of books and a desk overflowing with papers. We don't go into the dining room at the rear of the house. Instead, we double back and climb the set of stairs leading to the second floor.

"In here," Seth says, and pushes open a door. His room is neat for a boy's, much tidier than mine with my stacks of dog-eared books and accessories forever strewn about my dresser.

I gasp when my eyes land on the surprise. It sits in front of the tall, multipaned window, marked with a big red bow.

"So, you like it?" he asks hopefully.

"Oh my God! Seth, this is the Celestron NexStar 102 SLT telescope! I've been lusting over this model for months!"

"I know. The guy at Stargazers said as much. You're supposed to be able to see the lunar surface and everything."

My hand traces the compact cylindrical body of the

telescope in wonder, before pausing at the computerized keypad. "This is too much, Seth." I shake my head. "Way, way too much." It pains me, but I distance myself from the beloved telescope. "I'm . . . really sorry, but I can't accept this."

"Yes, you can," he urges. "Look, don't worry about the cost. If it makes you feel better, we'll call it a Christmas gift."

"It's June."

"An *early* Christmas gift." Seth crosses the room, looping his arms around me. "Let me do this for you, Wil." He tucks a finger under my chin, tilting my face to his. "Just say yes. What good is having money if you can't share it with the people you care about?"

Guilt vacuums the air from my lungs. Which is why it takes a moment for me to respond. I place my hands on his chest, feeling the beat of his heart. "Seth, this is so amazing and generous. I'll think about it, okay?"

Translation: *I will think of a million reasons why I can't accept this gift, starting with your brother. And ending with my deceit.*

He adds with an impish grin, "Did I mention the ten percent restocking fee if I return it?"

"No, you didn't." I toy with one of the buttons on his shirt, avoiding his eyes.

"Something else wrong? Or is it just the nerves over meeting my family?"

My gut twists and my heart spastically *ca-thud*s in my chest. And I'm fairly confident my palms have sprung leaks and are misting like the Walkers' sprinkler system.

"There's something I need to tell you." I try to measure his response, but his brown eyes are guarded.

"Yeah, actually"—he rubs the back of his neck—"there's something I've been wanting to talk to you about, too. I'm, uh, hoping we can laugh about it."

Laugh about it? Now I'm totally perplexed. If it's funny, it must not have anything to do with Grant and me, because there isn't a snowball's chance Seth would find anything remotely funny about that.

"You go first. What is it?" I sink my teeth in my lower lip to stop my own avalanche confession.

"Not now. After dinner, okay?" Seth kisses the top of my head.

"Okay," I reply, relieved to have bought more time.

That gives me appetizers, a main course, and dessert to formulate a concrete plan. And how I'll manage to keep any of that down with Grant seated across the table will be the greatest feat of them all.

chapter 18

Mrs. Walker hums while arranging the enormous white flowers in the table's centerpiece. No mystery where Grant gets his talent for music—her voice is like honey. And with her flawless olive skin, and hair that ripples past her shoulders in a river of chocolate, it's also easy to see where both boys inherited their good looks.

"Mom?"

She startles at Seth's voice, plastering a hand to her silk blouse. *"Seth,"* she breathes. "I didn't realize you were standing there." Her wide eyes bounce immediately to me. "And, Wil, welcome! My goodness, you are every bit as lovely as Seth said you were." Mrs. Walker rounds the perfectly set table boasting enough china and greenery to make Martha Stewart seem like an underachiever. "I have been *so* looking forward to finally meeting you."

I shift nervously from foot to foot. "Um, thank you, Mrs. Walker. It's a pleasure to meet you, too." And I mean it, despite the phony smile and fraudulent circumstances that have delivered me like a Trojan horse into the Walker estate.

She envelops me in the kind of hug that makes me instantly miss my mother. I push down the surprising stab of emotion. "Oh, please, no need for formalities. Call me Charlotte." Pulling back, she gives my shoulder a little squeeze. "I suspect we'll be seeing a lot of each other."

Accurate statement. Because if Charlotte ever finds out about my lip-lock with her eldest, she'll probably hunt me down and mount my head on the wall. I'll be a cautionary tale for all the future Walker girlfriends.

Seth stands proudly at my side. "Told you she'd love you," he says quietly in my ear.

Yeah, *now*. "These are for you, Charlotte." I hold out the irises, which she accepts with a smile.

"They're exquisite. How very thoughtful, Wil."

"She brought dessert, too, Mom," Seth beams. "Chocolate cupcakes. We put them in the kitchen."

"They're dark-chocolate espresso cupcakes. My grandmother's an incredible baker. I hope you like them."

Charlotte's golden-brown eyes light up. "Mmm, I bet they're positively sinful." My eyes flick down to my chest, where I half expect a large scarlet *A* to be blinking. "Why don't you both sit down while I grab a vase for these?"

Seth gives me an encouraging nod and pulls out my chair. "Where are Dad and Grant?" he calls out as I murmur my thanks.

I can feel the rush of color to my cheeks at the mention of Grant's name. I'll need to do something about that—like dump the crystal carafe of ice water on my face. But at least the brothers have reached a fragile truce. Seth didn't go into the specifics of the newfound treaty, but I wager it'll have the shelf life of a ripened pear—several hours, tops.

Charlotte returns, placing the irises on a small corner table. "Oh, your father's still on a conference call. Grant called and is stuck in traffic, so unfortunately, he'll be late." She shakes a finger at Seth. "And how did it slip your mind to mention you'd invited Wil tonight? Maybe he would've left a little earlier if he'd known there'd be company."

I *highly* doubt it.

My hand begins compulsively smoothing the cloth napkin on my lap. Seth stills my fluttering by lacing his fingers in mine. "Relax," he whispers. But the chances of that are about as remote as me Hula-Hooping the rings of Saturn.

Our attention shifts as Mr. Walker bursts into the dining room, jerking loose his tie and clapping his hands. "We did it, Charlotte! It's finally official. The deal is done!"

She jumps to her feet. "It is?" she squeals. "Oh, Jackson, that's fantastic!"

Seth's dad is what Irina would refer to as a silver fox—tall, handsome, and no hint of a saggy middle-age gut. He closes the gap between him and his wife in a few long-legged strides before scooping her up in his arms. "We did it," he repeats in elation, and kisses her.

Seth leans in. "Dad's been working on some big merger thing. Guess it worked out."

"Mmm, Jackson"—Charlotte gently disengages and nods in my direction—"we have a special guest tonight."

He turns around with a fleeting look of embarrassment. "Ah, yes, of course. We have lots to celebrate, don't we?"

"Congrats, Dad. This is my girlfriend, Wil."

"Carlisle, correct?" his father asks. "Hard to forget a last name like that."

It takes me a beat to recover from Seth's use of the word "girlfriend." "Uh, yes," I belatedly answer.

"I'm Jackson." He stretches across the table to shake my hand. "Pleasure, Wil."

"Likewise," I reply as we separate. "And congratulations on the good news."

He smiles, revealing two snuggling front teeth—a carbon copy of Grant's. "Well, thank you. And I must say, you're certainly living up to your glowing reputation. I can see why my son's so taken with you. Which leads us to the obvious question . . ." Jackson clears his throat and takes a seat. "Just how did Seth blackmail you into being his girlfriend?" He winks.

Seth wads up his napkin and launches it at his dad. "Very funny, old man. Just because Mom lost a bet and had to let you take her out doesn't mean Wil did." He pauses at my dropped jaw and chuckles. "It's totally true. Tell her, Mom."

Charlotte shakes her head and sets down her wine glass. "It is. And if I were a better bowler, I might've ended up with Keith Bronson."

With undisguised laughter, Jackson adds, "And your children would've had enormous heads."

She frowns. "Come to think of it, he did have a rather large head, didn't he?"

Seth and his dad continue joking about heads large enough to eclipse the sun. And I try to keep up with the easy banter, I do, but with each passing minute, my breath gets harder and harder to pull from my lungs. My airway narrows, not only anticipating Grant's arrival, but because . . . I really like the Walkers. Really, *really* like them. And it makes sitting at their family dinner table somehow blasphemous.

Charlotte brings a platter from the kitchen. "Crostini, Wil?"

"Thank you. They look delicious." And I bet the fresh tomato, basil, and mozzarella on crispy bread *would* be delicious . . . if my stomach didn't feel like it was in a perpetual state of free fall. I force myself to take one and pass the platter to Seth's dad.

"So, how did you two meet?" Jackson asks, helping himself to several of the appetizers.

Seth stretches his arm across the back of my chair. "Absinthe. A combination of fate and footwear brought us together." He grins. "Then she started talking about Egyptian deities and I was a goner." He gives my leg a squeeze under the table.

I gulp what has become a starchy, flavorless ball of paste in my mouth, and chuckle weakly. "Yes, well, your son was nice enough to offer me his seat. And I was grateful because my shoes don't love me nearly as much as I love them."

"Ah, yes." Charlotte offers a sympathetic nod. "It's true what they say—beauty is pain."

Seth's hand inches higher up my leg. No, mostly this evening is pain, but I certainly can't say that. I mumble my absolute agreement before taking another bite, and nonchalantly adjust the trajectory of Seth's hand.

As if on cosmic cue, Grant bursts into the dining room. "Hey, sorry I'm late."

The crostini goes sideways down my throat, triggering a violent coughing fit.

Grant dumps his messenger bag on the floor. "Accident on the highway had everything . . ." I sense he's frowning at me but don't look to confirm it.

Seth claps my back a few times. "Baby, you all right?"

My head bobs up and down like a sewing machine as I dab at my watering eyes with my napkin.

"Are you sure? Maybe you should drink some water," Charlotte frets.

"Oh, I'm fine," I reply hoarsely. *Pull yourself together, Wil!*

Her concerned gaze veers to Grant. "Well, we've barely made it through the appetizers. Enough time for you to go upstairs and change, honey."

He glances down at his ragged jeans, and pulls at his

T-shirt. "What's wrong with this?" Her expression says exactly what's wrong with it. Grant, in response, plants a kiss on her cheek. "Guess it works out that you look stunning enough for the both of us."

His mother softens and shakes her head. "Frightening what charming boys we've unleashed on the world, Jackson." The couple goes on to quibble over whose genes were responsible.

Grant nods stiffly at Seth before acknowledging me as he sits. "Wil." Our gazes lock for the first time.

He speaks my name, and suddenly I'm having flashes of last night. Of rolling in the dewy grass and tasting his sweet lips. How his T-shirt bunched in my hands as he cradled my head and made me forget the rest of the world existed.

I replay all of it in a matter of seconds. I grab my water glass and drink, hoping the cold will extinguish my rising temperature and the flush creeping from my neck to my face. Grant and I put down our glasses in tandem, eyes flicking toward, then even more rapidly, away from one another.

Stars above! Did Grant's *mother* just see that? And what was she just saying? Something about leveling the male-to-female ratio in the house. There's a pause before the corners of her mouth lift, dispelling the worry from her features. "Well, like I said, I'm sure Grant will find someone soon enough."

"Sure, Mom," he says flatly, taking a bite of his crostini.

The invisible noose on my neck wraps tighter.

"Dude, maybe if you sprang for a new pair of jeans, ran a comb through your hair, and covered those tats, you'd quit scaring the girls away."

Scowling, Grant replies, "And if I wanted your lame advice, I'd be asking for it."

And it's funny. All the things Seth's listed are things I've come to love about Grant. Oh my God! *Love?* Did I just use the word "love" in my head? Color bombards my cheeks, and my heart gallops like a herd of wild horses set free.

Seth opens his mouth in argument.

"Boys." The warning in Jackson's tone is clear. "Whatever's had you at odds the past few weeks can be set aside for one night. Got it?" His chair scrapes the floor as he rises to collect the appetizer plates.

Charlotte absently twirls a spring of parsley while watching me.

This is too much. "Uh, if—if you'll excuse me . . ." I push away from the table, clearing my throat. "I'm sorry, where is the bathroom again?"

"Second door on the right," Charlotte answers, concern scrawled over her face.

Seth scoots back and starts to rise. "I'll show you."

I place a hand at his shoulder. "No, please . . . I'll find it."

Once I'm in the safety of the bathroom, I suck in a huge breath.

Whatever I do, panicking is *not* an option. Also under the nonoption umbrella: replaying my garden tryst with Grant. It was an accident. A mistake.

Why do I want to do it again?

Oh. God.

I brace my palms on the cool granite countertop. The face in the mirror is undeniably flushed and her lips faintly puffy. How does one go from celibacy to kissing every Walker in the damn east-side directory? *How does that happen?!*

Exasperated, I take out my compact and dust powder on my nose and cheeks. It mutes the flush, but not the jarring realization.

Owning up to last night isn't enough to right this wrong.

I have to break up with Seth.

Tonight.

I push the penne and artichokes around with one of my twelve forks. Unfortunately, I don't believe any of these knives possess a blade sharp enough to cut the tension. Grant hasn't spoken or made eye contact with me since I returned to the table. And then there was that moment when I was recrossing my legs and my foot inadvertently bumped against him. Grant's knee banged the underside of the table with so much force it spilled several of the water glasses.

Jackson peppers the uncomfortable bouts of silence with funny anecdotes. Like when Grant was seven, and convinced all the neighbor kids to petition the tooth fairy to get their teeth back. Or the time Charlotte forced Grant to go to bed with Vaseline on his fingers and socks on his hands to keep his skin from splitting when he practiced guitar too much. There are stories of Seth, too. . . . I just . . .

Why can't I remember them?

Dinner wears on and Seth's anxious glances become more frequent. And I can't tell you what Charlotte's doing. I'm too afraid to look her in the eye for fear of what I'll see.

Which leaves me . . . *dying.* The emotional, not to mention *astrological,* fallout of ending my relationship with Seth has me about fetal. And Seth deserves better. How can I have taken so long to see that we will never work as a couple? My hopes and dreams have turned me into a complete fraud. I don't love Seth. And I never will. My eyes begin to water.

"Hey," Seth whispers, "your eyes are really red. Are you still feeling sick from last night?" You could say that. He rests his hand at the nape of my neck, pulling me completely back to the present. "And you barely touched your food. If you don't like it, I'm sure we can get you something else."

My eyes scan the table and discover everyone's plate is fairly empty, except mine. "No, the food is great," I whisper back, making a concerted effort to push down the despair with another bite of pasta. I chew and realize it's pointless. If I continue force-feeding myself, I risk vomiting over the exquisite china—all seven penne noodles and three quarters of a crostini.

"Ahem." Charlotte sets her napkin over her plate. "Why don't the ladies get some fresh air and the guys handle clearing the dishes, all right?"

My eyes widen a fraction.

Gosh. I hadn't thought there could be a worse sentence than this meal. Turns out I am wrong—alone time with Charlotte will be its own circle of hell. Looks like I'll pay my penance starting now.

"Great," I say with as much brightness as I can muster.

I follow her down a hall that leads to the patio and swimming pool out back; the walls are decorated with rich, vibrant paintings that bear her initials. I'm about to ask her about them when a small cat darts by, letting out a gravelly meow as it paws at the sliding door. Impatiently the feline doubles back and rubs against my leg. I bend down to scratch its one ear since the other is partly missing. It purrs and raises its kinked tail in appreciation.

"That's Bob, Bob Dylan. We let the boys get kittens, oh, maybe ten, eleven years ago. Seth's cat, Spazz, ran away after a couple of years." She chuckles, turning her eyes on the blue-gray fuzz ball. "Leave it to Grant to pick out the most damaged but resilient kitten at the shelter."

"My grandma's allergic, so we've never been able to have them. But Bob seems like a very sweet kitty," I say, stroking his velvety fur. He purrs to the point of rattling his organs.

"Well, he is, and he'll probably outlive us all." Charlotte tilts her head. "I can see you've got a soft spot for those damaged, resilient types, too."

"I guess I do." I rise, brushing the cat hair from my hands.

She slides open the door. "Off you go, Bob." He shoots out the door and vanishes under a trellis of climbing roses.

We step outside. Charlotte kicks off her jeweled sandals,

then glances where I stand unmoving. "You know, the water's a lot nicer with your shoes off." She bends, rolling up her linen pants as I panic over whether she's about to fit me with cinder blocks. The indecision must be a neon sign on my face. "Unless you'd rather go back inside?"

Um, no. Actually, I'd rather stick a hot poker in my eye. Repeatedly. So I take my chances with the cinder blocks and slip off my shoes.

There's the soft plunk of her feet submerging in the pool; she looks up expectantly.

I settle beside her at the pool's edge, sucking in a breath at the chill of the cool water contrasting with the balmy air.

"Refreshing, isn't it?"

"It is," I answer, my head tilting upward. But the cloud cover's too dense to know what the stars are trying to tell me, leaving me abandoned in my hour of need.

"They've said that about you. . . . Your interest in the sky," she says, and swishes her feet in the water. Crickets in the nearby shrubs continue their cadence. "Seth mentioned your mother was really into the stars. Astronomy? Or was it astrology?" She pauses, waiting for me to interject.

But I don't trust myself to speak, because even though I'm not wearing cinder blocks for shoes, I suddenly feel like I'm drowning. Swirling in a torrent of emotions.

"I—I didn't mean to pry. It's just . . ." Charlotte hesitates. "I remember when it happened, the accident," she clarifies. Much of Carlisle did. Eleven years ago the tragic car crash was all over TV and the newspapers Gram had tried to hide. "I'm sorry, Wil. I imagine you must still miss her terribly."

I nod, staring at my pale feet as they churn the water.

Charlotte tips her chin upward. "I can understand why the stars would be important to you."

"Yes."

The grief builds in my chest, threatening to crack it open and make itself known. But I won't let it. I've spent too many years keeping it in check. Too many years believing there *must* be a divine reason behind everything that happens.

"You're a sweet girl, and you deserve every happiness in life." She lets out a weighted sigh. "Just like my boys."

Her boys? I snap my gaze to hers. But her golden eyes give away nothing. I wonder what she sees in mine. Regret? Sadness? Does she see that my presence could never deliver happiness—for either son—no matter how hard I wished it could be different?

"Charlotte, I . . . I want you to know that I—" At that moment, the patio door slides open, and as it shuts, so does my mouth. A prickle of anticipation crawls over my skin.

Charlotte peers uncertainly over her shoulder. Her teeth catch and hold her lower lip, until finally, she speaks. "I'm sorry. If, uh, you'll excuse me, Wil, I believe I'm needed inside." The percussive sound of her wet feet slapping against the concrete accentuates the speed of her departure.

And I feel his advance the way I always do. Take away

all of my senses, and I could still detect the very second Grant Walker came near.

"We need to talk." His voice is stony.

"You said you didn't want to." I wipe a renegade tear from my face, and draw my feet from the cold water. Which has left me numb, or maybe it's more the certainty of my actions that's left behind this cold dread. I stand, slowly turning to face him.

Grant stops twisting his leather cuff. "I didn't . . . I don't, but . . . Wil, *what are you doing?*" The question is far from simple, but I treat it as though it were.

"Nothing," I say dully. "I have to find Seth." Because I have to end this, finish it quickly, like the ripping of a Band-Aid. I move toward the house and Grant catches my arm. His touch feels like its own tattoo on my skin. It always has.

"So, what . . . you're just going to carry on with him? Like nothing *happened?*"

"No! I—"

"Do you have *any* idea how messed up that was? Sitting across the table while my brother whispered in your ear and put his hands on you. Watching while you smiled and played the part of his girlfriend. Knowing less than twenty-four hours ago, you were in my arms"—he slaps his chest—"*my* arms, Wil."

I jerk free of him. "Do you really think sitting at that dinner table was *fun* for me, Grant? Because if you do, then you don't know me at all." But anger doesn't cleanse the anguish from my tone, the hurt that he could think

I'd take pleasure from this kind of pain. "I'm finding Seth and doing what I should have done weeks ago."

He crosses his arms. "Yeah? And what's that?"

"I'm walking away—from you, from Seth, from your lovely"—my voice breaks—"family. Because there is no other way for this to—"

"Bullshit. You're running." He blocks my path, taking my face in his hands. "Wil." He pauses. "Goddammit, I told myself I wouldn't do this. But . . . look at me right now and tell me you don't want me. Tell me you don't think about how right *we* are together. Tell me every second together hasn't been the most amazing—"

"N-no, no, you're wrong." I shut my eyes, because when I see Grant, he makes me doubt every truth I've ever believed. He makes me doubt the stars above.

"Look at me, Mena"—he gently draws my face closer, stroking my cheek—"and tell me you don't feel something *real* for me. Tell me that—and *I'll* walk away."

What do I say to that? I'll never know. Because when I open my eyes . . .

Grant's not there.

Chapter 19

"You backstabbing son of a bitch!" Seth shouts at the sloshing water. He circles the pool, where he's shoved his brother in.

Grant explodes from the water's surface, flicking back his hair. He draws a ragged breath and coughs. "I'm the son of a bitch?" He wipes a hand down his face. "Do you ever, for one second, think of anyone beside yourself? Huh?"

Seth is positively seething, clenching and unclenching his hands, itching for a fight. "You swore you wouldn't talk to her anymore! Promised you'd leave her alone! Admit it, Grant"—his voice a low growl—"you've been wanting my girlfriend from the minute we started dating."

"You're wrong," Grant sneers. "It was way before that.

But you were too selfish and blind to see it. So?" he taunts. "What are you gonna do about it?"

"Bastard," Seth hisses, and dives in the pool.

"No!" I scream. "Stop it!" I race to the water's edge as the punches start flying. The sickening smack of flesh on flesh overrides the peaceful night sounds. "Stop!" I shout at the top of my lungs. They ignore me, going about beating the tar out of each other.

Lunacy! Grabbing a neon-green pool noodle, I dive into the chilly water and commence whacking the living daylights out of both of them.

We are all shouting at each other—so loudly I don't know who's saying what. And my pool noodle's whistling through the air as it slaps their bodies in a vain attempt to end the madness.

"Enough!" Charlotte's cry carries over the mayhem. We freeze, soaking and gasping for air. Under different circumstances this might be comical. But no one sees the humor in it now. *"What* has gotten into all of you?"

I'm first to speak as the guys work to regain their breath. Grant has a thin stream of blood at the corner of his mouth, and Seth has the makings of a shiner coming on. "Sorry," I wheeze, "it's my . . . I'm so sorry." My dress feels like fifty pounds of sopping material as I trudge through the waist-deep water toward the steps. I hold my arms over my chest since the fabric has become embarrassingly sheer.

A deep frown mars Jackson's face as he takes in the scene. He drags his gaze from Seth and Grant, who are doing their own damage assessments as they slog from the pool. Opening a colorful beach towel, he wraps it around my shoulders. I clutch the fluffy cotton to my shivering body. It smells like dryer sheets—like Grant.

"Wil, please accept my apology for both my sons' behavior tonight." He tosses a towel to each of them, which they clumsily catch. "I expected a lot more from you two."

Seth peels off his soaked dress shirt, flinging it over a nearby chair. "And I expected more from that lying sack that's my brother," he retorts in disgust.

Grant glowers as he dabs at his mouth with the bottom of his wet T-shirt.

Charlotte tilts Seth's head into the patio light to inspect his eye. "I said enough, Seth, and I mean it."

He winces, pulling back. "I'm fine, Mom."

"So is anyone going to explain what started all this?" Jackson asks.

After a quick glance in my direction, Charlotte shakes her head at her husband.

There I stand, still shivering in my shell shock. Weeks of mounting pressure have finally given way to a mass explosion. And my presence tonight all but pushed that button. I break from my trance.

I move as silently as my sodden dress allows, collecting my shoes and purse and briskly walking toward the gate. Jackson continues giving the brothers an earful while Charlotte assesses Grant's injury, allowing me to slip away undetected. Until the hinges of the wrought-iron gate let out a rusty cry.

Damn!

I take off at a run. The towel billows like a cape in my wake.

"Wil!" Seth hollers.

I pick up my pace along the winding sidewalk lined with cypress trees. The Buick is now within my sight.

Keep moving. Keep moving. Keep moving.

Footsteps rush up behind me. "Hey, wait! Hold on!" Seth grabs my shoulder.

I whirl around to face him. Tears sting my eyes; I'm not strong enough to dam them for much longer. "*Why?* Why would you want me here? All it's doing is tearing up your family!"

"Wil, it's not your—"

"Look at you! You have a black eye—from your own *brother.*" As long as I'm standing here flayed and mortally wounded, I'd rather bleed out completely than suffer a slow death. "I can't . . ." A sob breaks loose. I cup a hand to my mouth, choking and swaying my head. I try one more time. "I'm sorry. I can't be with you, Seth. Now . . . or ever."

Seth looks gut-punched as he swallows. "No, you don't mean that." But his tone is unconvincing. "You're just upset. Come here." He tries to pull me to his chest, but I recoil. "Baby, I'm sorry, that was stupid. Grant and me . . . I don't know—we'll figure it out. We *will.*"

And I believe him. Just not with me in the picture. I place a shaking hand to his warm chest, and gaze up through blurry eyes. "Do something for me?"

"Name it," he whispers, wiping the tears trickling down my cheeks. "I would do anything for you."

The part of me wanting to confess what transpired in the gardens is dominated by my awareness of the self-ishness of the action. Unburdening myself at this point would only be cruel.

I pull Seth close enough to lay a kiss on his chlorine-scented cheek. "Forget me." The two words escape like wisps of smoke; the tendrils of their meaning hold Seth in suspended animation.

Dropping the towel, I wrench the Buick's door open, then slide behind the wheel, pulling the door shut and hitting the auto lock.

Seth pounds on my window. "Don't do this! You're upset . . . you . . . *don't leave like this*! You don't mean it! Come back, Wil!"

The floodgates open. Hot, salty tears cascade over my cheeks and fall to my chest. I throw the Buick in reverse, peeling out of the driveway.

The last image is of Grant in my rearview mirror, bare-foot, his wet clothes clinging to his body. He stands beside a cypress tree under the glow of the porch lights, and watches me fade into the night.

Something's wrong. Gram never sits idly on the porch swing without a book, or crossword, or a notepad where she's scribbling down her latest confectionary stroke of genius. And more unsettling—she sits in darkness. I recheck the time before getting out of the car. I'm not late, even with my aimless driving and gas station pit stop. I must've punched that hand dryer button twenty times to get my dress somewhere in the vicinity of dry.

I gather the wads of napkins I've been crying in from the passenger seat, shoving them in my purse. The half-moons of mascara remain stubbornly beneath my eyes. But between night's veil and Gram's questionable eyesight, it's likely she won't notice anything amiss in my appearance anyway. Which is good, because I'm not ready to talk about it.

The front steps protest with their usual groans when I climb them. "Gram? What're you doing out here in the dark?"

She doesn't glance in my direction. Instead, she fixes those steely blues on the tinkling wind chime hanging from the porch ceiling. "I'm sitting here wondering where I went wrong with you, Wilamena Grace."

"I—what?" Okay, that is about the last answer I expected, and the first to strike a whole lot of fear in the worn-out organ miraculously thumping in my chest. And she used my middle name—*Mama's* name. That heightens my alarm more than any line on her face could. My mind flips through the possibilities like the rapid shuffle of a card deck.

She gently rocks in the swing. Patient. Waiting. Confident I'll unpuzzle the meaning of her words. And still, she doesn't look at me.

Then it clicks. Oh . . . *no*.

"The dress," I blurt, drooping against the porch railing. In my mind's eye, I see the balled-up green dress carelessly left in my overnight bag along with all the other damning evidence.

Gram ceases her rocking. "Course, I've gotta ask myself what a girl who's having a sleepover would need with a fancy dress. Do you know what I came up with?"

The question's unwinnable. So I don't answer.

"There *was* no girls' night in. Was there, Wilamena? You lied to me. I trusted you, and you broke that trust with your lies."

Beneath my haze of exhaustion are the fiery sparks of anger. I push off from the rail. "But . . . you went through my things! How can you sit there lecturing me about trust?"

"Child, don't change the subject!" Gram booms.

"But—"

She holds up a hand. "No!" She takes a steadying breath. "Wilamena Grace, you are *grounded*. So grounded you'll be tasting the dirt through summer's end. Do you hear me?"

My anger ignites. "You can't! Gram, you have no idea what I've been through tonight! None! And I'm practically eighteen! I have a right—"

"You've got a right?" Gram rises, her displeasure polluting the air. "Your rights ended the second you stepped foot from this house last night!" Her fists land stubbornly on her hips. "Not another word on this tonight. But believe you me, starting tomorrow there'll be hell to pay. Beginning with the attic."

How I'm not exploding under the duress of this injustice is an effing wonderment. *And cleaning the attic?* The cobwebby, musty, crusty attic? Good Lord, you'd think I committed murder! I toss up my hands. "So, I'm just condemned? No discussion at all?"

"You wanna keep going? Because this can get a lot worse," Gram snaps.

I jerk open the screen door, then let it slam behind me.

Balanced high atop the ladder, I jab and sweep the broom along the corner rafters, removing an abundance of webs that coat the bristles like icky white cotton candy. I got an early jump on cleaning this morning because come noon, it'll be hotter than Mercury's core up here. It's not like I was getting quality sleep anyway. I spent the bulk of the night rehashing every traumatic detail of the Walkergeddon family dinner. Maybe today, if I wear myself out physically, I'll pass out the second my head hits the pillow.

I climb down off the ladder, nudging a box of multi-sized Styrofoam balls painted to look like planets out of my path. I got an A on that project and had it hung in one of the showcases at school. Gram made me Cherry Chip cupcakes in celebration.

Things were so much simpler then.

The scent of something baking drifts through the circular attic window from the kitchen below. My grandmother's up, but we haven't spoken. She's been clattering around making breakfast. But I'm too mad to talk and too nauseated to eat, so I keep working.

Another hour passes. If I squint I can almost see progress up here. *Almost*. I heft a couple boxes, cautiously picking my way through the maze I've created. But caution only gets you so far in an attic packed with mementos that better serve as booby traps.

I trip. The precariously stacked boxes tumble from my arms. *"Ow!"* I rub my stubbed toe. Wiping the sweat from my forehead, I glare at the sheet-covered rectangular object responsible for my klutz attack.

Irritated, I give the cotton material a forceful tug. Dust immediately kicks up, forming a cloud in the air around me. I cough and fan my face. And just as the allergen particles settle—*I see it.*

Gram's old cedar chest.

My gosh . . . I haven't seen this trunk in ages! Not since I was little and she kept it at the foot of her bed. She was always shooing me away from it.

But wait a sec. Didn't she tell me she got rid of it?

Then why is it still here?

Dropping to my knees, I run my hands along the surface of the chest, the smell of the pungent wood beckoning me. How many times had I sat as a child, wondering about the treasures . . . or secrets locked inside this mysterious trunk?

And now here it is, having magically appeared in the attic.

I frown, wrestling with my conscience. Breaking into the chest would be a *total* invasion of her privacy. And yet according to Gram, this chest shouldn't even be here. Which makes it somewhat fair game, doesn't it?

Well, that settles it.

I find a box containing old hardware, screws, and random tools, and set about jimmying the lock. My heart slams harder as I work to spring the old padlock, inserting one metal object after another to no avail. I try jiggling a bent nail in the keyhole, shifting it this way and that. "Come on," I hiss through gritted teeth. And then . . . the unmistakable click, and the lock drops open.

I blow out a breath, rubbing my hands back and forth on my paint-spattered overalls before easing back to sit on my heels.

This is it. The moment of truth . . .

I open the lid and peer inside. Carefully I sift through the contents, mindful of their original placement. I take out stacks of old letters—many from my grandfather, who died before I was born. The envelopes have begun to yellow and the ink bleeds. I find a copy of the Old Testament, a locket with a stern and weathered face I don't recognize, and a handkerchief with the initials *AEC* stitched in blue. And there are photos—lots and lots of photos—depicting a past Gram rarely revisits.

I dig and dig and dig until I am near the bottom of the chest. And so far, I have found *exactly* what you'd expect in an old trunk—precious keepsakes. Family heirlooms. Nothing more, nothing less.

I pinch the bridge of my nose to stave off a looming headache.

What am I doing? There's no mystery in this chest. Here I am picking locks and pawing through Gram's personal effects, and for what? To satisfy some silly childhood obsession?

Well, mission accomplished, and I still feel like crap.

Folded at the bottom of the trunk, I find the peach-colored blanket Mama and I used to lie on when we watched the sky. I pull it out, holding it under my nose, breathing in the sharp cedar scent. Of course there's no lingering trace of my mother in the fabric. But I try to find it anyhow. Try to catch even the faintest whiff of that soft floral fragrance that used to perfume her hair and skin.

Nothing. I feel a pang of emptiness. It would be unbearable if not for the stars. Because at least they tether my mother and me in a sacred bond. A bond that transcends even death.

I lower the blanket, glimpsing the last remaining item in the chest—an old hatbox. Pulling it out, I sit cross-legged on the attic floor and lift the lid. I expect more letters from my grandpa.

I don't expect to see stacks of letters addressed to me. I blink in disbelief, fingering through the colorful envelopes interspersed with official-looking bank letters.

What? Why would Gram have kept these from me? Why would she bury them at the bottom of her trunk? Why would—?

I shake my head. There's only one way to make sense of this.

I pull a pink envelope randomly from the pile. There's an Arizona return address and my name scrawled in sloppy writing on the front. I tear into the paper. My stomach clenches at the sound, a cold sweat cropping up at my hairline.

It's a birthday card decorated with bursts of metallic stars. A twenty-dollar bill floats to the floor as I open it.

Happy Birthday, Mema!

I don't know if this card will ever reach you, but I continue to send them in the hopes that one day they will. My birthday wish for you is the same as it always is—I wish for your happiness.

I smile as I imagine you blowing out those birthday candles and wonder what you're wishing for. Do you have a favorite cake? A favorite ice cream? You must be such a big girl by now. And every bit as beautiful as your mama was.

There's so much I wish I could tell you. There's so much I wish I knew.

Maybe someday I'll have that precious chance.

But no matter what, I will always love you, Mema.

Daddy

The attic swirls around me; the high ceiling presses down. I close the birthday card Gram never intended for my eyes and, with trembling hands, reach for another.

It's more of the same. Wishes of happiness and second chances and wanting to be here in some big or small way.

I rip through more envelopes, devouring every word.

Year after year of birthdays and holidays blur together. Lost years. Lost wishes.

Lost.

And I find myself gravitating to one card more than all the others, like the magnetic needle of a compass pointing due north. I pick it up again; the glitter sticks to my sweaty fingers. It's the card where my father tells me how pretty I looked with the purple ribbons in my hair.

Except . . . we've never met. So then, when would he have seen me? And when was the last time I wore purple ribbons in my hair? Not since I was little. Not since . . . It hits me and the card drops from my hand.

I wore purple ribbons to Mama's funeral.

And just as I sprang the lock on the chest, so springs a sudden memory buried so deep I nearly forgot . . .

Gram holds me in her arms, sobbing over Mama's grave sprinkled with sunflowers. I feel so small and helpless, and the world feels big and confusing.

I kiss Gram's wet cheeks and tell her it will be okay. I tell her Mama promised on the necklace she will never, ever leave. I'm so sure she will come back. So sure. I can't understand why this makes Gram cry harder.

Then the cemetery is almost empty. Except for a tall man in a dark suit. He wears a tie the color of sunshine—

Mama's favorite color. And his eyes are large and full of tears.

When he approaches, Gram sets me down, pulling me behind her. I cling to her leg, trying to peer around at the man as he weeps and begs for forgiveness. But Gram curses him. Says all sorts of forbidden words. I've never seen her so angry.

"Come on, Wilamena," our neighbor Mrs. Rowan says, scooping me into her arms. She usually smells like cheese. Today she smells of fake roses. "Let's get you a ginger ale. You like that, don't you, sweetheart?"

The man with sad eyes watches. Watches the distance between us growing wider.

And I never see him again.

All these years Gram has known the truth. Known my father—whatever his crimes—has been desperately reaching out. Through his unopened letters and deposits to a savings account opened in my name that I knew nothing about.

Gram has kept it all locked in a trunk, wedged in the attic, and hidden beneath a sheet—never to be discovered.

Gram refills her coffee mug. Like any other day on any other morning—except it isn't. Because I know all the other days were steeped in lies.

I sway in the doorway, clutching one of the cards from my dad.

"Heard you up early. Biscuits are still warm in the oven. There's quiche, too. You should eat something before . . ." She turns. "Mena? Child, you look positively ill. And you've been crying up a storm . . ."

She knows this is more than the grounding. Much more. Hustling over, she puts her hands on either side of my face. "Honey, what happened?" I can't find my voice. "Now you're scaring me, Mena, what is it?"

I swallow. "How *could* you?" I seethe, pushing away her hands and taking a backward step. "How could you purposely hide the truth from me?"

Gram knows. She knows I mean my father. She turns to peel off her apron, but not before I witness the fear flicker in her eyes. It takes only that second to confirm the truth.

"*You knew!* You knew my dad was out there! I thought he didn't care, that he abandoned me! But he *did* try; he reached out. And you took all those letters—letters addressed to *me*—and you hid them! *Why?*" The rage in my voice blisters and pops in the air between us. "Well?" I pound my fist on the fridge. "Say something!"

Gram flinches. Her face is ashy and she rubs a hand over her stomach. Taking a dish towel from the counter, she pats it to her forehead. "M-Mena, I was going to talk to you about your father. I was going to give you those letters, along with the others I've saved for you in my room. But . . . when you were old enough to hear the whole story, to try and understand. You have no idea how difficult things were."

My nostrils flare. "You're right, I don't. Because *you*"—I

274

jab a hostile finger in the air—"never told me. So? Am I old enough now?"

"I was going to tell you. I was . . ."

I wait for more. I wait for *something*. Some *rational* explanation why Gram saw fit to barricade my father from my life. How she justified her bold-faced lies.

I am hurt, betrayed—but of the myriad of emotions, I cling most fiercely to anger. Because anger keeps me standing. Anger's what pulled me up from the attic floor when I wanted to curl up and die. Anger will deliver me the entire truth.

I slap the card on the island between us. "You owe me an explanation."

Gram's jaw clenches as she dabs the towel again at her forehead. Her tearing eyes fasten on the hypnotic paper.

"Yeah," I sniff. "I'd be sweating too if all my deepest, darkest secrets were staring me in the face." I plant my hands on either side of the card. Leaning across the counter, close enough to smell her cinnamon-infused skin, I whisper, "This isn't over, Gram. You say I broke your trust, but all those cards and letters . . . they broke *us*." I storm from the kitchen.

I don't turn to see how the pain sets the crow's-feet deeper at her eyes, or how the faint lines at the corner of her mouth extend lower.

I don't need to.

chapter 20

The shower washes away the attic grime, yet I still don't feel clean. I go through the motions of setting my hair into waves. I put on a dress without registering the color or if my shoes match. I'm putting on my Parisian Pout and then stop, dropping the tube without recapping it.

As I gaze at my reflection, my mother's blue eyes gaze back. My hair is the same as hers, too—dark, wavy. Is there any of my father in my features? I don't know. And if Gram had her way, I would probably never find out.

And that, *that* is what makes me angriest of all.

Gram instilled the value of honesty and trust when she raised me. But apparently, those virtues were bendable. *For her.* The hypocrisy is mind-blowing.

My thoughts are a jumble as I descend the stairs, the questions compounding with my footsteps. However,

I'm clear on two things. Gram *owes* me—answers and apologies—and I won't let her timetable dictate when those come.

I shove open the kitchen door, prepared to wage a war that would put Ares to shame.

But the second I see her curled on the floor . . . my rage disappears.

"Gram!" I scream, falling to my knees. *"Gram!"* My hands are trembling as I push aside the silvery hair pasted to her forehead. I shake her. Her eyes are rolled back and vacant. I start to cry as I shake her again. "Wake up! You have to wake up!" My tears are dripping all over the shirt with itty-bitty daisies. "Please, Gram," I whimper, "come back to me."

I press my ear to her unmoving chest, but it's hard to hear anything over my panicked sobs. Gram is my sun and my moon and my stars. If anything happens to her, then . . . my world will collapse into darkness. Emptiness. A black and hollow hole.

I stumble to the phone and dial 911.

The woman on the line is walking me through CPR and I do my best to follow. I perform compressions on her chest soaked with my tears. I would give her my heart—my life—if I could. Because my life doesn't have meaning without her. She can't leave me and not know that.

And she can't leave thinking . . . thinking we are broken. Beyond repair.

I don't know how long we're on the kitchen floor before the paramedics arrive with their gadgets and machines.

I bury my face in my hands as Miss Laveau's words rasp in my mind. *An end . . . possibly a death. The outcome is so fixed . . .*

But this is more than I can bear. It's asking too much of my soul to carry.

I will shatter without her.

We are in the ambulance now, and I refuse to let go of Gram's cold hand all the way to the hospital. People are asking me questions and I must be answering. But I don't know what I've said. There are only whirling lights and horns honking, and an IV, and an oxygen bag being rhythmically squeezed over her nose and mouth.

The siren screams, and I want nothing more than to join it. To scream as loud and as far as my cry will carry.

"Honey"—one of the female paramedics pats my hand that holds on to Gram's—"is there someone we can call? Your mom or dad . . . another relative?"

The reality punches through me with the force of a wrecking ball. I may have a biological father, but he isn't my family. He's a stranger.

My mouth quivers and I shake my head. "She's all I've got. Please"—the tears that stopped come back full force—"you have to fix her." I struggle to draw my breath. "You have to bring her back."

The woman squeezes our clasped hands. "We're gonna do all we can to make that happen. But, Wilamena?"

My sight's completely blurred by my tears. I wipe them and the paramedic comes into focus. The woman's eyes are concerned and kind.

"I need you to be strong," she says. "Hold together, all right?"

"I'll try," I whisper.

One hour. That's how long I've been at Gram's bedside. Although the duration of time she spent in the cath lab makes it feel like an entire lifetime has come and gone.

Gram's condition has been stabilized, but she's as pale as the linens on her stark hospital bed. The intermittent beeps serve as a reminder that she's still alive.

I pull the chair up to the bed so I can hold her, and when that isn't enough, I climb into bed with her.

I tell her how sorry I am for lying, for the terrible things I said when I was angry and hurting. I'll make it up to her. She can ground me for eternity if she wants—I don't really care. I'll do manual labor. I'll pull out every dandelion in the whole damn state if it'll bring her back. And that's a shitload of dandelions.

It's not right—the things Gram kept from me. But I know she loves me. Would do anything, including laying down her own life for me, just as I would for her. So we'll find a way through this. We have to.

Gram has beautiful eyelashes. They are long and dark even though the rest of her hair's gone all salt-and-peppery. I tell her so. I tell her she's beautiful, eyelashes and all.

"Wil?"

I sit up to find Irina standing at the door. She draws her

hand to her mouth, bracing her other hand on the door-frame. "Is she . . . is she?" Her eyes well up.

"She's stable. They have her heavily sedated because they had to . . ." I can't even say the word *intubate* without crumbling again. "We were fighting and then I left her. I could tell she didn't feel well but . . ." I look down at Gram again. "But I didn't know she was having a heart attack. No"—I shake my head, recalling fragments of the doctor's explanation—"*worse* than a regular heart attack. It was called a STEMI, I think. Iri, her heart muscle was actually *dying*. I didn't know. I didn't realize. Until I found her on the floor and—" My words are cut off by another sob.

"Shh." Irina winds her arms around me. "Shh," she croons. "It's not your fault, Wil." She keeps an arm around me while taking Gram's IV-free hand. Her voice is a shadow of a whisper as she murmurs something in Russian. She repeats the phrases, over and over like a prayer. Whatever they mean, I find them soothing.

And for a time we sit, clinging to Gram's life and each other.

"Wilamena? I'm Dr. Gaultier, the cardiologist who treated your grandmother." He pauses to punch something into the tablet he carries.

"Will she be okay?"

The middle-aged doctor removes his glasses, tucking them into the breast pocket of his lab coat. "We are doing everything we can to help her to recover. Your grandmother suffered an inferior wall S-T elevation myocardial infarct, or what we call an N-STEMI. When she arrived, she had an acute blockage of the right coronary artery. This complete blockage also triggered the arrhythmia, resulting in her loss of consciousness. We've performed an angioplasty with stent placement of her right coronary artery to regain proper blood flow back to the heart.

"Now, Wilamena, we've run all the preliminary tests, and there's nothing that suggests your grandmother has experienced brain damage. However, because it's unclear the amount of time she was unconscious before you began CPR, we won't know if she's completely neurologically intact until she wakes up. It's possible there could be some memory loss, personality changes—"

Iri finds my hand and squeezes it. And as the doctor continues his explanation of Gram's status and care, I can't unstick myself from the words "brain damage" and whether or not my grandmother will be "intact." Those are ugly phrases with uglier connotations because it robs people of who they once were.

What if Gram isn't Gram when she wakes up?

What if she doesn't remember me?

What if, what if, what if . . .

I stare down to where Irina's hand clenches mine. My fingertips are mottled red and white. I feel nothing.

Dr. Gaultier's still speaking, but I haven't heard anything else.

"I'm sorry." I rub my swollen, tender eyes. "How long will she have to be on this breathing tube?"

"Currently the ventilator is doing much of the breathing for her. We can, however, monitor when she instigates her own breath. So until she's able to spontaneously breathe on her own, we'll need to keep her vented and sedated." He rests a hand on my shoulder. "It's important to have faith, Wilamena. As I've said, we've opened up the blocked artery, so she's getting the blood her heart needs. But your grandmother's been through a tremendous trauma. Her body will need time to recover."

"Thanks," I say as the doctor exits the room.

Irina's phone chimes. She lets go of my hand and frowns as she reads the message.

"What?"

"It's . . ." She offers a pleading look. "I, um, wasn't thinking clearly on the way here. I got a call and might've mentioned you were at the emergency room with Gram."

"Who was it?" I ask before blowing my nose into one of those scratchy hospital-grade tissues that offer all the comfort of tree bark.

"Hey, I got here . . . as quick as I could." Grant's standing there breathless, cheeks flushed with color, hair disheveled. "What can I do? How can I help? Or . . . do you want me to call Seth instead?"

"I'm sorry"—a panicked Irina looks to me—"I didn't know he would actually come."

Grant's head snaps to Irina and then back to me. "I—I can leave. Or wait downstairs? Or, um, you can send me on errands. I'm good at following directions."

I can't believe he's seeing me at my emotional rock bottom. And he sees Gram with all her awful tubes and breathing devices and . . . he's not flinching or turning away. If anything, he seems desperate to stay. I can't understand it. And I can't understand why I'm not immediately telling him to go.

A nurse pokes her head in the room. "I'm very sorry, but we can only allow two visitors at a time. One of you will need to go to the waiting area."

I give Irina a slight nod. That's the beauty of best friends—talking without words. She can read everything from the tilt of my chin to the expression in my eyes.

"Well, I was about to pop down to the crap-a-teria anyway. Earl Grey sound good?" Irina asks me.

"Please," I answer.

She kisses the top of my head and slings her bag with the metal rivets. "You'll stay with her while I'm gone?"

"Of course," Grant answers.

Irina squeezes his arm as she passes. "You're one of the good ones."

I toss my mound of tissues into the trash while Grant walks uncertainly closer. "Am I overstepping? Because you can tell me to leave. I mean, with everything that happened the other night . . ."

"I just don't understand why you'd want to stay."

Grant pulls the chair closer to the bed and sits down. He reaches through the space in the plastic rails to find my hand. It's warm and gives me more reassurance than

283

any doctor could. "A few years back, I had this friend who was in trouble. I should have done more to help. I won't make that mistake again."

I let my thumb stroke the ripple of tendons across the top of his hand. "What happened?"

He doesn't let go but shifts back against the chair. "Not now, okay?"

"Well"—I swallow the ever-present sadness in my throat—"thank you for being here."

"Thank you for not making me leave." He squeezes my hand. "But I meant what I said . . . if you want me to call Seth, I will."

"Is it wrong that I don't want you to? That I don't want you to call? I just . . ." I gaze back to my grandmother, sleeping deep inside herself.

"There's no right or wrong, Wil. So, what are the doctors saying? Unless . . . you'd rather not talk about it."

I'm shocked to discover I do. Grant listens and nods and asks all the right questions. And then Irina returns and someone has to leave. So Grant squeezes my hand one last time before walking out the door.

It's gotten late. I'm so exhausted I'm seeing double. Visiting hours are over but I'm told I can return tomorrow morning.

Irina's skipped work to be with me, but I know she needs the cash. Even with her latest pool hustling, she's still short on enough funds to move out of her *tetya*'s.

"I'm just gonna crash tonight," I say to Iri for the umpteenth time. "You might as well get a few hours in at Ink-

porium." We navigate the busy ER waiting area, where a baby is wailing and a haggard old man reeks of pee and alcohol.

"Uh-uh, I'm not leaving you alone tonight." She puts her arm around me, guiding us around a rambunctious kid who is not the least bit slowed down by whatever's stuck in his nostrils.

"Baba, why does that guy habe silber tape od his shoe?" Plugged Nose asks.

"It's not polite to point," she scolds. "And it's that finger that got you into this trouble in the first place. Whatever possessed you to shove raisins up your nose?"

My heart is leaping in my chest. I'm flooded with hope that it's *my* guy with the silver-taped shoe. And it is! Grant's slumped half-asleep in a chair too small for his long body. His elbow slides beneath him, causing him to jolt awake.

"Hey." He rises. "I, uh, wasn't sure if you'd need a ride." Grant crams his hands in the pockets of his jeans. "But Irina's probably gonna take you, so I'll go . . ."

"Actually," Iri says, checking her cell, "I was due at work a while ago. I'm sorta hurting for hours, so if you don't mind, maybe you could take her?"

"Yeah, sure. Whatever you need."

Irina hugs me goodbye. "Did I read that right?" she whispers.

Honestly, I don't know what I want. But I nod into her shoulder, because sorting out my messy feelings is too much work.

I promise to call if I need anything, and she promises to meet me at the hospital first thing tomorrow.

Grant takes my hand and for the briefest second, I forget the anguish of the day.

"Let's get you home," he says.

chapter 21

I wake up to the feeling of movement. We're in Grant's pickle wagon, and my head is cradled in his tattooed arm. I take a deep breath, inhaling his laundry smell, and my stomach grumbles at another smell . . . food.

"You're home," Grant says quietly. "I didn't want to wake you, but I stopped at Spoon & Ladle and got some takeout. I know, probably dumb to get soup in the summer."

I sit up woozily. "No, it smells good."

"I wasn't sure what you'd want so I got four different kinds."

"I'm not really that fussy." My attempt at a grin doesn't carry the grace it should. "Thanks."

Grant parks the wagon and follows me up the steps.

I unlock the door and can hardly believe this is the

same house it was this morning. Now it is unwelcoming. Cold. We kick off our shoes on the mat beneath the bench.

"Where should I put these?" He holds up the soup carrier.

"Living room is fine." I tuck my hair behind my ear. "I could use a shower if you don't mind. Maybe a change of clothes."

"No rush," Grant says.

But it isn't long before I'm padding back downstairs, clean and in my silk pj bottoms and worn constellation T-shirt. My cheeks seem to have permanent stains of pink that look like rouge gone wrong. Simply put—I'm a disaster. And too tired to care.

Grant's laid out spoons and napkins on the coffee table, and lined up all the soups in a neat row. "Okay, what's your poison? Broccoli and cheddar, tomato bisque, hearty chicken nood—"

"Stop, just . . ." I sit down beside him on the couch and bury my face in my palms.

"It's too warm for soup, isn't it? I can run out and grab something else. Whatever you want—"

"No! It's . . . if you do or say one more sweet thing, I might fall apart." I choke back a sob. "Why are you still here? Why do you keep doing all these things for me?" I close my eyes and slowly open them. "Grant . . . what do you want?"

He takes his time setting down the soup lid, training his eyes on it. "Is it that you really don't know? Or you want me to say it out loud?" He swallows before looking at me when I don't answer. "You should eat your soup before it gets cold." He passes the cup of chicken noodle, which I wordlessly accept.

A stupid movie plays, filling the conversation void. When I can't withstand another second of mindless chatter, I shut it off.

"I broke up with Seth," I say. "That's part of why I didn't want you to call him."

Grant rubs his furrowed brow. "Last night wasn't exactly a shining moment for any of us, Wil. And . . . I think he'd take you back in a heartbeat if you asked him to. If"—he pauses—"that's what you really want."

None of that eases my conscience; it makes me feel worse. "You know why I was with him in the first place?" I let out a morose laugh. "Because he's supposed to be perfect for me according to our astrological charts. He even had the exact birthday of the person I was looking for. Seth is my cosmic destiny. And right before my mom died, she had me promise to—"

"Wil, you don't have to do this now. You've been through enough."

"No, I do, because you should know. I'm not a nice person. I'm a rotten person."

"I disagree. I think you're an incredible person who's had rotten things happen to her."

I whip my head away, staring at the afghan Gram knitted eons ago. Anytime I was sick or upset, she'd wrap it around my shoulders. But she isn't here to do that now. "You're wrong, Grant."

"Well, then, you don't know the girl I do." Grant slides closer. In response, I move closer to the armrest. "Wil, stop trying to push me away, or trying to make me think you're a bad person—you're not."

"Nice people don't agree to dates and meeting parents and hot-air balloon rides because of the day someone was born. Seth has been nothing but sweet to me, and . . . and . . ."

Grant slides his arm over my shoulders. I give up fighting it. "And what?"

"I don't love him," I finish hopelessly. "I don't. I never will, not the way I should."

All the air rushes from his lungs as he pulls me tightly to his chest.

My eyes water, spilling their sorrow all over again. "God, what if I really *am* broken? What if all this loss . . . destroyed my ability to really love the way a person should?"

"I don't buy that for one second, Wil. I *see* you," he says fiercely. "I *see* the love you have for Irina and your gram." He dabs my wet cheek with a napkin. "You're bruised . . . not broken."

My shoulders shake with another sob. "Gram's my entire universe. Without her, I have nothing—*no one*. I can't lose her, Grant. I just . . . *can't*."

"*Shhh, shhh,*" he croons. His arms embrace me, holding me together, while the rest of me falls spectacularly apart.

I slide deeper into my chasm of sadness. And he lets me. Lets me cry until I'm emptied of tears and quiet again.

I sniffle in his T-shirt. "Grant?"

"Yes?"

"Why did you climb the water tower when you're afraid of heights?"

"What?" He stills the hand rubbing my back. "I told you, we thought you were going to jump."

"But . . . there was something else"—I peer up— "wasn't there? There had to be."

"Wil, sweetheart—"

"Call me Mena."

Grant tucks the hair behind my ear. *"Mena,* it's not a story for tonight."

I find his hand, drawing it into mine. "Would you tell me anyway?" And I can't explain why it is so important for me to hear his story. Maybe it's being here in his arms, soul stretched and bare before him, that now makes me desperate to know the parts he hides.

Indecision wars on his face.

I squeeze his hand. "Please?"

His hand instinctively moves over his tattoo. "It's . . . it's because of the friend I was telling you about earlier. Her name was Anna—Anna Rodriguez." I startle at the last name. "Yeah, Manny's cousin—my girlfriend sophomore and junior year. She was this totally incredible girl who wasn't afraid of anything, and there was a line of guys dying to date her, but she picked me. Out of all of them, she picked me." A sad smile lifts the corners of his mouth. "She taught me how to dance, how to speak Spanish." He quiets for a moment. "She taught me a lot of things. For a while . . . it was great.

"But Anna had these dark moments, too. Her home life sucked. Manny tried like hell to get her to leave and come to his family's house, but she wouldn't. Wouldn't dream of abandoning her mom—even at her own expense. Not that her mom was around much, since she worked two jobs just to make ends meet. Which *killed* me because we had more than enough.

"And then her stepdad"—Grant gives his head a disgusted shake—"he was a heavy drinker and pissed away any earnings on the bottle and gambling. She denied there was any abuse, but I think by the time I came into the picture the damage was already done. All her scars were on the inside. I wanted to fix it—make her better. I wanted the happy girl I fell for to be there all the time. But I saw her less and less. The past has a way of catching up to us, you know?"

I do. More than I'd like to. I draw a breath to speak, but Grant has already moved on.

"So we broke up. I broke up with her. I was sixteen and my overprivileged ass didn't know how to deal with the way her past was eating at her. Anna got mixed up with a rough crowd of partyers and users. God, Manny and I did *everything* we could to get her out of that scene. But she kept migrating back—over and over.

"Then she called me one night—drunk, high, maybe both—begging to get back together. I said no."

The sadness percolates from somewhere deep inside him before he continues. "I knew she was upset, but I also knew there'd be no reasoning with her when she was that messed up." Grant's fingers pass over the inked musical notes on his arm. "Anna died that night."

"Oh, Grant." I push back from his arms, seeing the pain cut across his face. "What happened?" I whisper.

"Sometimes they partied at construction sites. She, um . . . she climbed up some scaffolding to one of those metal beams, lost her footing, and . . ." His voice thickens with emotion. "It was pretty much instantaneous."

I wrap my arms around his waist and lay my head to his chest. "*God.* I'm so, *so* sorry."

"Me too. I played back the last time we spoke again and again and thought of a million different things I could've said, I could've done."

"You know it wasn't your fault."

"Maybe, maybe not. But there isn't a day that goes by when I don't wish I had done more, tried harder, listened. I don't know."

I sigh into his chest. "That's why you climbed the tower, isn't it? You were rewriting history . . . by saving me."

Grant nods and then continues. "After the funeral, I went into my own tailspin. Staying out late, drinking, finding excuses to get into fights.

"One night at a party, a guy got rough with this girl. I found her on her back, dazed, nose bloody, and I just . . . *snapped.* Ended up beating the guy so bad he spent several days in the ICU. He filed charges, and if it weren't for my parents and the lawyers, I would've stood trial. So they saved me."

He shifts uncomfortably in my arms. "But besides the drinking and fights, I was also sleeping around—*a lot*. Anything to make me forget about Anna and how I could've been the one who made the difference between her living and dying. You can't imagine the weight of something like that."

My hand finds his; our fingers lace together. I caress my thumb over his skin. "What brought you back?"

Grant lets out a sorrow-filled chuckle. "Manny. He knocked the self-loathing out of me—I mean that literally . . . he punched me in the face. Told me how pissed Anna would be at the way I was throwing my life away. So . . . I just immersed myself more and more in my music. It gave me an outlet for the grief, the anger, all the helplessness. It's when I wrote 'Anna's Song'—the tattoo." He lifts the inked arm, trembling when my finger runs over the musical notes. "It helped me get through."

I understand loss. We are intimately acquainted. I understand the way it can hollow you if you let it. How something so simple can be so devastating. My mother going to get maple syrup, Anna's single misstep—events that could've played out in countless, impermanent ways. But instead, they ripped away the people we loved.

He's watching me, gauging my reaction. His jaw is tight and lines appear on his forehead. I think he worries he's said too much. He hasn't.

Grant's watering eyes fill with more emotions than the English language is equipped to describe.

I take his arm, pulling it closer, kissing his tattoo, kissing away the hurt, the way Gram has done on so many skinned knees and elbows. I don't want him to bear the burden alone anymore. Pain is something we can share.

I smooth the lines above his troubled brow. Just as I'd wanted to that night at Absinthe that now feels decades ago. My head tucks back against his chest. His breath is hot on my scalp, making me forget our hurts. Making me forget everything.

And, I know, the smallest movement would change everything. If I lift my chin, then our lips will almost be touching. Almost . . .

His heart beats faster as if he's sensing my thoughts. The cotton of his T-shirt brushes softly on my cheek as I slowly, slowly lift my head. Half-lidded eyes gaze back, matching my longing.

I touch my mouth to his and hear the sharp intake of both our breaths. In that second that our lips meet, all the aches and pains of living . . . vanish. I know they aren't gone forever, but for now . . . I don't feel them. I only feel Grant.

We are still except for our breaths and our hearts. My hand, feeling the stubble on the side of his face, hasn't moved, and neither has his arm that curls around me. I am surrounded by "Anna's Song." I'm sure it's as beautiful as she was.

I pull back and we stare at each other in wonder. It shouldn't be wondrous.

Because we are doomed.

But for tonight, for *one* night . . . I will imagine I can rearrange the stars.

I drop my hand, which carries the heat from his face.

"I can't go back to pretending. I don't ever want to pretend with you, Mena—*ever*. You're all I want. All I've wanted since the moment we met." Grant takes off my glasses, which clatter to the coffee table. He leans closer, eyeing my lips. "Tell me to stop."

I say nothing. Grant may not want to pretend, but I do. I want to pretend there is nothing but us—no vows, or charts, or lives hanging in the balance. Because this ache I have for him is unlike anything I've ever felt. It's all-consuming.

Suddenly Grant pulls me into his arms and kisses me. *Hard.*

I gasp and we fall back into the couch cushions. His lips move frantically over mine, and I match his need with my own. All the emotion I've pent up, all the memories of that night in the gardens—it's my undoing. The kiss deepens as our bodies recall the way we fit. The way our contours shape against one another—puzzle pieces waiting to be joined.

I tug the back of his T-shirt until it's bunched at his upper back, scratching him with my haste. I murmur my apology against his mouth as his shirt is tossed to the living-room floor.

I don't know what I'm doing. I can't *believe* what I'm

doing. I've practically torn the shirt off his back and all I can think is . . . *please, oh please, don't stop.*

Once again, our lips collide like bits of heaven bursting through atmosphere. We gain speed with our fall just like heaven's debris.

And I am in flames. Ignited by the way his lips and hands move over me.

I cross my arms at my torso, reaching for the bottom of my shirt. I don't want anything between us. I want to feel his heart, his skin molded to mine. I want the physical connection to match the emotional one.

"Mena." Grant pulls back, bracing himself above me. His bare chest rises and falls erratically, his hair even wilder than usual.

"Not sex," I breathe. But I can't define what I want. Connection? Closeness? To feel something worth remembering?

"No, this wasn't"—he stalls and licks his lips—"this wasn't why I came to the hospital. Or why I came here tonight. You're hurting. The last thing I want is to comp—"

I still his mouth with my fingers, and push down the grief that threatens to surface once more. "I'm not the only one hurting."

He gently removes my fingers and sits up. "That's different. Those are old scars." He drops his head to his hands. "I haven't been with anyone in a long time. I haven't really wanted to. But then I met you, and . . . *everything changed.*"

Quietly I echo, "It changed for me, too, Grant."

Now, sitting beside him, the taste of him on my lips, the scent of him on my skin—I realize why no one else has awakened me quite this way.

Because no one else . . . was Grant.

My hand trembles as I turn off the lamp. It's easier to be bold in darkness. "I've never really wanted to be with anyone. At least, not the way . . ." But then my voice fades along with my nerve.

"Not the way?" he prompts. Grant cups my chin, turning my face toward him. "It's me. Mena, there's nothing to be afraid of."

He's right. And the *rightness* of being with Grant is pounded out in every beat of my heart. My fear dissolves. "I've never wanted to be with anyone"—I gaze into his darkened eyes—"the way I want to be with you."

Then I stand, the moon's caress at my back. This time he doesn't stop me as I peel off my T-shirt and toss it on top of his. The slamming inside my chest does little to mask the sound of his breath.

"You're so beautiful, Mena." Grant's voice drops to a whisper, "You make it hard to breathe. But I need to say, you need to know how much I lo—"

"Please, Grant"—I shake my head—"no more words. Could you just . . . find another way to speak?"

I see the outline of his throat tighten and relax with his swallow. He stands facing me.

Blood rushes in my veins and in my ears and in every part of me, reminding me I am alive. I am so very alive. I wrap my arms around him, pressing my skin firmly to

his. It is like holding fire, and looking into his eyes is like gazing at the sun.

When I finally let go, we collapse on the couch. I fall on top of him. His hands aren't as rushed as they were before, and they don't try to remove any more clothes than I have already.

Not sex. He honors this, even as I move desperately against him and fumble with the button on his jeans. It's a reckless move, and I haven't really considered what I'll do once the jeans are off. But I want to ease what he must be feeling. What *I* am feeling.

Suddenly I'm pulled beneath him. Grant's breath is ragged, and his body is shaking, but he sways his head back and forth when I grapple with the button of his jeans again. He pins my hand against the couch cushion. Our fingers intertwine; he kisses them.

Grant hovers above me now, head outlined in silver light. His face has that same euphoric look as it did the first time I saw him play. Except now I'm the guitar. And those talented hands play me much as they did his beloved instrument. Touching me like no one ever has. Then his mouth is on mine, kissing me until I can't form thoughts. And he tells me *everything* . . . without once uttering a word.

"Don't," he whispers when I start to roll away. He draws me back against him so we are chest to chest, hearts beating in time. "Stay with me."

299

I'm not sure how long we've been on the couch when I finally awaken. Long enough for the tingles to recede and for dawn's first light to pierce the living-room curtains.

My head feels stuffed with wool and my eyes are gritted with sand. Grant's arm is draped over my waist and his breath has the slow steadiness of sleep's rhythm.

I love Grant.

The thought startles me like a thunderclap. And I'm not joyous, or happy, or any of those things someone in love is suppose to feel. Instead, I'm terrified.

Because loving Grant compromises a lifetime of beliefs. Worse, it compromises my mother's legacy, the promise I made. I squeeze my eyes shut.

My God, what have I done?

The grandfather clock bongs, echoing six times through the house. Grant doesn't stir.

Carefully as I can, I roll out from beneath his arm and yank on my T-shirt. His lips are parted, head half-mashed into the cushion, deep in a blissful sleep. His breath is slow and even. I so badly want to kiss him.

But enough damage has been done.

Tiptoeing out of the room and upstairs, I get ready in record time. I've even put on the jeans I hate. Besides, it feels too wrong to put on one of my mother's dresses after last night.

I let out a quiet exhale when I see Grant hasn't moved. Crouching down, I flip over some junk mail and scribble out four words:

I'm sorry, I can't.

I bite my knuckle to keep the sorrow from emerging, before adding one last line.

Please forgive me.

And I don't give myself time for second guesses. I bolt for the door, and quietly shut it behind me.

chapter 22

Irina arrives at the hospital and doesn't ask a single question about what transpired between Grant and me. She does food runs and coffee runs, and I have to practically shove her out the door to get her to go to work.

I fritter away the time reading to Gram, playing solitaire, and watching TV. Eventually I'm so restless I'm ready to crawl out of my skin. Her lovely lashes don't flutter. Hope is such a fragile thing. And mine becomes increasingly delicate and breakable with the passing hours that Gram is under sedation.

The doctors still say she's stable and breathing more on her own, but we won't know until she's awake if there's neurological damage the tests don't show.

I hug her and kiss her good night before I go. And pray tomorrow will be different and I'll have my gram again.

My mind is a puddle of mud. I can't remember where I've parked and end up wandering aimlessly until I spot the Buick in all its Buicky glory.

But some part of my brain must be functioning, because I find my way home, and when I do, Seth's parked at the curb. The streetlights are on and glance off the spotless, shiny Lexus.

My foot barely touches the ground and Seth is already out of the vehicle striding toward me. I plant my feet, preparing for the worst.

Seth's pace loses steam and he slows. He gnaws his lower lip. "Jesus, you look like hell."

"I know."

"Listen, Wil." He jams his hands in his pockets, then takes them out. "I'm so sorry about everything. I would've told you, I swear. In fact, I was gonna tell you after dinner the other night." His eyes beg for understanding.

I adjust my glasses, totally thrown by whatever it is he's trying to tell me.

"I was wrong, okay? It was totally messed up and I was wrong. I can see that now. If I could go back in time, I would've done things differently. But when you told me those things about your mom . . . *shit.* I just lost my nerve. I—I couldn't."

He was wrong? How can he be wrong if *I'm* the one who spent the night with Grant? I don't follow. My thoughts are so scrambled, it's possible these things should make sense and I'm just not connecting the dots. I fold my arms over my chest. "Seth, I don't—"

"I *know* I shouldn't have lied to you, but you were turning down every guy in the club! And then that chart was just hanging out of your purse so . . . I looked. I figured it was the only way you'd give me a shot. I thought if you got to know me, my sign wouldn't matter. Because you'd see how amazing we were together. How much fun we could have."

The asphalt shifts underneath me, making everything go lopsided. I brace a hand on the Buick's trunk. "What?"

Seth nervously rubs at his neck. "I assumed Grant told you, and that's why . . . that's why you . . ." He curses under his breath. "I thought that's why you weren't returning my calls."

"No . . . I've been at the hospital." My voice is eerily calm when I rediscover it. "When is your birthday?"

"Wil, it isn't important. What's important is how you feel about me and—"

"Yes!" I explode. "It's important, Seth! Tell me your birthday!"

"A-April eighteenth," he stammers.

And I can't move. I can't stop the high-pitched ringing in my ears. The world is no longer lopsided. It has completely tipped over and crashed down in a way I cannot make sense of. "So you're not . . . you were never . . ."

Seth was never a Sagittarius.

My paralysis breaks long enough for me to stagger to the porch steps. I sink down, dropping my head to my hands.

"You're an Aries," I whisper dully.

Dear God, I got it wrong. I had it all wrong. I saw what

304

I wanted to see in Seth. I wanted to fall in love with him. I wanted him to be my Sagittarius. *Desperately.*

Could the same be said of Grant being a Pisces? Was I only seeing what I wanted to see because it kept him unattainable? Is it possible I've gotten his sign all wrong, too? But no, I had proof. I—

These questions make my head hurt. And there's already a surplus of pain competing for my attention right now.

Seth slides next to me on the warped step. Desperation clings to his words. "Please . . . talk to me, Wil. Let me try to make it up to you. Give me one more chance. Because what I feel for you . . . I've never felt for anyone."

I wipe the tears from my eyes as Seth tries to put a consoling arm around me. "No"—I shrug away—"don't. You won't want to touch me when I tell you this." I hug my knees. "Gram had a severe heart attack the other night; she's still in recovery. That's why I was at the hospital."

He rubs a hand over his face and moans, "Oh man, and I dumped all this on you tonight. Tonight when you're dealing with everything else." Seth lowers his hand. "But why didn't you call? I would've come. You didn't have to do this all on your own."

"I didn't. Irina came and so did . . . Grant."

"Grant knew?" Seth's nostrils flare. "Well, why the hell didn't *he* tell me?"

"I asked him not to," I reply quietly, and tilt my head skyward. There is a clear view of the Milky Way tonight. The shimmering band is as far away as I wish I could be.

Anger rolls off Seth in suffocating clouds. "So Grant

was there for you at the hospital. Was it *just* the hospital or something else?" I can almost hear the enamel being ground off his teeth as he waits for an answer.

"Seth, don't. Don't put the blame all on him. It was my—"

"Stop looking at the damn stars and talk to me, Wil! Did Grant stay here last night? Is that why he didn't come home?"

I fix my gaze on Seth and steel myself for the wrath sure to follow. "Yes."

But what follows isn't at all what I expect.

Seth's eyes glisten. He looks completely and utterly . . . crushed. I expected the anger, the rage, the injustice of it all. But I didn't expect this, to see him so, so *wounded*.

My heart folds in on itself; my body follows suit. And if it is in the realm of possibility to feel worse, then I do.

He pushes the heels of his hands into his eyes. "I knew it!" He drops his hands. "So, how long has it been going on? How long have you been sleeping with my brother?"

I hug my legs closer. "We didn't sleep together."

"Wow, well, that's a *huge* relief," he says wryly. His hands hang limp between his knees. "You know what's ironic? *I'm* usually the one who struggles with being faithful. Do you have any idea how many girls throw themselves at me at the club? Hell, I don't even have to try. Fish in a damn barrel! But for the first time, I didn't even see them, Wil." He lifts his shining eyes. "I only saw you."

I nod, completely gutted. "I disappointed you." I rise,

gripping the railing like a lifeline in a sea of grief. "But you disappointed me, too. I guess neither of us is what we thought we were." I turn to the front door.

"So we're done? That's it?" Seth barks, anger catching up to the shock.

My body crumples with exhaustion. "Seth, what else is there?"

He's looming behind me, and while his movements were quiet, the subtle scent of his cologne gives him away. "I need to know, Wil. I need to know if I was just some guy who fit the mold . . . or if you actually ever even cared about me."

"I cared," I rasp. "Of course I cared."

"But you love him. You *love* my brother, don't you?"

Streetlights glance off the house key in my hand, calling to mind the little silver key Grant once gave me. *As long as you don't go losing your heart, you'll always know where to find it,* he said.

I swallow. "I love Gram. And right now she's lying in Carlisle Community Hospital."

"I'm sorry." His words are laced with shame.

"Goodbye, Seth."

And for the second time today, I am closing the door on a Walker.

Morning comes. The sun spills across the skyline, warming the city of Carlisle. And the one person I'm desperate to talk to can't even hear me. But I talk anyway, all

Wednesday morning and afternoon, like Gram's hospital room is a friggin' confessional. I pour everything out to her. The glorious mess I've made, my ramshackle Fifth House, and how I'm tempted to ship myself off to a deserted island and avoid all this in the future.

Eventually I nod off in the chair, my arm slung across her middle, head down on her bed. I've napped long enough for my arm to fall asleep and my neck to develop a hellacious kink. But neither of those discomforts are what cause me to stir. It's the hand on my head, light as a feather, stroking my hair.

I jerk upright. "Gram? *Gram!*"

She can't speak. Too many tubes run in and out of her. I punch the call button eighty times, laughing and crying at the sight of her sparkling blue eyes. Not just the sight of her eyes, it's what's behind them. *Recognition*. And I don't need a single test to confirm what my heart already knows.

Because I see Gram—*my* Gram.

I am whole again.

At the end of this week from hell, Gram's finally back home where she belongs. Recuperating, and wondering why in blue blazes the kitchen door is scratched up. The EMTs ended up taking it off to fit through with the gurney. Of course, I had it rehung before she got home, but leave it to Gram for no detail to go unnoticed.

While there are still plenty of follow-up appointments, those are small potatoes after the scare of almost losing her. It's a miracle to have her back at all. The doctors believe she must have lost consciousness just moments before I found her. The CPR saved her from the damage that might've been. So her mind remains sharp as ever.

I bake three dozen cupcakes and deliver them to the 911 dispatch office, and another three dozen for the hospital staff. It's not enough to pay back what they've done. But it's something. I've also signed up for CPR certification at the community center.

Tomorrow I will make my last and final *X* on the calendar. The close of June brings the close of my auspicious planetary alignment. Three weeks ago this would've thrown me into a tizzy, but in light of everything, it seems almost . . . ridiculous.

I haven't heard a peep from Seth. Naturally, he sends the most extravagant get-well flowers to Gram, but otherwise, his silence says more to me than any words could. I understand. I've forgiven his lie (including swiping the *exact* birth date of my match off the chart), even if he hasn't forgiven me.

The brass mail slot clinks softly, odd because today's mail has already come. I take the teakettle off the stove before moving to the hall, where I immediately spot a manila envelope on the floor. I know that neat, compact writing—it's Grant's.

My pulse quickens as I pull back the curtains, just in time to see the flash of his taillights at the end of my street.

And then he's gone. I suspect he and Irina have been in contact, but she'd never give me a straight answer. I guess it's her way of protecting me.

With shaky hands, I tear open the envelope, finding two regular-sized ones inside. One labeled: *Open first.* The other: *Open second.*

I've been so preoccupied with Gram that I haven't allowed myself time to miss Grant. But as I unfold the first note, the ache of his absence levels me.

Dear Mena,

Know you've been in my thoughts every second of every day since we saw each other. Iri has kept me updated on Gram's condition (please don't be mad at her). I can't tell you how glad I am to hear she's finally home.

But I've kept my distance, because the last thing I wanted to do was add more turmoil to an already difficult time. And, in fairness, I don't believe Seth did either. But there are things that (selfishly) I do not want to go unsaid.

I don't regret one moment of our time together. Even if that's all it will remain—a moment. I will treasure it. Always.

Now for the selfish part. I miss you. I miss your smile and your laugh. I miss the way you always know what the sky is saying when no one else does. I miss the smell of that soap you use—the lavender vanilla one. I miss teaching you guitar and wish I could have

*taught you more. I miss the way your tongue sticks out
when you concentrate. I miss all the ways we fit, even if
your astrology says we don't. I could write thousands of
songs about all the things I miss. And so, I'm going to
say the thing you wouldn't let me say before....*

I love you, Mena.

I stop reading to wipe the tears from my eyes, and take
a deep breath before continuing.

*You asked me once what brought me back from
my darkness. It was music. But more than that, it was
putting my faith in people again.*

So I put my faith in you.

*With me, or without me, you will find your way.
Because you shine too bright not to.*

Yours,

Grant

I rub the splotchy tears from my lenses and pick up the
second envelope, flipping it over.

Everything you wanted to know but never asked.

I hold it to my chest—Grant's astrological chart. It must
be! And he's absolutely right, I never asked because I was
so positive I already knew.

"Mena?" Gram calls from her bed. "Mind bringing that
tea for me?"

I tumble back to reality and try to pull myself together. "Sure," I croak, ducking back in the kitchen.

A few minutes later, I enter Gram's bedroom with her favorite chamomile in hand.

"I think we're overdue for a chat," she says in a serious tone.

I put some powder under my eyes, attempting to hide the redness, but maybe it wasn't enough. Maybe I appear as shaken on the outside as I feel inside. "You've been through a lot, Gram. You're supposed to be resting." I set the mug on her nightstand.

Gram frowns. "And yet you're the one who looks worse for wear." She pats the spot beside her on the bed. The color is back in her skin and that determined flair is returning to her gestures. Even with her illness, I know arguing is a lost cause because Gram will win. Every. Time.

I crawl in next to her. She takes my hand, sandwiching it between her own. "We need to talk about what you found in the attic."

"Later we will—I *want* to. But when you feel better."

She shakes her head and gives my hand a weak squeeze. "No, *now*. It's a conversation we should've had years ago but I was too afraid. Interesting thing about almost dying"—she pauses for a sip of tea—"it makes you question what kind of living you've done. What I did, I did out of love, you see? Doesn't make it right. Doesn't mean you'll forgive me . . . or understand, but—"

"Gram, I—"

"Hush now"—her wrinkled hand pats mine—"please. I need to say this."

Gram pauses, lifting the photo of my mom from her nightstand. The frame is decorated with tiny shells I collected from our beach trip together, messily glued around the edges. Gram's finger traces the image of her happy daughter, smiling wide for the camera, blue eyes dancing with innumerable dreams.

"Grace was just sixteen when she met Jonathon Markham. Handsome boy. Ambitious. She fell for him hard and fast as young girls so often do. And I believe Jonathon was equally smitten with her." Gram smiles sadly. "Should've seen the way he watched your mother speak. Looked at her like she'd hung the moon." She sets down the photo with a soft sigh.

"A year later she found herself pregnant. My Grace was sure he'd support her, be there in her time of need. Except . . . Jonathon had just learned he'd received a scholarship to an elite college out west. One his family could never have afforded. It was his dream. A dream he was more driven to fulfill than owning up to his responsibilities as a man. As a father.

"So Jonathon left. Left your mama—pregnant and scared and brokenhearted. Sure, he sent money as he could. But once he was gone, I don't believe he set one foot back in Carlisle. Until the day your mother was laid to rest."

I'm still—even more if that's possible—hanging on Gram's every syllable.

"The day I buried my only child, I made her a promise." Her teary eyes find mine. "I promised that I would protect you. Always. And from that day forward, you were my world, Wilamena. While I couldn't shield you from the pain of losing your mama, I'd do everything in my power to keep you from the pain of others. So when Jonathon showed up after six years seeking forgiveness and wanting to be a part of your life—I just . . . *couldn't.*

"Besides protecting you, it also felt like a betrayal to Grace, if that makes sense. Like . . . forgiving him would make what he did okay."

I open my mouth to disagree.

"I know, child, I know. That's not the true nature of forgiveness. But I was hurting and angry. I wanted someone to blame, and for more years than I care to admit, that person was Jonathon.

"Still, I had another reason for keeping you apart." Gram gazes at me again, and as she blinks, a magnified tear tumbles from beneath her glasses.

"Why else, Gram?"

Her voice cracks. "Well, I'd already lost my daughter. I suppose I was afraid . . ." Then Gram sobs, her body shaking with sorrow.

"You were afraid you'd lose me, too," I whisper, piecing it all together. How could she think I'd ever leave her? I've decided I will reach out to Jonathon when I feel ready. But he could never be what Gram has been to me. No one could.

"No," I murmur. I wrap my arms around my grandmother, surrendering to my own tears. "Love doesn't work that way."

She chuckles midcry. "Sixty-eight years of age and it

takes my granddaughter to teach me that. Ah, Mena." She rubs my back in little circles the way my mother used to do. "I'm so sorry for all I've kept from you. But I promise, from this day forward, no more secrets, okay?"

No more secrets? But that means . . . *Fuuudge*. I still have one secret to unload. One big thing I've kept hidden.

I push from her arms. "Um, Gram, I . . . kind of have a confession."

She takes a tissue from the box before passing it to me. "Well, let's have it." Then her swollen eyes somehow widen. "Lord in heaven, tell me you're not pregnant!"

"*No!* No, it's . . . I study astrology," I blurt. "For a while now." I sneak a sideways glance, but her face tells me *nada*. Why haven't I inherited her poker-face gene? I'm more transparent than a freshly cleaned window.

"I suspected as much. How long is a while?"

"Oh," I blow out a breath, "I'd say eight years now. And I *might* have a dozen or so astrology books under my bed."

Gram's eyebrows slowly ascend to her hairline. "*A dozen or so?*"

I twist the tissue in my hands. "Specifically, twenty-three. Twenty-four if we count the collectible hardcover edition of Linda Goodman's *Sun Signs*. Which, um, should be arriving in the next four to six business days."

My grandmother then does the most unthinkable thing . . .

She laughs. No. She *belly-laughs*.

"But . . . you're not mad?" I ask bewildered.

"For what?" Gram replies once she's caught her breath. "Being your mother's daughter? I know I can be a stubborn and opinionated woman, and maybe in this case, to a fault." Her grin fades. "I think I was *so* fixated on all the other studying and extracurriculars you might be sacrificing by devoting yourself to this star business that I never once stopped to see what you gained. But, Mena, I understand now. And the last thing I ever meant to do was to come between you and something special you shared with your mama. Even if *I* think it's—" She bites her tongue.

I chuckle, resting my head on her shoulder. "Oh, Gram, just say it."

"Cosmological hooey." The smile in her voice matches the one on my face.

Some things will never change. And I'm okay with that.

I'm having a stare-down contest with the number-two envelope when Gram pads into the kitchen early Sunday morning.

"What are you doing up?" I ask, hiding the letter behind my back.

But she's already spotted my futile action. "What have you got there, Mena? Better not be another speeding ticket, so help you." Gram snatches it from my hand quicker than she should be capable of moving.

"It's from Grant."

"Ah." She slides it back onto the counter and turns to pour herself a cup of coffee. "But I see you didn't open it."

I wring my hands, itching to tear into the paper. "I think it's his astrological chart."

"Think or know?" Gram asks.

"Ninety-nine percent sure." I pull up a stool and resume my stare. "A few weeks ago I would've opened it quicker than the speed of light."

"And now?"

"Now . . . I don't know. He says that"—my eyes flit to her thoughtful expression—"he says that he . . ." Why can't I spit it out?

"I believe the word you're looking for is 'love.' Grant Walker *loves* you."

My eyes bulge. "How did you know?" The letter is upstairs in my bedroom, underneath my pillow. Gram can't quite make it up the stairs yet, and anyway she'd never read something so personal.

She chuckles, giving her head a little shake. "Because my eyes were open, Mena. 'Bout time you opened yours. You want to know the secret to life?"

My head bobs.

"There *is* no secret. You can't shortcut living. I know your mama wanted to protect you when she asked you to make that promise about following your star chart. But people make mistakes—clearly the Carlisle women are no exception."

I slide the amethyst stone back and forth along its chain. "So, you really think she'd want me to break my promise to her?"

Gram's face softens. "What I *think* is that she'd want

you to be happy. That would be more important to her than anything else."

I mull over what she's said. Her words carry a ring of familiarity. My father wished for my happiness. And while Gram was a staunch loyalist of Team Practicality, I knew she wanted my happiness, too. Oh my gosh! Yes, and *Charlotte*. Didn't she say exactly that about Seth and Grant?

Happiness.

Why *wouldn't* my mother have the same wish for me? After all, she told me she'd love me for longer than the stars would shine above.

And as quickly as the thought forms—the crushing weight from the guilt of betraying my mother, the profound fear of losing what has bound us—it vanishes. Because it isn't the stars keeping us together, it's . . . *love*. And it always will be.

So, could honoring her memory really be as simple as being *happy*?

Gram must see the revelation in my eyes because she nods, a contented smile playing at her lips. Then her gaze drifts to the envelope I clutch in my hands. "Honey, the answers you're seeking can't always be found in the heavens above. Sometimes life requires a leap of faith. For you, maybe, just maybe—that leap means staying right here on the ground." She kisses my forehead before shuffling out of the kitchen.

I sit, blinking. "But . . . what does that even *mean*?" My grandmother is a fortune cookie, a walking, talking cookie. What am I supposed to do with that? I drop my head to my arms.

Suddenly Gram's voice, clear as a bell, chimes from the hall. "It means if you love him, you'll get off your duff and tell him. Child"—she chuckles again—"they don't call it falling for nothing."

Then it all clicks. And I know exactly what to do.

chapter 23

Lucky day, my foot. First, I lose hot water midshampoo after my morning epiphany with Gram. And now—*arg!* I lay on the horn behind the line of unmoving cars. Yes, I'm being one of those annoying people.

Hilarious that I've waited all these weeks to acknowledge that I am head over heels in love with Grant, and now a little log-jammed traffic is making me lose it. But it's not the traffic; it's knowing that only a mere mile or two stands between us.

I could run there faster . . . in Irina's heels . . . *uphill.*

"Oh, come on." I slap my hands on the wheel. "What is the holdup?" I check my hair and lipstick and puff out another impatient breath. I dab my underarms with the remaining napkins I find in the glove box. All I need is to start pitting out while declaring my love to Grant.

Traffic finally starts crawling across the bridge to the east side.

I whiz by one ginormous house after another, my anxiety growing with the size of the homes. I spot the familiar line of cypress at the end of the cul-de-sac and pull into the long drive.

I want to throw up. Instead, I pop a mint and try to focus on the words that will come out of my mouth when the door opens. What will I say?

Hi, Grant, the lobotomy was a success and, ha-ha, turns out I was in love with you all along.

Or maybe something straightforward like: *Feel free to ignore the kiss-off note I left while you were sleeping on my couch.*

Well, there's no denying it. I suck more than a black hole.

My mind is reeling all the way up until the front door is yanked open.

"Um . . . hey." Which is the best I can come up with, now that my tongue has triple-knotted itself.

Charlotte stands in the doorway wearing a splotched painter's apron, hair piled atop her head. "Wil?" She blinks. "Well, this is certainly a surprise." But the shock of finding me on her doorstep quickly fades. "Sweetheart, we're so relieved to hear your grandmother is home again and making a full recovery. You must be overjoyed."

"Oh, yes, thank you. She's getting stronger every day." My grin wavers. "Charlotte, er . . . I was actually hoping to talk to—"

"Grant?"

My eyes round. "H-how did you know?"

Charlotte takes a paint rag from her apron pocket, wiping at a smear of crimson near her temple. Her lips lift in a sad little grin. "I think you may have been the only one who didn't. But"—her frown deepens—"he just left. Didn't he say goodbye?"

"Left?" I echo.

"Yes. He wasn't planning to head up north until August, but then—"

"Wait! He's . . . gone?" I blink.

"Well, yes, but he'll be—"

"What about Seth?" I ask, realizing I didn't see his car in the driveway either.

"He's staying with a cousin in Chicago for a while. Things have been . . . difficult." Charlotte places a gentle hand on my shoulder. "Honey, it was an impossible situation. Someone was bound to be hurt." She lets go. "Maybe it's for the best that you all take a little time and gain perspective. You've been through quite an ordeal this past week."

But I don't want perspective; I want Grant. My heart deflates. Grant's gone and I never got to tell him how I really feel.

"Um"—Charlotte's brows draw together—"can I ask why you're carrying a bouquet of Brussels sprouts?"

"They're for . . . no reason," I finish quietly with a shake of my head.

Her lips purse as if working through a complex equation. "You really care for him, don't you, Wil?"

"Yes," I murmur, rotating the sprout bouquet in my hand. "But I guess it's too late, isn't it? Everything's just so mangled and . . . I'm sorry to have bothered you, Charlotte." I turn and start back to the car. Clamping my lips together, I swear not to bawl hysterically like the last time I left the Walkers'. *Don't cry.* And with each footstep I chant: *Pillar of strength, pillar of strength, pillar of—*

"Wil! Wait!" Charlotte calls, jogging from the veranda. "Look, I don't know if this helps, but Grant did say something about stopping at that Italian sandwich shop downtown."

Perking up, I feel my first glimmer of hope since arriving. "Valentine's?"

A tiny smile appears. "Yes, I think that's the one."

"*Oh!* Then . . . I—I have to go." There's still a chance! If I drive like a maniac, there's still a chance I can catch Grant. Sunday is a busy day at Valentine's and the line is usually epic. I have to catch him.

But before I do, I launch myself into Charlotte's arms, almost knocking her over. "Thank you," I gush into her hair. *"Thank you, thank you, thank you."*

Charlotte matches the force of my embrace and then stiffens. "Oh, Wil, the paint." We separate, both inspecting my yellow dress.

"It's okay. I'm clean."

Charlotte doesn't look convinced. "No, it's in your hair. Shoot! I'm so sorry. I must still have vermilion on my face. Let me get a clean rag from—"

"There's no time, I gotta go! Thanks, Charlotte!" I holler over my shoulder.

I dive into the Buick, then perform the worst three-point turn in the history of driver's ed. Nothing will stop me from getting to Valentine's in time. *Nothing.* Most of Carlisle's construction is happening on the south side, so I'll have a relatively clear shot downtown. This should be a piece of cake. He can't be that far ahead if he's just left.

These are exactly the thoughts one should never have.

The sun beats at my back as I size up the enemy. Plural—*enemies.* I'm paralyzed by fear; perspiration dots my hairline. The low, rhythmic pounding of a drum moves about a quarter of the speed of my thrumming heart.

A grease-painted monster with a rainbow Afro passes by holding a sign that reads:

SQUIRTING FLOWER CLOWN TROUPE—SHOWERING THE WORLD WITH HAPPINESS

No. Seriously. No.

This isn't funny.

I pace back and forth at the parade's sideline like a caged animal. How could I have blanked that it's Carlisle's annual Summer Sun Parade? With many of the side streets barricaded, finding parking was a freaking miracle.

Still, I'm losing precious time. And these clowns are blocking my path to Valentine's—as if my hate for them needed more fuel.

Dozens and dozens of painted monsters parade over the hill and down the street with their squawking horns and noisemakers. I decide this must be karmic hell, and the only explanation is that I was Genghis Khan in a previous life.

I force one heel in front of the other, ignoring the constriction of my throat, ignoring the dark spots speckling my vision. I will channel Athena. I will rise to the challenge. And unlike Jessica Bernard's seventh birthday party, this time . . . I will *not* wet my pants!

My pace quickens until I'm in a flat-out run, hurtling toward the carnival procession.

"Move!" I thrust my sprouts and charge the clowns. I don't look at their faces. I'll lose my nerve. I look only at their baggy trousers and striped socks. *"Outta my way! Outta my way!"* I shriek, only to discover the clowns are practically tripping over their floppy shoes to avoid the produce-wielding psychopath.

Emerging on the other side of the street, I barrel into Valentine's, gasping for breath. Mouths hang agog as I frenetically scan the little corner deli. I feel the stare of customers questioning my bizarre state and the parade bottleneck I created.

That's *all* I need, for Gram to witness this on the six o'clock news. Her poor ticker couldn't take it.

But my hope and the adrenaline start to wane when I don't find Grant among the queuing patrons. I check the bathrooms. Nothing. I even ask the deli dude if he's seen a tall, really attractive guy with music-note tattoos, wearing a gray T-shirt and Chucks with duct tape. He looks at me like I'm an extraterrestrial fresh off the mothership.

As I glance down at my battered Brussels sprouts and re-call the red paint in my hair, I guess I can see his point.

My shoulders droop. He probably never even came, what with all the chaos of the parade.

It's over. I let out a shuddery breath.

My chance with Grant is done.

Gram's fine—I've called twice, which wasn't easy since pay phones are more elusive than wormholes in space. Of course I've forgotten to charge my cell . . . *again*. A lady from Gram's garden club has brought over a casserole—the Midwest equivalent of flowers—and is keeping her company. And since Gram sounded so chipper, I'm not inclined to go home and taint the mood.

So I drive across town to Inkporium.

"Hey, Bo Peep, how's the—" Crater breaks off, grin faltering. "What's wrong?"

"Huh?" Worried my eyes have taken to spontaneously leaking, I wipe underneath them. But no, I'm not crying. I'm done crying. Life will go on. That's the way it works, I'm told. And I've survived worse.

He flicks the hair from his eyes as he examines me. "Man, you look so sad, like someone stole your sunshine."

"Oh, rough week," I reply vaguely. "Lots of clouds."

Crate nods, "Yeah, they kinda come with the whole package, don't they? Heard your gram's doing better, though. Helluva silver lining."

"It is." I grin, mirroring his hopeful expression. "Um, Iri still here?"

"Yep, and crabby-assed as ever. Tell her if she wants to cut early she's got my blessing. I'll make sure she gets the full hour of pay."

"Thanks, Crate. Really."

He blanches. "Jesus, you kidding? You're doing *me* the favor." He jerks his chin toward the back studios. "Now go release the Harpy."

Irina stares at her phone, her lip curled in a sneer. She glances up, startled. "Oh, hey! I wasn't expecting you."

"I, um . . ." I notice the cactus beside the sink, sitting shriveled and dying. "Did you forget to water it?"

She crams the phone in her purse and picks up the withered cactus, tossing it in the aluminum trash can. "Jordan Lockwood turned out to be a complete douche bag. Turns out the Suit came with an engagement ring."

"Say again?"

"Meaning he was *engaged*. Can you believe it? I was going to be the last wild fling before wedlock. I'm just glad I waited and . . ." A string of Russian profanities follows.

"So . . . you didn't have sex with him?"

She shakes her head. Her eyes turn glassy, pooling with tears. "I really liked him. I wanted it to be spe—"

"Irina Dmitriyev." I place my hands on her shoulders. "Douche bags don't deserve tears. Especially not yours."

She swallows hard and nods. "I know. *Chert poberi!* It's just . . . allergies—damn cottonwood."

I hug her, murmuring just how unworthy Jordan the Jackhole truly is. Then I spot an exotic-looking plant on the other counter. "But who gave you the Venus flytrap?"

She sniffs into my shoulder before pulling away. "Manny. We've been hanging out." It's impossible to hide my shock. "Not *that* way. When he came in the other day, he saw the cactus and said it was totally lame. He bought me this instead." Iri produces a grin. "A carnivorous plant."

"He's something, isn't he?"

She offers a noncommittal shrug and then does a double take. "Are you aware of the red paint in your hair?"

"Long story. Listen, would you do me a favor if you're up to it?"

"Sure. You know I will."

"Pierce me?"

Her mouth unhinges. "But . . . but you hate needles. Why?"

"Because. Then I can remember today as the day I faced all my fears. I battled clowns, tried to profess my love, and now"—I turn my back toward her—"I'm going to get my belly button pierced. Undo that hook, will you?"

Her hand hesitates before she undoes the hook. "*Dorogaya*, you don't have to do this."

I unzip the dress to my waist, pulling out my arms and positioning myself on the leather recliner. "Yes, I do. I want to. And then we're going to get a huge order of fries at Curio's and eat them until our fingers are so greasy we can't hold on to any more. Let's go, comrade, my fries are waiting." I grip the armrests. "Go."

She swabs my navel with antiseptic, looking down with concern. "Are you sure this is what you want?"

"Do it," I say firmly. I close my eyes at the sound of the drawer with the medieval tools opening. I feel the pinch of a metal clamp on my skin and suck in a breath.

"Easy, *dorogaya,* don't move. And don't worry—I'll be quick. I think Grant is gonna *love* this." She quickly adds, "Not that you're doing it for him."

"I'm not." My vision goes wavy. "Anyway"—the blood flushes beneath my skin, creating a hot-and-cold prickly sensation—"I lost him. Oh God." I stare, delirious, at the fluorescent lights on the ceiling. "Is it too late to change my mind?"

"Wil! Wil!" Irina's echoing voice bounces around my brain. "Don't you pass out on me!"

I lift my woozy head from the table. "Am I done? Am I pierced?"

"Er . . ." Irina peels off her gloves and elevates the headrest. "No. Why don't we save piercing for another day, hmm? Now, what's this about losing Grant?"

The room gradually comes back into focus. I tug on my dress. "He left early for college. He's gone."

"Funny"—she lifts a brow—"he called half an hour ago looking for you."

"He . . . he did? But how's that possible?"

"You really think he'd skip town permanently without a word?" Iri rolls her eyes. "You forgot to charge your phone again, didn't you?"

I hop from the chair. "*Oh my stars!* I—I have to find him! I have to tell him!" But now I'm torn because my friend is in need and I won't leave her high and dry. Not when she dropped everything to be there when my world collapsed when Gram was hospitalized.

"I'm good, Wil," she says, reading my mind. Her phone chimes. She holds it up, facing it toward me. "It's Grant. What should I tell him?"

"Tell him . . . don't leave. I really want to talk, but first I have a friend who needs me."

Iri's lips curl into a devilish grin as she taps out the message.

"What? Why is your face doing that? Iri!" I wrestle the phone from her grip and read the message that's just come in. "What? What does he mean by 'I'll be there'?"

"Grant needs you. More than I do right now. I'll come over tomorrow for breakfast and we can have girl time then. You can bake me muffins of gratitude."

"But . . ."

"Oscar!" Irina calls.

Footsteps sound in the hallway, and the door cracks open. Oscar's wary face pops in.

"Do you like French fries?" Iri asks, like it's the most natural question in the world.

"Sure." Oscar lifts a shoulder. "Who doesn't?"

"Want to grab some? Wil doubled-booked herself and I hate eating trans fats alone."

He lifts his heavy brows.

"Strictly platonic," Iri clarifies.

"You know"—Oscar folds his arms—"I am capable of friendship. But you wouldn't know that because you've been avoiding me for weeks."

Iri puts her bangle bracelets back on her wrist and smiles. And it's dazzling. "So, that's a yes?"

A quiet laugh rumbles in Oscar's chest. "Yes, my Lady of Strange. The answer is yes. Let me go clean up my studio, okay?"

"Take your time," Irina replies.

When Oscar turns around, we spot yet another dog-eared copy of Shakespeare sticking out of his back pocket.

"Sweet boy"—she turns her gray eyes on me—"but I want to go it alone for a while. Figure out what I want."

"I think you are wise, *dorogaya*."

"You know, Wil, June's not over yet. Technically, there's still a few hours left."

"So?"

"So the planets are still aligned and blah-blah-blah, and I told Grant you would meet him at the tower."

"You did?" I squeeze her hand. "Irina Dmitriyev, you really do believe in love, don't you?"

She holds her index finger to her lips. "Shh, don't tell."

Chapter 24

The stars beckon me to gaze upon them. I can feel them winking. Tugging at my hand like billions of impatient children vying for my attention.

But I don't. I won't look up.

Because I can't tear my eyes off the image of Grant sitting on the bumper of his pickle-green station wagon. His lean body is hunched, his eyes staring at the ground. When I slam my door, he looks up.

And that lift of his chin fills me with all the courage I need.

I take off in a sprint, my dress rustling and puffing out with the rapid strikes of my knees. But these shoes don't let me move with the speed I desire. I kick them off and surge ahead.

He stands motionless. And he feels as hopelessly far as the celestial bodies shining above.

But finally, *finally,* I reach him and skitter to a halt. Totally out of breath. *"I . . . love . . . you,"* I wheeze.

Grant tilts his head up to the sky. I see the overlap of his teeth when he brings his handsome face down again. He's smiling, *beaming.* It's the warmest, happiest, loveliest smile I have ever seen in all of my life.

I spring into his arms and he laughs while I cry.

"About time you figured that out, Songbird." He's still chuckling when he puts me down. "Aw, and you brought me really sad-looking Brussels sprouts." The poor sprouts have been to hell and back, but that's a story for another day. "I keep wondering if there's ever gonna be a time you don't surprise me. Seriously, you're the most unusual girl I've ever known." He works his fingers through the dried bit of paint in my hair.

"But you like unusual, right?"

"No"—Grant shakes his head—"*I love it.* What's that?" He nods at the white rectangle sticking out of my dress pocket.

I let go of his hand. "It's . . . it's for you." I pass it over.

He unfolds the envelope, peering at me, then back at the paper in his hands. "You didn't open it. But . . . I thought this was important. I thought you needed to know."

"It was, but then"—I drop my shoulders—"I went and fell in love with you anyway. So I guess it's pointle—"

Grant kisses me. His mouth is fierce. And even though his letter expressed how terribly he's missed me, his kiss tells me more. He lifts me up, setting me on the hood of the station wagon, never once allowing his lips to leave mine.

I'm breathing like I've run another sprint when he does

break away. He rests his forehead against mine, letting out a breathless laugh. "You know, you're going to find out my sign soon enough. My birthday's—"

"No!" This time I cut him off with my own kiss, and he gives up talking for a while.

A long while.

Grant lies on his back on the wool blanket covering the crabgrass and dandelions at the base of the tower. I am nestled on my side in the crook of his arm. The warm summer night surrounds us.

"Are you going to keep staring at me all night like that?"

"No." I smile. "I have to be home in an hour. Anyway, I have to get my staring in because you'll be leaving for school in August."

He rolls his head back and forth. "Yeah, and where did you get the idea I'd leave for school two months early?"

I lift a shoulder. "I was in a panic. Your mom said you headed north; I just assumed it was to Michigan." I assumed wrong, of course—a skill I've been mastering at an alarming rate.

While Seth might've preferred to disappear into the bright lights and big city of Chicago, it turns out Grant sought peace and solitude. So he packed up his guitar with every intention of leaving town for the family's lake house—five hours north. Fortunately for me, Grant didn't make it beyond the city limits, because his mom called.

And I would buy a star and name it Charlotte, because whatever she said had him careering across traffic and straight back to the heart of Carlisle.

Back to me.

Of course, things were still rocky between the brothers when Seth left town. Especially when Grant found out how Seth had manipulated me. I can only hope, with a little time and distance, the fractured relationship will heal. I believe it will—one day.

Grant turns his head so he can look at me, and pushes a wavy lock back from my cheek with his free hand. "You know I'll come home every weekend I can, and all the holidays. And you can come see me whenever you can get away."

"You might get sick of me with an open invitation like that."

"Get sick of my muse? Are you kidding?" He smiles. "I'm going to create beautiful music because of you."

That is another huge change. Grant is going to major in music. *Not* business.

Once Grant leveled with his parents that he was pursuing business out of a sense of duty, and not any real desire, bye-bye business degree. Because no way would they continue to allow their son to feel beholden to them for simply doing what any good parent would. They had preserved his future by saving him from his past. As to the shape that future would take, well, that would be entirely up to him.

Grant continues stroking my cheek. I love that he can't

keep his hands off me. "So, you really aren't the least bit curious about my sign?"

I roll my eyes. "Course I am. Just because I see the error of my ways doesn't mean I've forsaken astrology completely. But"—I frown—"there is something that still confuses me. Your key chain has the date February twenty-third. I assumed that was your birthday because—"

Grant laughs.

"What's so funny?"

"That's my *car's* birthday. Anna made me that key chain to commemorate the day I bought the green beast."

My mouth forms an O of understanding.

"Well? Any educated guesses? I think we can safely eliminate Pisces." His fingers tease like his words, gliding down my throat and across my chest, where they follow the swell of my breasts.

My heart rate accelerates enough to break the sound barrier. "Uh-uh. *No way,* no more guessing."

"What if I whispered it in your ear?"

I grin and tilt my head. "Go ahead, tell me."

He whispers the word and I shiver with the hush of his warm breath.

"Stars in heaven, that's almost as bad," I reply, straight-faced. Then burst into giggles when he nips at my ear.

Grant rolls back again and we lie in silence as he stares at the sky. "Hey, isn't that the Milky Way?"

"Probably," I answer, without an upward glance. Because I'm too busy admiring what's amazing here on Earth. The crinkle of his eyes as he grins, the fan of his lashes as he blinks, the way his lips move to form the words "I love you." Again and again and again. The joy, the beauty of it is too much to hold.

I prop up on my elbow, gazing down. "Do you remember what a supernova is?"

His brow quirks. "A star that explodes, right? Next one might happen in fifty years."

"Uh-huh." I run my fingers over his tattoos. "And it can outshine an entire galaxy and is one *billion* times more luminous than the sun."

He takes my hand, pressing his lips to the inside of my wrist. "Sounds breathtaking."

"Yes." I nod. "You certainly are." I'm about to carry on with my explanation of supernovas and how gloriously rare they are—the last one being seen in our galaxy in the 1600s—but then Grant quiets me with another kiss.

He briefly pulls away. His thumb brushes along my lower lip. "Mena, my Mena, no more words." Then my sweet and steadfast Capricorn whispers in my ear, "Find another way to speak."

And I do.

Acknowledgments

They say it takes a village. For me, it took a global metropolis. Which is to say I have everyone in the world to thank! An impossible task that I'll inevitably flub, but here we go . . .

First, enormous thanks and a lifetime supply of grilled cheeses to my CPs: Rebecca Campbell, Bria Quinlan, and Jenn Stark. Your clever insights breathed life into this story, and on more than one occasion resuscitated me. Xs and Os to infinity. You are emosewa.

Endless thanks to my extraordinary agent, Catherine Drayton. Would that I could, I would name galaxies of stars in your honor! But I could only afford one (star, not galaxy). Still, I like to think it is the brightest and shiniest—just like you.

Thank you to my utterly amazing editor, Emily Easton. You have gone to the ends of the earth and back again for Wil and Grant, and for me. Great. Now I'm weepy. Because how can anyone find the words to thank the person responsible for their happily-ever-after? I owe you one . . . million.

I'm drawing teeny-tiny hearts around all my wonderfully supportive RWA friends: the Starcatchers, my Lucky

13s and Savvy 7s, MMRWA, and YARWA. Not to mention the *infinite* others! Gobs of gratitude to my snarky soul mate, Tracy Brogan, for believing I would go places despite my ability to get lost in a paper bag. And to Rachel Grant for her chocolate martinis. Because.

Heartfelt gratitude to the entire team at Random House Crown BFYR! Because of you these pages shine. Also to Samantha Gentry for the acknowledgments mulligan and more!

Big squishy hugs of appreciation to my comrades and clients at Douglas J—with extras to Carole for the astrology books. You guys keep me tethered in the best of ways. Thank you also to my BFF Elizabeth—I love that our auras have merged! Thanks to agent William Callahan for graciously lending his eyes so that I might see. And a mighty thanks to Dr. Rishi Kundi for his MD prowess.

Last, but eons from least, thank you to my family. Because of you, I know what it means to love and be loved. With special thanks to my parents, for nurturing my belief that the worlds I imagined were real. (They still are.) And to my husband, David—it *all* begins and ends with you. Loving you has been the ultimate adventure.

Finally, thank *you,* dear reader. Turns out, astrology is *unbelievably* complicated. So please forgive any mistakes and liberties I've taken in this work of fiction. I hope you've enjoyed this book, and that perhaps your heart is smiling because of it. That is my sincerest wish.

Group hug.

About the Author

DARCY WOODS has held an eclectic mix of professions—from refueling helicopters for the U.S. Army to recharging bodies and spirits at a spa—but her most beloved career is being an author. She is a happily-ever-after addict, and finds all things metaphysical endlessly fascinating. Wil's character inspired her to discover why a girl would place astrology above all else, including the desires of her own heart. She lives in Michigan with her husband and cat. The Golden Heart® Award–winning *Summer of Supernovas* is her first novel. You can follow Darcy on Twitter at @woodswrite.

THE OLD ONES

THE OLD ONES